GIFTS

IN

BROWN PAPER

PACKAGES

BY

S.P. BROWN

Gifts in Brown Paper Packages© Copyright 2017 By S.P. Brown

Published 2021

New York, NY, USA

ISBN E-book:979-8-9852684-2-3

ISBN Paperback:979-8-9852684-0-9

ISBN Hardcover:979-8-9852684-1-6

Library of Congress Control Number: 2021923364

Acknowledgments

*All my gratitude and honor to Almighty God for swaddling me
and bestowing blessings upon my life that make this journey possible.*

*To my Olympic intertwining sister spheres hailing from my varied walks of life,
my bench — you know who you are! You encourage, inspire, and encircle me with
your ears, shoulders, hugs, discerning words, and unequivocal, unwavering support.
A special shout out to DRB for the dialogue that birthed the title
of this narrative.*

*And to my husband, Al Brown, the epitome of "ride or die," who, for over three
decades, has been the gift that accepts and loves me with all my flaws
and has never left my side.*

TABLE OF CONTENTS

PROLOGUE

"Forgive them Father" - Lauryn Hill

The sun had begun its sluggish descent as she crossed the border where Prince Georges County, Maryland, became the outskirts of Southeast Washington, DC. She was mesmerized by the transformation of the sky's complexion, God's reminder every twelve hours that he controlled every moment in case anyone had the temerity to doubt his hand. A chiming tone directed her gaze to the blinking gas symbol on the dashboard.

"Dammit, I have to stop!" she exclaimed out loud to the empty car.

She pulled into the next service station she came upon. As the attendant pumped the gas, she noticed a group of young men standing around eating out of white cardboard Chinese food cartons just beyond the entrance to the gas station. Gregarious tones and trendy colloquialisms floated through the air. The unapologetic exuberance of their youth and experiences made her nostalgic. She stared at them, wondering what they had going on in their lives as she pulled out of the station and heard the familiar sound of an abbreviated police siren. Peering out of her rear-view mirror, she watched two uniformed officers jump out of their car and approach the young men, hands resting on their hip holsters. She sucked her teeth in annoyance. There it was, she thought, the characteristic that rang true in both black and brown communities and upscale ones alike; cops policing what didn't need policing, black and brown boys and men minding their own business.

She turned the car back onto what had become Pennsylvania Avenue, Washington, DC, and her frustration deepened. This was such an important night for her, and she was now late. The traffic was thick, and the pool of contradiction in DC was equally dense and so putrid to her that wading through it was nauseating. Driving from Prince Georges County into DC from the Southeast entry point, the poverty was almost confrontational as Route 4 crossed into DC. The downtrodden are sudden fixtures on corners and in front of neighborhood liquor stores.

She turned up the volume of the car stereo to distract herself from both her thoughts and her tardiness. Sade's velvet tones filled the car, seemingly pleading with her to answer the question about crime and its correlation to love. She sang back to Sade, her voice rich and melodic, and she matched Sade note for note, her vibrato doing its job as it disconnected her from the uncertainty and tension consuming her. Music always had the power to collect the pieces of her and make her whole again, soothing her body, mind, and soul. As she sang the notes, the lyrics and rhythms safely delivered her to a peaceful place outside of herself, a conduit for her pain and the forceps for the pleasure deep within her and coaxed out through her song. Singing was God's way of speaking to her, shielding her, keeping her, loving her.

As Sade ended her serenade, she brought the car smoothly to a stop at a red traffic light, feeling more at ease than she had felt even five minutes prior. She breathed in deeply and flipped through the satellite stations in the BMW rental to find something else to listen to, passing popular selections that she certainly appreciated and would normally thoroughly enjoy. Beyoncé & Ed Sheeran convincingly crooning the definition of perfection while challenging musical collaboration norms; Bruno Mars tirelessly pumping twenty-four karat magic in the air and Kendrick Lamar brilliantly pontificating about royalty in his DNA and sounding as angry as she often felt. None of those selections would help her at this moment, she surmised. She connected her phone and adeptly tapped her Spotify playlist, and within seconds, the 'Miseducation of Lauryn Hill' filled the car. She knew every word of every song of this album. Its music and rhythms were timeless. Many of the selections spoke to her in the way she once needed back in 1998 when it was first released and likewise today in 2021. She went quickly to her first desire.

"Ahhh yeahhh," she murmured as the first chords filled the car, and Lauren's opening rap accompanied it. She bobbed her head and sang the poignant rhythms of "Forgive Them Father." Night had finally blanketed the car and her surroundings. She glanced at the clock on the dashboard. She was not obnoxiously late but just late enough. She was supposed to be at the venue thirty minutes prior to the event starting, and instead, her ETA was right around the start time. That was going to have to be good enough.

A short while later, she entered the ballroom of the Washington, DC Four Seasons. All eyes turned to follow her as she strut, aplomb with the certitude of her presence as well as how striking she looked. Her gown was made by an unknown designer, a close friend of hers to whom she was eternally grateful and in awe of his talent. The gown swaddled her muscular lithe frame like a fleece blanket comforts a newborn. It was a glittering platinum, strapless, the bodice covered with minuscule hand-sewn pearls and crystallized sequins, each gem and crystal as brilliant as a star in a midnight sky. The balance of the gown was taut along the length of her long slender torso and shapely rear end, unencumbered by any additional adornment to avoid distraction from the compliment of the fabric's perfect fit to her curves. Just beyond the knee, it flared into billowing layers of silk and sheer chiffon, completing the upscale princess aesthetic. Her hair was cut close, its tight auburn dipped curls lending to the accentuation of her blemish-free dark brown skin, chiseled cheekbones, full lips, and brown eyes. She walked through the massive room like an international model walking a runway, through the socially distanced numbered tables, easily finding the one where her husband was waiting patiently for her. As she sat down, her gaze swept the room, a thorough review as she copiously sought to take it all in.

This was the first of such events she had accepted since the Covid-19 pandemic had shut everything down, from schools to flights and large gatherings like this one for well over a year. Given this one had

3

agreed to donate a large portion of its proceeds to a domestic violence agency she was a board member of and required negative Covid-19 tests from attendees, she had agreed. The fundraising auction was the first item on the program. She watched silently as trivial items like star basketball players' sneakers, tickets to music, and film award shows complete with meet & greet backstage passes, and expensive golf outings were the subject of good-natured bidding wars, the participants nonchalantly raising their paddles driving the prices into the many thousands.

She suppressed the building annoyance at the lack of humility required to participate in such an exercise. "Look how financially secure I am," it seemed to scream. It was for a good cause, she thought. She was happy about that, but ironically, it also saddened her. She couldn't attempt obliviousness to the reality that many children from her old neighborhood could have eaten for a month for the cost of one of these golf outing bids. The abject poverty just a few miles away in this very same zip code but yet so very far in reality from the pristine opulence and buttoned-up aristocracy was heartbreaking. It was the apparent normalcy of those contradictions to so many around her, which deeply irritated her. She yearned to understand how the lawmakers who walked the prestigious halls of the nation's capital also drove through the city's impoverished neighborhoods and failed to make the demise of the poverty-stricken communities its mission. In fact, many failed to even acknowledge it or recognize the very irony that the President of the free world slept in a masterful White House built by slaves, and just a few blocks away, descendants of those same slaves could be found replete with desperation.

While she was proud to be in the room, she cringed at the opulent display of philanthropy. She didn't judge, but she opted to give back in ways that were shrouded in discretion. She decided that she was a spectator to it all, present in body but only half in spirit and not at all in soul. She was accepted into this community but not really a member. The HBCU and Ivy League graduates, the Greek sorority members, the Links, and Jack & Jill legacies…none of that was really her experience. She could look and sound the part; the east coast lilt to her dialogue was cultured to the point that her actual origin was not immediately discernible, at least not until one got through her walls.

Sure, she could talk the talk to a point, but she never felt like she was really a member despite all of the accouterments. Her scrutiny of the ballroom continued, the smiling faces, the raucous laughter. "Get your head right; you are in this room this time for a purpose," she told herself. As she continued to digest the room and the enormity of her task, she turned inward and queried, *"How did I get here? Does my story matter to these folks? Do they really see me?"*

PART I

IN UTERO

[\in-you-te-ro\]
Adverb or Adjective **In the uterus: before birth:**

Merriam Webster

*While in utero, the fetus forms, coveted,
protected from all ills while it grows and
develops to full term and is ready for birth.*

CHAPTER 1

Cornered

"Black Butterfly" - Deniece Williams

Whack! Kyrie was always startled when the flame erupted on the side of her face as if she had no awareness that such pain was a possibility. Like a toddler's response to a seemingly innocuous match igniting fire, her immediate reaction was generally wonder. How was it possible that a person would seek to cause another being that level of pain? She thought a lot about that very question. What she knew intrinsically was the pain, although it was the kind of pain that permeated her mind and body in a way she couldn't really articulate.

Kyrie's hand sprung upward to meet the sharp burning sensation and felt the weal forming on her cheek. She struggled against the bilious churning in her gut and fixed her eyes on the roach, obliviously making its way across the ceiling behind his head. The sting of the slap was quickly sharing its favor with her eyes and the back of her throat, and she willed herself to defeat the sob and accompanying tears threatening to escape the confinement of her body.

Kyrie closed her eyes momentarily and then quickly reopened them to find the purveyor of her pain had not, through some miracle, been vanquished. He was still there. Sometimes she imagined that if she concentrated hard enough, she would conjure up some unperceived powers and make him disappear, like the powers that surfaced just when the heroine needed them in the fantasy novels she routinely devoured. He was so close to her. Her nostrils discerned the evidence of his evening's activities. Hennessy. She wrinkled her nose in distaste. The thickness of his speech suggested maybe he had been sniffing too, although that usually made him paranoid and distracted from her. Given he was screaming in her face at that very moment, his attentiveness was assured. Perhaps there was no money for the white powder this night.

"Where the fuck were you?" Man screamed into her face. She flinched but didn't answer. The roach had reached the crease between the wall and the ceiling and was now crawling back and forth in the corner as if it were confused. Stupid roach. Could it hear? Could it think? Was it drunk with confusion because of the screaming going on beneath it, or was it only aware of the seemingly impenetrable corner? Kyrie stared at it. She resented its presence, so nonchalant in this hell she was living. Not to mention, it was gross, she thought. *I hate roaches.*

Whap! Like the first, this slap was delivered with surprising force. Kyrie's head knocked into the doorway she was standing in as she staggered backward. She needed to answer him, she knew that, but the fear that her words might exacerbate his agitation silenced her. She never really knew what to say in these instances besides "I'm sorry," and that usually didn't help. She also couldn't decide what was worse: the screaming anger spraying spittle in her face continuing for hours, or a few blows peppered with some finger jabs to her forehead combined with sharp words, which sometimes ended the assault quickly.

"Answer me, goddammit. Where the fuck were you?" She flinched again but remained quiet in the moment. Shit, her face was wet. Her tears had betrayed her with the second slap. She always attempted to appear unaffected, denying him the satisfaction of feeling any power over her emotions. Like today, she often failed. She hated him so much in those moments that even if he spared her the physical onslaught, his angry denigration in her face was usually enough to draw the ire in her belly that only flowed freely through her tears.

Through her sobs, she began to rattle off incoherent strings of words. "...to work... to class after... was at my friend's house until late... I'm sorry I didn't call..." Kyrie's voice trailed off, and she tried to swallow her sobs. Sometimes he got angrier if she was crying.

Whap! This blow was to the other side of her face.

"You fuckin' little lying bitch. You were with that skinny mother-fucka! I told you to bring your ass straight the fuck home! You are going to learn that you are not in charge in this motha-fuckin' house." Kyrie balled her fists tight and stared at the wall trying hard to find the roach through the haze of her tears. Unable to do so, the words came cascading from her mouth in torrents.

"I don't understand why I am in trouble...why are you so angry with me for hanging out with a friend after class?"

Man's eyes flashed, and he moved closer to her, bringing his face within inches of hers. "I'll tell you why — because I run this motha-fuckin' house. Neither your little bullshit job nor you being 17 means you're grown! You think you don't have to do what the fuck I say? If it wasn't for me - staying -in -your- little – ass- you- wouldn't -have – even - graduated – from- high - school."

Each word was punctuated with a pause before the next and a jab with his forefinger to her forehead. But more than the fact that he was touching her with his finger, the weight of his presence was enervating as if every ounce of him was sitting on top of her chest, suffocating her.

Man stood about 5'11" inches tall and weighed about 225 pounds. He was broad-shouldered and muscular. His skin was the color and texture of smooth bronze, without a blemish disturbing it. Kyrie spent years thinking about how attractive his complexion was; not light at all, but also not dark. She had heard enough that she was "too dark."

For years, Kyrie had lamented why she hadn't been born with his skin color since he was just a tad lighter. It was quite ironic to her since she knew she looked more like him than she did her mother. He had nice facial features, striking bone structure, a nice, wide yet smallish nose, and deep chocolate eyes set just the appropriate distance apart on his face. However, what stood out the most was his head. He wore his head shaved bald, which was the only way that Kyrie ever remembered it. She had heard stories that when he had allowed it to grow in his younger years, it was a crop of copper curls, setting him apart from many of his peers. Those curls earned him the nickname "Red" as an adolescent.

As an adult, he wore his hair clean-shaven bald from an early age, and for as long as Kyrie could remember, her mother shaved it for him at least once a week. "Pam, I need my head shaved today." Regardless of what she was doing, her mother would oblige; that was who she was. He would sit in a chair in the living room with a towel around his neck. Her mother would set up a folding card table with one of their larger kitchen bowls filled with cool water. She would stand behind him, spray white foam all over his head, and move the blade from front to back very methodically. Like a farmer tending to each row of harvest, she'd shave row, after row, pausing only to clean the blade in the bowl of water after each row, the shaving cream disappearing little by little until his head was clean-shaven.

Kyrie would marvel at her mother's patience and kindness when the shaving expedition took place in close proximity to Man slapping her mother around. Kyrie would take a seat with her book in the kitchen area so she'd have a good view, just in case this would be the day that the blade would slip and her mother inadvertently slit his throat. That never happened. After she was done, he would go to the bathroom sink, rinse the shaving cream residue off, and reappear with a gleaming head. That bald head, combined with the broad, muscular build and a perpetual scowl on his face, created a foreboding presence. Then there was the brooding silence or the gruff, commanding, and oftentimes bullish tone, plus the quick temper and even quicker hand that would strike another seemingly without regard for relationship or consequence. All of those personality elements resulted in an overall persona of meanness. When Kyrie first heard the term "angry black man," she thought for sure it was created for Man himself.

The spittle drops had intensified, which meant he was leaning in closer. "You graduated! Shiiiit! Barely graduated........cutting – fucking – class – every- fucking – week. You must have a short memory…forgot about the yellow truancy cards that came in the mail all the time? Failing your classes because you were doing WHAT? WHAT?" He screamed the last two words in her face. "Running around with that fucking stupid looking motha-fucka! I don't give a fuck that you graduated. I'll still kick his ass and yours up the damn hill if I catch you with him! You got that?"

The tears were flowing freely by now, although she swallowed the sobs the best she could. Her voice was not to be trusted. A slight movement caught her eye in her peripheral vision. There it was -- the roach. It was still seemingly confused in the corner of the ceiling. In the minutes before she had located it again, it had traveled the width of the wall at least twice, lost maybe? Her face was so wet now, and her sobs uninhibited. She knew not to attempt to respond anymore.

The present line of questioning was rhetorical. A response would almost certainly trigger either another slap or an extension of the berating, and tonight, Kyrie felt that she could bear neither. She could not bring herself to look at him in his face, fearful that the lack of respect she felt would certainly be unmasked in her eyes, even through the pool of tears. She began humming the words of the song that was permeating her consciousness at the moment, but it was not Deniece Williams' voice in her head. It was her own voice, softly crooning her own rendition of a black butterfly's journey to freedom.

She sang in her head. Anything else would assuredly earn her nothing less than a full-on ass-whipping. Man had also threatened her with kicking Shane's ass if he caught them together for the last two years that she had been seeing him. But Shane was one of her few opportunities to escape this hell, which is why she had resorted to cutting school to be with him. Shane had graduated two years before her and was working and going to college at night. Since she wasn't allowed to spend time with him openly, she only had a chance when she was supposed to be in school.

School made her feel bad because she struggled in every class except English, so she had certainly participated in a fair share of truancy. Man was right about that. Kyrie had also graduated by the skin of her teeth, plus a year of simultaneous night school classes and summer school after her June graduation. Man was also right about that. But he was wrong about his "staying in her ass" being the reason she graduated.

Kyrie was very clear about what she wanted, and that was the opportunity to eventually get out on her own. Staying behind in high school for a fifth year while all her friends were going away to college would not serve that goal. So, exactly when she needed to, she buckled down and enrolled herself in enough night school classes to make up for the classes she had failed over her four years and graduated on time. But none of that should matter now. She was officially a high school graduate at this moment, a year early because she skipped the fourth grade. Why should she have to sneak around with Shane? Why was Man still threatening to beat him up? Why was he always so angry with her? These questions ran through her mind, but she didn't dare pose them out loud. Instead, she sang in her head.

With the last unanswered question hollered in her face along with a forceful finger jab and spray of spittle, Kyrie forced her eyes downward. Man's voice had transformed into a growl-like stage whisper.

"While you live in this mother-fuckin' house, you will do what the fuck I say. And you wanted to go away to college! Shiiiiit! That's why you're not going away to no fucking college – that's right – staying your ass right the fuck here- so I can keep your ass in check. You didn't do shit but fuck up in high school anyway, so you better be lucky you were even good enough for the city college school you got into."

"Can I just move out on my own, then? I have a job." The trepidation she felt as the words slipped through her lips was unparalleled to any feeling she had ever encountered. The words had been delivered by an unknown sender. Move out? The idea was truly inchoate. Kyrie didn't have the faintest sense of where it came from. She imagined at that moment that the words had formed on her lips even before the conscious thought developed in her brain, but she knew that was impossible. And while the abject fear of Man's reaction was stifling, she was confident about her desire to disappear from this space, however impromptu the idea.

Man reached out and grabbed her shirt collar and pulled her close. She could really smell him now. She tried to hold her breath to reject the odor invading her nostrils. "Let me tell you something, you little ungrateful bitch. You're not going anywhere! You ever try to leave here, they will find your ass in the bottom of the Hudson River. Now try me on that." He released her, shoving her indiscriminately, and walked into the bedroom that he and her mom shared, slamming the door behind him.

Kyrie turned and stumbled into her room. Her body wracked with sobs and torpid, she crumpled to the floor. She hated this place. Home? She couldn't even remember if she ever felt like this was home. She sat on the floor, her back against the wall, and allowed the sobs to overcome her, swaying, self-pity rocking her violently and completely to her core. She felt helpless and alone.

After some time, her sobbing subsided, and she laid down on the floor and tried to gather her thoughts.

"What am I going to do?" she asked the room around her.

"Leave." This was the response that remained with her.

"Can I really do this?" She continued the conversation with herself.

She thought about the Hudson River, which was right below their apartment since they lived a few hundred feet from Riverside Drive. It wouldn't take him long to dump her body. Would anyone notice that she was gone? Sire would. He was annoying as hell, but he loved her. Shane would. What they had was good. She wished she could call Shane now; he would listen to her cry and tell her it was going to be all right. But no, she couldn't risk tiptoeing to use the wall phone right past her parents' room, by the front door. Anyway, it was the middle of the night. Shane's mother would have a fit if she called at that hour, and he might not even be home.

"Try me on that," he had said.

"I don't have a choice," she thought to herself.

She would acknowledge later that it was fear of Man combined with the challenge in his very words that had propelled her forward. She didn't know how long she stayed there, drowning in the enormity of her thoughts.

At some point, Kyrie got up slowly and stood in the center of her room for several minutes, her eyes closed. Then, it was as if she stepped outside of herself because she was no longer thinking about her actions. She started…moving. She grabbed her backpack with her textbooks and added only a few bare necessities; a couple of pairs of panties, one pair of jeans and two shirts, two work outfits. She couldn't take much; she needed to put the backpack on her back as she went down the fire escape.

"The fire escape?" she said out loud to the empty room.

"Yes," she thought.

That is how she would do it. She could not confuse this momentary courage with stupidity. Stupidity would be attempting to walk past her parents' bedroom and her little brother sleeping on his make-shift bed on the living room sofa and out the front door of the apartment. No, she could not be bold in the execution of this risky decision. Instead, she would make her egress through her bedroom window and down the fire escape like a thief in the night, but this time claiming ownership of herself. The fire escape was where she spent a lot of time. The wobbly rusted metal platform with the thick chipping beige lacquer-like paint had seen a lot of Kyrie over the past five years of living in the apartment. The window faced the back of the tenement building around the corner, which had a fenced courtyard filled with abandoned furniture and garbage. It was a mess to look at, but it was sufficient outside scenery to trigger Kyrie's imagination on most days.

16

Climbing out of her window to sit out there reading her library books for hours at a time had been as much of an escape for her as when she realized that she could climb up and down the structure and disappear into the night undetected, for hours on end. The latter was almost as exciting to her as escaping inside the fantasy worlds that her books offered.

Sneaking out nights, challenged by the fear of being caught by Man and the adventure of freedom, she captured some semblance of control. Man didn't generally allow her to leave her block when she wasn't going to school or to work. Even after she was in high school, she could go no further than the front stoop or the park at the bottom of the block, and she always had to take Sire, her little brother, along with her.

Since she had turned 13 and realized that she could pilfer the time and freedom to go wherever she wanted in the still of the night, the fire escape became her solace, her real escape. She would climb gently out of her window, down the ladder, and softly drop the few feet to the courtyard below. Some weeks, she would go out every night. In the summer, she would jump in a taxi and go to her girl Lisa's block on 110th street. Sometimes they would just hang out in Lisa's room, talking. Sometimes they would go to a house party. And sometimes, they would jump on the subway, go down to Times Square and walk around amongst the grown folks and the bright lights, stopping to take pictures in front of the decorative backgrounds for $5.

Sometimes, she would go to Shane's place. Shane's bedroom was right near the front door of the apartment where he lived with his parents. His parent's bedroom was in the back of the railroad-styled apartment, making it easy for him to let her in at night, his slumbering parents oblivious to her presence. It was with Shane that she felt the most free, at first just being with him.

The audacity of this very grown-up decision, to spend the night with a guy in his room, was extremely empowering. He was so very nice to her; although quiet, he liked to listen to Kyrie talk, had an awesome smile, and above all, told her he loved her. He also liked to kiss, and she loved kissing him. Sometimes they would kiss for hours,

17

with him caressing her softly and patiently. When she felt like she couldn't take it anymore, she would tell him to stop, that she wasn't ready. He always listened and would then just hold her.

Eventually, after over a year of her denying his soft pleas for more than just kissing and touching each other, she obliged to what she soon realized was the glory of lovemaking, and then that became a favorite pastime for both of them. She was 15 by then; he was 17 and really experienced for his age, at least in her eyes. She had kissed and petted with other guys, even a few older than Shane, but never felt even the least bit interested in letting them take it all the way.

One guy had called her a "dick tease," but that didn't bother her in the least. Shane later told her he had first had sex at age 11 with a girl a few years older than him, so he had been practicing for several years by the time Kyrie came along. Shane made her feel amazingly beautiful, both inside and out. Afterward, she would lay wrapped in his arms, feeling loved and safe. Yes, tonight, the fire escape would provide for her the exit to freedom that it always had, but it would be her last drop.

Kyrie was accustomed to the short jump to the courtyard below, but the big bag on her back was cumbersome and made her movements clumsy. She climbed out of the window and paused, kneeling on the iron grating, listening intently for any movement inside the apartment. Her tears had dissipated in her earnest preparation to leave, but the sound of her heartbeat was strong in her ears. The September night air was silent and brisk around her, and besides her heavy breathing, she could hear only the traffic sounds from the street.

"Yes, I'm really doing this," she told herself. "If he comes after me after he realizes I'm gone, I can always call the cops." Would she really do that? Her mother would never speak to her again. She wasn't even sure that she had a legal right to be on her own. She had attended her high school graduation ceremony that previous June, enrolled in summer school for the months of July and August to complete the remaining credits she needed. She had received her actual diploma a few weeks before. She was only 17 and, technically, still a minor. She wouldn't turn 18 until the following May.

She pressed down on the window to close it gently, hoping to seal the doubt in her decision in the room that she was leaving behind. She gazed through the dirty pane into the space that had been her resting place for so long. The apartment building was one of many rent-stabilized dwellings in Harlem.

Like her mom, many of its inhabitants received some portion of public assistance. It had been newly renovated housing when they had moved in several years prior. However, such housing wasn't generally well maintained by the building management, and her mother could barely keep food on the table, much less worry about general upkeep. The scuffed-up walls were in desperate need of a paint job. There was a thin sheet-less mattress on bedsprings with no box spring to support it. She had stopped sleeping on it long before because of the sharp metal springs that had become dislodged and had begun protruding through the old and tattered material in various places. The self-made pallet of old blankets on the floor was what she slept on. It was far from the teenage girl's rooms from the pages of her novels, but it was all she knew.

She assumed her mother loved her because she was supposed to and she told her so, but then she would stand by and allow Man to slap Kyrie around and talk to her like she was an enemy in the street. Kyrie shook her head hard and focused on obliterating the creeping uncertainty encroaching her sensibilities. *Where am I going at 3 am?* She closed her eyes briefly to block out the window in front of her and then quickly flung her leg over and began her backward descent down the side of the structure, swinging with ease over to the ladder. Then, she froze, her eyes trained on the living room window of the apartment where she thought she saw movement. She remained still in the darkness, praying the dog in the courtyard across from the window would not emerge and start its barking.

Kyrie made out a small face and eyes peering out at her. It was Sire, her 11-year-old brother. Sire. His name raised eyebrows and provoked discussion all the time. Respect. Man would generally remain stony-faced when questioned about the origin of Sire's name, only explaining himself if he was so inclined. Her mother, who was more verbose with strangers than her husband, would proudly launch into the explanation that he had been named intentionally so that he would always be greeted with respect as a black man. Kyrie used to think it was cute to have a name that always piqued interest and elicited conversation. Right now, she thought, there was so much irony in this story. The fact that Man would require something from others for his son, that he never indulged in a practice of disseminating himself, was the epitome of irony.

Kyrie stared at Sire through the darkness. Of course, he was up; nobody could sleep through all that racket that had transpired a few short feet from where he lay. She put her fingers to her lips, silently motioning a plea for him to remain quiet and not expose her. He nodded his concurrence. He would assume that she was coming back. She suspected that he had uncovered her secret of sneaking out before and just never said anything.

Kyrie pulled her eyes from his, guilt engulfing her. She was leaving him here, and that didn't feel good. She turned her gaze back to her bedroom window again and caught a glimpse of the roach. She thought it odd that she actually saw it in the darkness of the night around her and through the dirty window pane. The roach had worked its way out of the corner and was crawling quickly down the wall. She smiled slightly, released her fingers, and dropped to the cement below. Her feet hit the ground, her body in a crouch, and she took off in a sprint.

As she ran underneath her parents' window, which was slightly ajar, and through the courtyard gate, her thoughts were consumed with one thing only. "I am cornered no more." As she ran, she sang about the black butterfly, sailing across the water, triumphantly.

Kyrie was 17 years old.

20

CHAPTER 2

Bus Ride

"Ain't No Mountain High Enough"
- Marvin Gaye & Tammi Terrell

The upstate bound bus had its own story, its pages bound by the hot burning rubber on the interstate, the words shared up and down the pavement amongst the passengers who rode. Conversations between family members and strangers and unspoken apprehensions made up the chapters spewed by the plethora of riders that boarded and unloaded over the years. Tattered and soiled vinyl upholstery lined the seats where narratives mixed with the inadvertent splashes of bad coffee, Utz potato chips, rest stop sandwich droppings, and Little Debbie pastry crumbs were carelessly ignored and left forgotten in the seams.

The passengers were the mothers, fathers, girlfriends, spouses, and friends that traveled to a designated pickup destination or depot and then boarded the buses for the overnight or 4 am rides to arrive at correctional facilities for their visits. They all shared the corpulent weight of fear or just discomfort about the impending visit to their loved one tucked away in their hearts and minds. A stew of questions ut incarceration filled the crockpot of uncertainty for the family members and friends visiting. Regardless of whether the rider was looking forward to the visit, the bus ride was unpleasant for most, but particularly the young children who really didn't understand much about it. Notwithstanding her precociousness, Kyrie was no exception. She listened to it all and was constantly reminded that the destination was not a place she liked to go.

Kyrie tugged on her mother's sleeve to grab her attention from her fixation out the window. Kyrie wondered what she was thinking about.

"Mommy, Mommy, Mommy!"

"Yes, baby? What is it?"

"Are we leaving New York?"

"No, we are traveling to upstate New York, but we are not leaving New York."

"What's the name of the town we are going to, Mommy?"

"You know the name, Kyrie. It hasn't changed since the last time we came. Plus, I know you read it on the bus sign because you read everything."

"It's Mount Hope!"

"That's right, Mount Hope. So if you knew, why did you ask me, silly!" Pam grinned at her and returned to gazing out of the window.

"Where are we going in Mount Hope?" Kyrie fidgeted in the seat next to her mom. She had to pee. Again. She would hold it until the bus stopped again so as not to make her mommy mad.

Her mother sighed heavily before responding, which was contradictory to the forced cheery tone of her response. "To see Daddy, baby. You know I told you that several times now."

"But how long is it going to take Mommy? I don't want to be on this bus anymore. It's stinky. How come I couldn't stay with Grandma?"

"You know why, Kyrie. The same reason you couldn't stay with Grandma the last time we came and the last time you asked. Because I said so! And that is not a nice thing to say! You see your grandma every day."

"Well, how long is it going to take to get there?"

Her mother sighed. "Not long. Maybe three hours, depending on the traffic."

"Why does he live in Mount Hope? Did he ever live where we live? I don't remember Daddy living where we live." She tried hard to remember, but her only recollection was visiting him upstate.

"Yes, he did for a little while after you were born, but your Daddy will be living in Mount Hope for a while."

Kyrie fiddled with the end of her cornrows. There were two of them, which her mom tidied or re-braided every day. Her signature style, her mom told her. She liked her two cornrows today. She started to pull at the ends, which a casual observer might assume she was doing absentmindedly since she was simultaneously staring expectedly into her mom's face, thinking of more questions to ask her.

On the contrary, her actions were quite intentional. Her thoughts had shifted to how much she wished for the ends of her cornrows to hang onto her shoulders, like the little girl not much older than Kyrie sitting a few seats away. Her mommy always told her that her hair would not hang down like the little white girl's hair did on T.V., but she noticed that this little girl a few seats away was brown like Kyrie, and her braids hung past her shoulders. Kyrie's braids curled under without the aid of any curling agent or rod. While she was interested in the answers to her questions, she was equally intrigued by the stubborn attitude of the braids on her head and figured her questions would distract her mother from her own hair stretching experiment. She peered around the bus seat quickly to try to catch another glimpse of the little girl and her perfectly cooperating hanging cornrows. She couldn't see her. She settled back into her seat. Maybe if she pulled harder, it would work.

"Stop pulling on your hair Kyrie before you make your pretty barrettes fall off. Your daddy misses you and can't wait to see you. Plus, we are going to have such a good time." Her mother's voice was still high-pitched and cheery. That was Kyrie's cue to continue her present line of questioning and hair stretching experiment.

"Well, how come he doesn't live at home with me, you, Grandma, and Granddaddy then? Can't we really have a good time all the time if he was home?" Kyrie really didn't like the long bus rides they took to see Man. She knew she had to call him "Daddy," but she liked calling him Man. That's what her mom called him, so it was also what she called him in her mind. Her mom didn't answer her questions. Instead, she turned her head back towards the window, closed her eyes, and began to sing a melody softly.

One of the hair barrettes had fallen to the floor with the last set of tugs. She glanced up quickly to see if her mother noticed. She was still staring out the window and didn't seem to be paying Kyrie any attention. Kyrie continued pulling, ignoring the discarded hair ornament. She didn't really like that barrette anyway. She turned her attention to a conversation going on between two women sitting two rows ahead of where she and her mother were sitting. One of them almost looked like her Aunt Michelle, but the woman had a scarf tied around her head. She giggled out loud; Aunt Michelle would never leave the house with a scarf on her head.

"So who you got at Otisville?" That came from the Aunt Michelle look-alike.

"My brother, girl. He's doing a 4-7 bid for third-degree robbery. He just got sentenced and transferred here about nine months ago, so this is only my second visit. I told him I would try to come every other month, but it's hard to leave my daughter, even for the day. She's only three years old, and I ain't bringing her to no prison. What about you?"

"My man. Drug charge. First-time offense. He got caught with a little bit of coke on him, but he got the minimum sentence of 2.5 years. His lawyer said he could get out in 18 months, though, so I'm just hoping he don't get into no shit while he's up in there. They got this job training program in there that he's been talking about if he can stay outta trouble long enough to finish it."

"Girl, you ain't lyin'. Last time I took this trip, Dre', that's my brother, got into a fight with some dude and was put into the hole. I found out after I got up here. I waited for almost two hours before the officers told me. And those assholes felt me up when they were searching me! My mama said she ain't coming up here to see his ass because she didn't put his ass in here. It's kind of messed up, but I don't blame her. She really don't need her blood pressure going up, and that is exactly what coming up here would do to her."

The other girl was nodding her head vigorously in agreement. "I know that's right! The way the CO's treat the visitors, you would think that we did something wrong just because we trying to hold these brothers down. It's creepy up here with these guards patrolling the grounds on their big ass horses. I just come to give him something to look forward to – you know it's hard in here. But I'm glad he didn't get sent to Greenvale. My cousin's baby father is up there, and she said it's worse than Otisville."

Kyrie turned back to her mother, bored with the women's conversation, remembering she was afraid of the big horses and wasn't interested in hearing why Greenvale was worse than Otisville. She didn't want to go to either place. Her mother was singing softly. She always seemed to sing when Kyrie asked a lot of questions. Kyrie leaned closer to her to catch the song.

"Oh, Mommy! You're singing 'Ain't No Mountain High Enough.' I like that song!" she squealed.

She started singing along with her.

"Gurrrl, you got a beautiful singing voice," a short thick woman sitting in the row in front of them said. The woman's girth took up both of the seats in the row she was sitting in, so while the bus was filled to capacity, the only empty seat was next to the woman. Kyrie wondered if it was ok that the woman used both seats for herself. She decided she would ask the bus driver if she remembered as they were getting off. The woman had positioned her body sideways so that she could peer at Kyrie and her mother through the gap in the seats.

"You should do something with that voice the good Lord gave you, baby. Yes Jesus! Voice of an angel, I tell you."

"Oh, I am a professional singer – but thank you," her mother replied. She kept humming, a little louder now.

Kyrie asked many more questions during the bus ride. How come Man stayed in Mount Hope which was so far away that it took forever to get to so they had to leave during sleepy time on the stinky bus full of strangers? How come they always came to visit him, but he never came to visit them? How come he never came home? How come he lived in that ugly brick building that was so tall and had hangers untwisted into loops on the roof? How come there were so many policemen with guns at Man's house, and he wore weird clothes, and a whole bunch of other men lived there with him? How come those policemen never smiled, and why did they look through all their bags before they let them see Man? And how come after it took them so long to get there, Man was never ready to see them when they got there, and they had to wait some more, sometimes for hours? Why was it that when Man finally came out, he always had on the same clothes as the last time, and he never smiled? Why must they sit in the same room, with nothing in it but grey metal tables? Why were the board games they kept in the big room always missing pieces?

Her mother just hummed her songs and smiled. Kyrie knew that nothing she said would convince her mother to abandon this trip. Eventually, Kyrie turned her full attention to her braids and books because she was a good reader and her hair was very important to her.

Kyrie was 4 years old.

CHAPTER 3

Free to Flee Home

"Home" - Stephanie Mills

It was 1989, and the Harlem streets were replete with drug pushing and petty thievery. Young people who had the means to don the latest fashion trends might find themselves victimized; their sneakers or suede Ballys stolen off of their feet while standing at bus stops, gold chains snatched at will. Sometimes the perpetrators of the criminal acts were other teenagers. Sometimes it was a crackhead resourceful enough to have a weapon and not desperate enough to have sold or bartered it yet for his next fix.

As Kyrie ran through the night, she was reminded by the foreboding darkness of the two times she had been robbed, both times at gunpoint. The first time, she was 15 and had been sitting at the playground with Shane while Sire played no more than thirty feet away. The gunman had crouched in front of the bench they were sitting on and held the gun trained on them while calmly instructing them to remove their jewelry and place it on the ground in front of him.

The playground was filled with people, and it was the middle of the afternoon, broad daylight. It was over within seconds, and the gunman was gone. The second time, a group of boys had cornered her on the block of her high school. She had been late, so the entire street was empty. One boy held the gun, and another yelled at her to empty her pockets. Both times were quick, and no triggers pulled. She considered herself lucky.

Shell top Adidas, leather bomber jackets, high top Reebok classics, and Gucci tote bags were components of the urban uniform for girls in Kyrie's circles, but she didn't have the money to keep up with these trends even though her Uncle Will did what he could to hook her up with the latest styles. On the night she left, an old pair of yellow Reeboks hit the cement under her window and carried her 110-pound slender frame sprinting from Broadway three avenues across town to St. Nicholas Avenue to the D train station. Reflecting on her appearance, she dismissed the lingering thoughts of danger; she didn't have on anything that would draw a thief's attention despite the 3 am hour.

As she passed Convent Avenue, she thought briefly about going to Shane's, but since she had not forewarned him to listen out for her, there was no guarantee that he was even home. In any event, that would probably be the first place Man would look when he came after her, and Shane's dad would not be a co-conspirator in her shelter. No, Shane's place was not an option – not even temporarily. He would probably think she had lost her mind, but he would support her decision; she was certain of that. She would call him when she settled somewhere. But where?

It wasn't until she was approaching the subway station that she stopped sprinting and began to digest what she had done. "I did it. I left my home." She repeated the words in her mind. But was it really home? She had always heard that home was where the heart is. Stephanie Mills, her most favorite recording artist of the time, had just released her cover of "Home" from The Wiz that past June. By August, Kyrie could mirror the rendition almost exactly. While belting it out might have been a painful reminder of what she lacked, the rhythms soothed her, especially Stephanie Mills' recorded rendition.

Stephanie spoke the first couple of lines before singing the beautiful melody with rhythms boasting all of the comforting characteristics of being home; an abundance of love, safety, and comfort. Kyrie loved the song, although her reality was the opposite. There was no love overflowing in her home, not that she could feel. She felt far from safe and could not recall when she had been comfortable. Now, she had fled where she lived, and it was not until she boarded a Bronx bound D train that she even paused to catch her breath. She sat down and immediately put her head between her legs in an attempt to calm the nausea. "The train is safe," she told herself. She was on her way, but to where? She had just started working and had only received one paycheck so far. She needed to buy some time to save some money, which meant staying with a friend. Kyrie began to mentally run through her options.

Kyrie's very first friend was Yvette. Kyrie and Yvette had met in the 5th grade at P.S. 154, her first foray into public school in Harlem. Neither really fit in, respectively, and had found each other quickly in the lonely space of ostracism, bonding immediately over the "brainiac" label ascribed to both of them by their classmates as well as their opposite physical characteristics. Kyrie had entered the school mid-year, subject to the typical peer scrutiny suffered by every "new kid" who moves into a new neighborhood in the midst of a school year after friendships and cliques have formed and the groove of the routine mastered. However, this was not a reality that she would have been aware of at nine years of age with no history of elementary school social constructs, so she was earnest and hopeful about the prospects of this new academic environment.

She had moved around a bit prior to that, and her mother promised she would remain in this school through the school year. She had not remained at her prior two schools for longer than a few months, so she was clamoring to finally make friends. To her dismay, she was instantly targeted, bullied at recess and after school by unkind classmates as early as the first day. The line of attack generally encompassed taunts about Kyrie's skinny frame, "toothpick" stick legs, awkward and less than trendy attire and hairstyles. Then, there was her instantaneous rise to the top of the class testing percentages for every subject, where Yvette sat perched comfortably.

29

Yvette was as chubby as Kyrie was skinny, and as far as Kyrie was concerned, both the smartest and the nicest girl she had ever met. Yvette had nice clothes, and her hair was always pressed really nice. Yvette was funny and confident, even though the other kids made fat jokes and called her "teacher's pet." Kyrie liked her instantly, and they began a comfortable friendship that carried them into junior high school together, where they both were placed in a special honors program and later both tested for the New York City specialized high schools, successfully gaining entrance together.

Yvette came from a large family that owned a popular neighborhood Harlem business, so she was rich by Kyrie's standards. Yvette's mom was really nice to Kyrie. She spent as much time as Man allowed, which wasn't much, at Yvette's apartment over the years of junior high school. During that time, they ultimately cemented their relationship with the comfortable adage of "best friends." Kyrie lamented that label and their recently dismantled friendship as she sat on the train that morning. The two had slowly grown distant over the prior four years of high school, acquiring different groups of friends and pursuing different interests.

Kyrie smiled wryly. She could acknowledge retrospectively that her tendency as a junior and senior to cut class to hang out in the cafeteria playing cards or just skip school altogether likely forged the distance between them. Yvette was still as smart as she had been in 5th grade and focused on her path to her bright future. Conversely, Kyrie's focus had since shifted to merely getting through the dismal nights at home. For her, being with Shane helped a lot. Cutting class became her way of dealing with the reality that she felt dumb and unprepared in school when she had spent the evening prior crying or writing to Malyka about what was going on in the apartment. She knew that what she should have been doing was her homework and trying to decipher high school algebra and geometry, but her brain just didn't seem to comprehend any of it at all.

The truth was Kyrie spent most of her high school years feeling like she really didn't belong in a school where everyone suddenly was smarter than her. Then, after exchanging angry words, Yvette stopped speaking to her in their junior year of high school after a disagreement.

Kyrie really thought she was looking out for her long-time friend's best interest but later decided that she should have just minded her business because she had lost her first friend. They had barely spoken since. So, Yvette was not an option. Even if they were speaking, Yvette had been accepted to a good college out of state and had surely left New York by now.

Her closest friend in high school, Malyka, was the person that she shared everything with for the last four years and vice versa. Malyka had her own dysfunctional family situation to deal with, starting with being raised by her older sister, a drug addict. Kyrie and Malyka spent their evenings almost since they had met in 9th grade, writing each other letters in which they shared details of their respective existences – every night. They exchanged the letters in school each day and made a gentle competition out of whose letter turned out to be the longest each day.

Unfortunately, the lengths of the letters were dictated by the drama each girl had dealt with the night before. A letter longer than five handwritten pages usually meant a bad night; a ten or fifteen-page letter meant all hell had broken loose. The letters and Malyka's comforting, low-key demeanor had kept Kyrie sane these last four years. But Malyka was gone now and had no more time for their childhood letter writing past time. Malyka had handled escape the right way; she had gone to class, achieved good enough grades, and did well enough on the SAT to make it out. Malyka was away in Massachusetts at Boston College.

There was Ariana, a 21-year-old single mom of the cutest 5-year-old daughter. Ariana lived in the apartment next door to Kyrie and was on her own, raising her daughter. Ariana and Kyrie had become close over the years, a relationship initially triggered by the proximity to Kyrie's apartment and the fact that Ariana heard a lot through the walls. Once Man became aware of the friendship, he forbade Kyrie from hanging out with her. Kyrie knew it was because Ariana epitomized independence and being grown, which was nothing he felt Kyrie should be exposed to, so she usually snuck to hang out in Ariana's apartment. Clearly, Ariana was not an option for her run-away shelter, she mused.

There was Lisa, her "uptown" road buddy, that she had also gone to high school with. Lisa was always good for a good laugh and a good time; she didn't let anything bother her and was really smart too. Lisa was attending a local college like Kyrie, but Kyrie didn't think she was an option. There were already a bunch of older siblings, some with their own children, living in Lisa's apartment where she lived with her parents. Anyway, Lisa practically lived with her boyfriend, who stayed in Staten Island.

There was Tasha, who Kyrie had met at her job at the donut shop in the South Street Seaport a few years back. Tasha was a few years older than Kyrie and from a rough part of Harlem. Tasha was street smart, extremely loyal, had plenty of mouth, and was not scared to fight. Tasha was like a big sister to Kyrie. She understood without having all the details of what Kyrie was dealing with at home. Still, like Lisa, she had too many "folks" in and out of her apartment for her place to be an option. Yes, although a new friend, Candisse was her best bet.

Kyrie had met Candisse in one of her classes in college just a few weeks before. Candisse had a rough exterior and didn't appear initially to be friendly or open to chatting, but something about her had drawn Kyrie to her, and she had kept talking. They went to a local pizza shop after class on that first day and sat and talked for hours. Candisse was someone that Kyrie had let in, and that didn't happen often. Candisse had actually told her just a few days prior, after Kyrie had stayed at her house for so long it was obvious she was avoiding going home, that if she ever needed a place to stay, she was welcome.

It was just Candisse and her mom in a big house in the Bronx, and Candisse assured Kyrie that her mom wouldn't mind Candisse "bringing home a stray," in fact, Candisse had done it before. Ms. Jackson, Candisse's mom, was warm and gruff all at the same time, cooked the best home cooking Kyrie had ever tasted, and always had a plate, a hug, and a sassy remark for Kyrie. By the time the train rolled into the station on 167th Street and Jerome Avenue, she had a plan. She would ask Ms. Jackson if she could stay just for a few months, during which time she could save her money to get her own apartment, or maybe even a place with Shane if he wanted.

The temp agency had just placed her at a fairly large, well-known insurance company. Although she didn't have any formal typing skills, Kyrie had managed a passing score on the typing test. They sent her to interview for an administrative assistant position, and she had gotten the job. She was articulate and confident in her presentation. Thanks to her avid reading over the years, she could easily pepper her dialogue with impressive words and enunciated well.

"You talk so white," people from the neighborhood would say about her.

Kyrie rejected that. "Why do black people that sound intelligent get labeled 'talking white?'" Kyrie would retort. "What does that say about black people's ability to read and learn to speak the English language properly – and just be smart? It makes us sound like we are normally ignorant sounding."

Her friends would laugh and tell her to shut up – she was being too serious. Anyway, she had taken her "white talking self" the week after her high school graduation and quickly registered with a temp agency in lower Manhattan. She was placed in the temp assignment full time after only two weeks, and it was going well. She was an administrative assistant for two managers, one black one and one white one. She pecked her way through the typing they gave her, and luckily, it was infrequent and the memos were short. She handled the phones and meeting scheduling exceptionally well, so they both seemed to like her well enough.

The person she was filling in for was out on maternity leave and scheduled to remain out for six months, so she had some time. She figured if she could keep the temporary placement and save most of her money, she should be able to get her own place in a few months and look for another job before this assignment ended. She had enrolled in Baruch College within the City College University of New York system and was taking her classes in the evening so that she could earn money working a full-time job during the day.

As she looked for a pay phone to call Candisse to let her in, her gait slowed. The fatigue, and the weight of her backpack laden with the clothing and her angst stuffed haphazardly inside, was catching up with her. She dialed the number and prayed Candisse would pick up the phone first and not her mom. What would happen in a few hours when Man realized she was no longer there? She sighed, listening to the phone ringing in her ear. She didn't want to imagine that; she just wanted to imagine a new home.

CHAPTER 4

Cloudy Day

"September" - Earth, Wind & Fire

Everything changed so quickly when Man came home from upstate. They moved from grandma's and granddaddy's house to their own place. Soon after Man returned, her mommy grew a baby in her belly for a long time. Then she brought it home from the hospital. Now it was always in their apartment, and usually crying. It was a boy, and they called him "Little Man," but his real name was Sire. Her mother constantly held him in her arms and didn't have much time to read to Kyrie anymore.

Kyrie was a little sad because she had gone to the nursery school that her grandma worked at for a long time, and suddenly that ended. She had liked it there; the teachers were really nice to her and told her in secret that she was the smartest in the class. Her mom had taught her to read already, so the ABCs and little words they practiced in class were really easy for her, so sometimes she helped her teacher lead the class. Her grandmother worked in the kitchen and was in charge of all the meals, so the food was really yummy.

Now, it was all different. Man was home, the baby was here, and she couldn't play with her friends in nursery school anymore. Her mom said that she had outgrown the nursery school because it only went up to age six, and she was already six years old. Her friends there talked about going to "real school." She had asked her mom whether she would get to go to first grade like everyone else, but she responded that it would be better if she taught her at home. She had heard her grandma and granddaddy argue with her mother about not letting Kyrie go to school. They also argued with her mother about Man. They didn't like Man because he was "no good," they said, which made her mother angry. Pam Graves didn't like it when anyone said anything bad about Man.

The one-bedroom was large, sparsely furnished, and the walls were bare and in need of a fresh coat of paint. A full-size bed sat in the middle of the room, and a tall mahogany bureau stood in one corner. The bureau was the most beautiful piece of furniture Kyrie had ever seen. Its color was dark and rich despite its weathered appearance; each drawer was adorned with massive brass ornate handles that revealed a cavernous interior when opened.

Her grandmother had given her mother the bureau and told her the day she and her grandfather had dropped it off that it had been her great-grandmother's and to make sure she took care of it. Instead of end tables, plastic bins that held the overflow of any belongings that didn't fit in the bureau also provided the counter space for miscellaneous odds and ends that accumulated. There was no crib or bassinet in the room, so Kyrie had been extremely confused about where the baby would sleep when he came home from the hospital.

There was a window in the room. It had no curtain to shroud the interior occurrences from the outside world, but usually, her mother hung a bed sheet to it. The bed sheet often became dislodged from its rudimentary fixture in the window, which Kyrie preferred because she liked having an open view of the sky.

"Where will we put it, Mommy?" It was a few weeks before Pam's due date, and Kyrie had been determined this day to compel her mother to answer her questions. She tugged on her mother's belt loop to get her attention. Pam was hurrying around the kitchen, preoccupied with what she was doing, so she had not heard Kyrie calling her initially.

Pam's belly was large, and she was irritable these days. She mumbled something about Man never being home that Kyrie could barely make out and didn't acknowledge that she had heard Kyrie's question. Kyrie tugged on her belt loop again.

"Where will we put it, Mommy?" she repeated.

"Put what, Ky?"

"The baby. When you get it from the hospital, where will we put it? I don't think it should sleep in the bed with me. I might roll over and smash it."

"Oh no, baby. Your daddy is going to get a bassinet this week. Don't you worry. If not, we can be creative. Those bureau drawers are just about big enough to hold you. We can probably make a bed for the baby inside one of them if we try. And a baby boy is a *he*, not an *it*."

And that is just what her mother had done two weeks later when the baby was born, and there was no bassinet by the time she and the baby came home. Her mother removed the contents of the bottom drawer, relocated the empty drawer from its home in the bureau, and placed it on the floor. She lined the empty drawer with a changing pad and cushioned it with blankets, and it became the baby's bassinet.

Kyrie was intrigued by her mother's ingenuity, and on this day, several weeks later, she was sitting cross-legged on the hard bedroom floor with her chin resting on her wrist, thinking hard. *What other items that were not made for a baby could actually be used for the baby?* She considered the possibilities as she stared at the little bundle sleeping peacefully, although Man's voice was elevated.

Man was arguing with her mother. He was usually yelling and cursing, and as usual, her mother wasn't saying much in response. Kyrie didn't understand a lot about what they were talking about. Although her mother didn't say much, Man kept yelling and saying bad words.

The yelling scared her. Sometimes he would hit her mother in the face. It wasn't like this before he was home when there was no yelling and hitting. Whenever Man hit her mother, Kyrie started singing softly; willing the sound of her voice to block out the words and images of anger in her mind.

The baby stirred. The window was ajar, and Kyrie could hear a familiar song playing in another apartment. Her mother and Man sang that song together sometimes when they were happy. Kyrie looked towards the sky, which was cloudy and becoming more overcast by the minute. He was yelling louder. Kyrie wondered if the cloudy sky made Man's anger intensify. Kyrie could hear the song, but she didn't know the words, so she sang the melody of the song until the chorus came. She knew the chorus, but most of all, she remembered that the clouds were chased away. That's what she wished for.

As she sang, she noticed a plastic dish rack on the floor not far from where she was sitting. Her mother had begun packing. Man said they were leaving town, and the dish rack was on the floor because of the packing process. Kyrie wondered if it would make a good bed for the baby; it looked just about the right size. Man's screaming continued from the other room. Kyrie kept singing. Her voice sounded nice in her ears, like her mommy's voice, which was really pretty.

Kyrie stood up and walked over to the baby and picked him up. She carried him over to the dish rack and laid him inside. The plastic grooves dug into his head, and he started crying. He cried louder than Kyrie's singing. Her mother came running into the room.

"Kyrie, oh my goodness! What are you doing? I told you not to pick up the baby when I'm not in the room. Why would you put him in there? That's not for babies. It's for drying dishes. You know that, Kyrie!" Pam scooped the crying baby up out of the dish rack and rocked him.

Man walked into the room with his belt in his hand and grabbed Kyrie roughly by the arm.

She closed her eyes and sang about chasing the clouds far away.

Kyrie was 6 years old.

CHAPTER 5

The Cool Blue

"Just My Imagination" - The Temptations

Pam Graves had skin that was smooth and dark round eyes that peered directly through your soul, so piercing they seemed to see the person standing behind you. People sometimes commented that she had Diana Ross-like eyes. She stood at average height for a female, 5'6 inches tall, was slender and toned, and wore her hair in a Caesar cut which accentuated her facial features in a very complimentary way. Most often, she spoke with a level of self-assurance, as if her notions were whispered in her ear by God himself, that is, except when she was talking to Man or being talked to by Man. Then, her comportment was deferential and submissive.

When she was not in Man's presence, she carried herself with the grace and air of someone who was well educated even though she had dropped out of high school when she got pregnant with Kyrie at 16. However, most people didn't know that to judge her, so people usually listened to her. To Kyrie, her mother was the most beautiful she had ever seen. For most of her young life, Kyrie also thought her mother was the smartest person in the world, particularly because she was Kyrie's first teacher. She taught her how to read and was always teaching her big words. One of her mantras was, "Words are power. You can speak into existence what it is you want and need."

"I'm hot, Mommy." The sun was hotter than ever that day, and the tag in Kyrie's shirt collar was itching her neck.

"It's mind over matter, sweetie. If you say you are hot, then you're going to be hot. Think cool thoughts, and you'll be cool." The response was offered with such conviction Kyrie believed it. Although it was summer and they were in a big backyard with nice lawn furniture and an in-ground pool, Kyrie started thinking about the snow. Her mother took her hand and walked her over to the edge of the pool.

"Just sit here, Kyrie. You can put your feet in, but that's it. And don't move." Her mother stood above her as Kyrie carefully removed her clear jelly shoes and sat them carefully next to her before walking over to the table several feet away where the adults were playing a card game.

The shimmering cobalt wrapped an intense coolness around Kyrie's feet and ankles, and she momentarily forgot the hot California sun's relentless attack upon her milk chocolate skin. She moved her feet from side to side, relishing the feeling and silently willing it to envelop her entire body while staring at the other children carefree and frolicking in the pool water. They ignored her. She was the new cousin they had just met in the previous weeks, and they had plenty of old cousins and friends that they had known all their lives to play with. There was no incentive to try to get to know her.

Kyrie wondered if she were prettier or more interesting if they would have an incentive to get to know her. She sat quietly, fully dressed with no bathing suit, her feet dangling in the cool of the blue, and she stared, mesmerized by the water's welcoming persona, intrigued by its mysterious character. It was just so hot here, and she wanted so badly to get in. The other kids seemed to be having so much fun. Her mother had told her just to sit there. She couldn't swim, and since all the grown-ups were playing cards, there was no one to go in with her. Her mother had told her that she could swim really well, so Kyrie wished she would get in with her. But Kyrie didn't think that would happen since she didn't even have a bathing suit. So, she just sat, with her legs dangling in the cool blue, and let her mind submerge and float away with the ripples in the water.

Kyrie wasn't sure how long it was since Man had come to live with them. Since she measured time now by the changes in baby Sire, who still couldn't walk or do much, it was probably within a few short months of Man's arrival. They had left New York fairly abruptly and had taken an Amtrak train to Southern California, and they were staying with some people Kyrie didn't know. These were Man's cousins, which meant they were her cousins too. "We are family," her mother repeated earnestly every time Kyrie asked why they had to live with people they didn't know. They were staying with the cousins until they found their own place.

Kyrie had noticed that most of the houses in this neighborhood seemed to have pools, so she hoped that meant when her mother found their own place, it would have a pool too, so maybe Kyrie could learn how to swim. Her mother didn't explain why they had to leave New York in the first place, and Kyrie didn't understand why they had left. Still, she had overheard Man telling Pam that he wasn't answering to any pig parole officer. Kyrie didn't know what that meant, but she did know that California was hot, and they didn't have a place to stay of their own yet, so they were staying with these cousins who had a nice house with a pool.

Kyrie really hadn't spent much time with the kids; they went to school during the day, and in the evenings, Man made Kyrie stay in the bedroom. Kyrie had spent a lot of time staring out the window at the pool since they had arrived, but this was the closest she had been allowed to get to it since they had arrived.

Her mother and Man were engrossed in the card game with the other grown-ups, laughing and having a good time. Kyrie hoped that maybe she would be allowed to attend school where she would meet some new friends. She wondered what the school would be like here. She really hoped her mother would change her mind about home-schooling her and allow her to finally go to school. Pam always said that she could do better teaching her at home than the free public schools, but maybe the free schools in California would be better.

Kyrie closed her eyes and envisioned the new friends, the school building, and the classroom. She had superpowers in her new school. She could read minds and control the thoughts of everyone that she encountered as long as she made eye contact with the person for at least five seconds. Kyrie smiled at this thought as she walked around her new classroom in her mind, stopping in front of each student to hold their gaze. While they were checking her out, she controlled their minds to make them think that Kyrie was pretty and know that she was really nice.

In her daydream, her hair was in the same two cornrows that her mommy did each day, but instead of the ends of her braids curling under, too short to hang, her braids hung along her back. Since the kids thought she was pretty and nice, they really wanted to be her friend. Laughter in her reality brought her back. She opened her eyes just a slit and saw the gaggle of cousins at the other end of the pool staring at her, their play paused and bodies shaking with mirth. She shook her head hard, attempting to release her daydream and, instinctively raising both hands to shield her eyes from the brilliant sun, and simultaneously lost her balance from her perch on the side of the pool, falling into the cool blue. As her head submerged and before the panic set in, she thought, "Wow, this really feels good, just like my imagination said it would."

Kyrie was shivering. She was wrapped in a thick fluffy pink towel, softer than any towel she had ever felt. She sat on the bed in the room that she shared with her mother, Man, and the baby, trying not to cry. The flurry of activity that followed her fall into the pool was exciting; grown-ups screaming, people jumping in to get her out. But after she was out and safe, Man was angry with her for falling in, and she knew that the only reason she didn't get a spanking was because there were so many people around.

Kyrie tried to explain that it was an accident. She told him that she had been pretending in her mind and lost her balance, but he didn't respond. He had grabbed her by her arm and yanked her into the house. The look he gave her when he closed the door of the room and left her was enough to express what would be coming later. She sat on the bed, cuddled in the towel, shivering in the air-conditioned room. She had taken off her wet clothes and put on the dry pair of panties, shorts, and T-shirt that her mother had given her before going back outside.

Her mother had been quiet. Pam never said much of anything when Man was mad at her. Kyrie wished her mother would help her explain herself to Man sometimes so that maybe she wouldn't always get into trouble, especially since her own words always seemed to be stuck in her throat.

The room she was in faced the backyard. Everyone had resumed their fun; the grown-ups had returned to playing their card game and drinking their grown-up drinks. The children were taking turns jumping into the pool. Kyrie wiped at her eyes angrily. She didn't want to be out there anyway, she thought. It was much better in the house, where it was cool.

She turned her attention to her baby brother, who was on the bed sleeping. He'd been sleeping on the bed for hours, it seemed, with her mother checking on him every so often from outside by peeking through the window. He was lying on his back, his little chest moving up and down. Kyrie sat staring at him; she really couldn't figure him out. He seemed so peaceful when he was sleeping, but when he was awake, all he did was cry, but he never got in trouble.

Man called him, "my little son." She didn't remember if Man had ever called her "my little daughter." Why was it that Man never seemed angry at Sire, even when he was crying for nothing? Kyrie stared at him, willing him to wake up so she could play with him, or maybe her mother would come in the house to change his diaper and Kyrie wouldn't be all by herself anymore. Staring at him was not working. Kyrie reached for the pillow behind her on the bed and placed it gently over his face, pressing down slightly. That should wake him up.

"Kyrie, stop it!" Pam was screaming at her from outside the window.

Kyrie moved the pillow, staring down at baby Sir, his chest rising up and down, eyes still closed. Running footsteps were approaching the closed bedroom door. She squeezed her eyes tightly and imagined herself submerged in the cool blue. A tear fell onto her cheek. She had no idea why she had done it, and surely, she was deserving of whatever she had coming. She shoved her head under the pillow to momentarily block everything out and while she searched for the song to press play in her mind. Enveloping her fears within the music in her head, she sunk deep into her imagination, her mind running away wherever it could go.

CHAPTER 6

Bullet in the Night

"Midnight Train to Georgia"
- Gladys Knight & the Pips

The house they rented in California didn't have a pool, but it did have a mango tree in the front yard. It was not a tall tree, but what it lacked in height, it compensated in girth and plentiful branches that stretched long and hung low under the weight of fleshy mangos. Sometimes Kyrie would watch her mother sit underneath it, her legs crossed, eyes closed. Meditating, she said. Kyrie thought for sure she saw her inhaling the tree, taking in its sweet scent with such deep respect and appreciation. The magnanimous trunk and shade-producing limbs provided many days of reading pleasure for Kyrie and sometimes an audience for Kyrie's one-girl concerts. For the little time they spent in the house with the mango tree, the mangoes made her mother happy; she picked them often, cut them swiftly, and ate them plentifully. However, Kyrie's introduction to the succulent fruit was also her last.

"That is a very pretty and ripe mango baby. It looks just right." Her mother was preparing some carrots for juicing while she watched Kyrie carefully arranging her first mango in the bowl in the first week of their residence there.

"It fell right into my lap while I was reading." She returned to sit under the mango tree to continue reading her book and quickly devoured the bowl of fruit. Within a few minutes, her body became a minefield of tiny ants tunneling miniature holes into her pores. She jumped up and ran into the house.

"Mommy, Mommy! My body is burning!" Her mother grabbed her and pulled her into the bathroom, peeling her clothes off of her as she tugged her. When Kyrie faced the bathroom mirror, she gasped at the image. Her body was covered in a sheath of large welts that itched and burned simultaneously. The welts lasted for hours. Her mother gave her medicine and lathered her body with the gel of the aloe plant also growing in the yard. That was the last time Kyrie had mango as a child, but it didn't stop her mother from enjoying the wonderful fruit.

The house was not sprawling like the cousins' house. In fact, it was small, and it didn't have a pool. It didn't matter to Kyrie; she was glad they had moved from the Cousins. It didn't feel normal to her that they lived with another family that she didn't know. She had constantly felt like she was under their gaze, her discomfort scrutinized by strangers. They looked at her funny, especially after the pool and pillow episode. Plus, she missed her grandma and granddaddy very much.

Her grandma hugged her and called her "Grandma's baby." Her granddaddy took her to McDonald's without her mother knowing because her mother didn't allow her to eat beef or fast food. Anyway, when her mother told her that they would be moving to their own house in SoCal, Kyrie felt happy. It was a house that would be all theirs, at least for the time being.

There was a large living room where Kyrie and her mother spent a lot of their time and one bedroom that they all shared. Kyrie liked the house enough, although it was lonely because there were no kids in the neighborhood. She did her schoolwork that her mother gave to her daily and read books, which passed the time quickly. At night she fell asleep to a book and usually didn't wake up until morning unless Man came in late making a stir; like the night they left the little house in SoCal and the mango tree.

"Pam! Paaam!!! Come out here! Shit! Paaaaam!"

Kyrie dropped soundlessly to the floor and crawled stealthily as a cat until she could peer through the cracked door that her mother had neglected to close tightly when she hurried into the living room to Man lying on the couch. She could see that the kitchen clock read 2:35 a.m. Man was yelling her mother's name so loud that Kyrie realized this had to be something altogether different from his usual agitation.

His face was scratched and bleeding. His breathing was heavy, panting. He seemed to be in agony.

"What happened?" Pam asked. "You're hurt. Oh God, you're bleeding, baby! What happened?"

"Arrrg! Dammit, Pam! I had to bust a cap in somebody to get out of a jam. They were chasing me…I had to run through the woods. Then I got hit! I got shot!"

"What! Oh my God, baby, let me see." Pam got down onto her knees to kneel in front of the couch where Man lay, writhing in pain. She quickly grabbed a pair of scissors lying on the nearby table and cut Man's jeans around his thigh where the material was bloody.

"Ok. I see it. You need a doctor."

"Are you fucking crazy? I can't go to the hospital. That will involve the cops, and I will wind up locked back up, this time in California." Man grabbed Pam's arm.

"Pam, look at it. How bad is it?" Kyrie stared through the slit in the door. As she watched her mother examine Man's leg, she realized that she was trembling. She was petrified.

"I think I can see the impression of the bullet in your thigh, so maybe it's not that deep."

"You have to take it out," Man said. "I don't think it's deep. Then wrap my leg up, and we need to get the fuck out of here."

Pam looked up at him in alarm. "What do you mean? Leave California? We just got here. We just signed the lease to rent the house…"

"Arrrg. Shit. This hurts like hell, Pam. I don't have time to explain. Just get this shit out of me and then pack up whatever we can so we can be on the first train out in the morning, or this heat will be at our doorstep. I got into some shit, Pam. We've got to go. These motherfuckers will find out where we live, and they will find me! We can lay low in Georgia for as long as we need to. I've got family there."

Her mother stood up without another word and walked hurriedly into the kitchen. She turned on the burner on the stove and began to boil water and gather towels, rubbing alcohol, peroxide, and a sharp instrument from the kitchen drawer, which she put into the fire. When she turned around, her eyes fell upon the door left ajar, behind which Kyrie was kneeling on the floor, still peering out. Their eyes met, and Kyrie quickly pivoted on her knees, crawled back to the bed, and jumped in just as she heard her mother's quick footsteps cross the floor and the door click shut.

Kyrie lay there in the bed, very still, afraid to move. Minutes later, she heard Man screaming, and she knew that her mother was doing what he had asked. Kyrie squeezed her eyes shut tight. She began singing softly and tried to escape to her pretend place.

It was sometime later that night when her mother shook her awake and told her to get dressed. Pam had already put all her things from the bureau into their suitcase. Kyrie asked no questions this time. As the morning dew was settling on the tree leaves, and the sky was parting to usher in the light of a new day, they walked through the front yard with the mango tree and made their exit into the waiting taxi.

A short while later, they all boarded a Georgia bound Amtrak train. Man was limping and wincing but walking, so Kyrie figured that her mother must have done good. Pam carried baby Sire in her arms, sleeping, unaware of the evening's transgressions that had produced a set of new circumstances upon their lives and a transition to yet another new beginning.

Kyrie had felt the California sun, dipped in the cool blue, and enjoyed the momentary shade of the wide, spanning branches of a wondrous mango tree. Then, as quickly as the journey had begun, she had ingested and was infected with its sweet fruit by day and glimpsed the impact of a lone bullet by night. Their time in California was short-lived. While they were headed to Georgia for a short while, they would eventually make it back to New York. She had prayed for something to happen to require them to leave California, and it did. She smiled. Maybe her mind powers worked after all. She decided that it didn't matter that they were leaving after midnight on a train to Georgia.

Kyrie was almost 7 years old.

CHAPTER 7

Heavy Air

"Wake Up Everybody"
- Teddy Pendergrass

A hug speaks volumes when words are either lost in the warm belly of love and affection or immobilized by a reservoir of anger, frustration, or disappointment. Kyrie would learn as an adult that reticence was often more productive than unleashing the litany of painful words upon the offender when it was the latter. When they returned from the brief but eventful stint in SoCal and short stay in Georgia, her grandma and granddaddy's hugs spoke abundantly to her. She knew that because she always remembered the hugs, despite how much time had passed. Her grandparents were happy and relieved to see her; the tightness and desperation in their grasp said plenty, even to a child who had barely seen seven years. Kyrie didn't remember much about their return to New York, but the hugs were so very satiating she felt them wrapped around her like a snug blanket in frigid weather.

Her granddaddy owned some real estate and managed other properties. They moved into an apartment building on Merrick Boulevard in Queens that he managed. Despite his intolerance of Man, her granddaddy always said that as long as he had breath in his body, his grandchildren would always have a safe place to live.

"I want the best for you, Ky." Kyrie loved when her granddaddy called her "Ky." The time in the apartment building on Merrick Boulevard was a blur to Ky. The days blended into months and perhaps years, but Ky had no sense of the passage of time except that she didn't attend school for most of it. Pam gave her lessons to do during the day. While Kyrie learned quickly, she didn't have any other children to play with until her introduction to Usian Shule.

"Your father and I have decided to send you to school." Kyrie was sitting on the floor, in between her mother's thighs while her mother cornrowed her hair for the week. Up until her mother's comment, she had been trying to keep herself awake. She perked up immediately at the mention of school.

"Yippee! Where is it?" Kyrie asked, barely able to contain her excitement.

"Usian Shule is a few minutes away, not far from your grandma's house, in St. Albans."

"Usian Shule! That's a funny name." Kyrie laughed.

"Well, Usian Shule is an independent school. My cousin, Kadiri, just opened it. He practices the right principles, and he plans to teach Swahili and some African customs and traditions. Usian Shule means wisdom school in Swahili."

"I didn't know you had a cousin who is a teacher, Mommy! That's so cool!"

"Well, Kadiri was never an actual teacher, but he has been researching and developing his curriculum for long enough, so I'm a believer."

"Are there going to be other kids there with me?" Kyrie asked.

"I don't know how many he will actually get to enroll, but he and Sabra have five children of their own, and they're all going to be attending. You've met them. They all have dreadlocks, remember? That's a classroom as far as I'm concerned."

Kyrie was ecstatic. Even if only two other children were in her class, it would be better than her current solitary academic experience. This plan to send her to Usian Shule seemed to be one that Man was supportive of. She overheard him talking to her mother about it later that evening.

"So Kadiri is actually doing it. Damn! A black man starting up his own school in 1979. Maybe we are actually getting somewhere." Man leaned back and took a swig of his beer.

"He did have some problems with the original space, but he was able to lease an even larger space up the street – you know the old community center down on Linden Boulevard, off of Farmers? That's where Usian Shule will be. It's a really nice space, big and open. He was able to get desks from a friend of his who was a janitor at an old public school that closed down."

"Well, if he sticks with the idea of teaching these kids about African culture and embracing African traditions instead of assimilating into white America's acceptable norms, Kyrie will be there front and center. We need to build self-esteem in who we are, and then maybe we will have some pride and be willing to take what is rightfully ours."

Man took another wig of his beer. "I'll take Malcolm's preaching of by any means necessary before Martin Luther King's marching for equality any day. Shiiiiit! Turning the other cheek and all that peaceful shit doesn't get black folks anywhere! Black folks walking around New York with amnesia about how our ancestors got to this country, robbed of our culture and freedom – and then they act like anything African is a disease they don't want to have anything to do with!

"Things are not going to get better for Black people until we take matters into our own hands. Like educating our children ourselves! Does Kadiri still plan to teach that tribal language? What is it? Swahili?" Man downed the rest of his beer.

53

"Yes. Swahili is like a first language in his house. Did you know that *kadiri* means capable in Swahili? I'm not sure what Sabra's name means, but it's also Swahili. He and Sabra changed their names, but all of their children have Swahili names from birth. And you know they dress in African print dashikis every day, and all those kids have dreadlocks. This will be a great cultural experience for Kyrie."

"This will be great for Kyrie because she won't be learning the white man's version of history before she learns something about her own culture. Shit, I told you before that you should have been teaching her about her culture already!"

Kyrie sighed. As usual, the conversation had turned to Man criticizing her mother for what she should be doing better. Kyrie had heard enough. She was satisfied that she would actually be going to Usian Shule because Man was in complete agreement. Kyrie didn't much care about all of the cultural stuff that her mother and Man were focused on. It was being with other children at Usian Shule that made going there exciting for Kyrie. Anything would be preferable to waking up in their apartment and remaining in that same space all day with only her mother for company and then reading in the evening. Swahili lessons were a part of the curriculum, which was interesting to Kyrie, although she did not retain much from her tutelage in her later years.

"Habari gani!" This was the greeting in the morning. Discipline was doled out at Usian Shule in a memorable way, but there were no beatings. Instead, if the students were goofing around and not being attentive, a common consequence was to be sent to the front of the room to "hold the air."

"Is that Kyrie talking when she's supposed to be completing her work?" Cousin Kadiri would say.

"But I wasn't doing anything," Kyrie would protest.

"Kyrie, to the front of the room and hold the air for 5 minutes." And to the front of the room Kyrie would go and stand with her arms straight out in the air, palms up as if she were about to do a jumping jack. Holding the air was funny at first. Kyrie giggled at the ridiculousness of standing in front of the room with her arms out.

After the first minute, the weight of her arms was not funny at all. Going into the third minute, it felt as though ten-pound bricks were resting on your palms. The air was heavy at Usian Shule, but it was not as heavy as Man's hand, so it wasn't bad for Kyrie, and she didn't complain.

Kyrie's time at Usian Shule took residence in her memory as one of the best times of her young life.

Kyrie was 7 years old.

CHAPTER 8

New addition

"Papa Was A Rolling Stone"
- The Temptations

The angry talk between her mother and Man was usually about there not being enough money. Kyrie called it angry talk in her mind because usually, when Man talked to her mother, his words were hard, and he sounded angry. He was often shouting, and he was telling her mother what she needed to do as if she wasn't a grown-up just like he was. Then Kyrie would hear the sound of the heavy hand meeting soft flesh. The sound sent Kyrie's face directly under her pillow to block whatever was coming next. Her mother would react then and try to reason with him.

The good thing was that Man was not home a lot. He stayed out late into the night. Kyrie heard him come in sometimes if he was loud. Kyrie didn't know what he did when he wasn't there, but she knew that he drank liquor and smoked weird cigarettes that he made himself by rolling little green sprigs into white paper when he was home. "Bamboo" was the name on the packaging, and it was always lying around the house. He called the finished product a "joint."

Kyrie was so confused about how he could smoke cigarettes and joints when her mother had a picture hanging on the wall from a magazine showing a healthy brain next to a cigarette smoker's brain. Kyrie would sit and gaze at that picture a lot. Her mother explained everything that was happening to the cigarette smoker's brain, and it was disgusting to Kyrie. Kyrie really couldn't understand how the cigarette brain continued to function at all, given how nasty it looked, but that didn't seem to bother Man at all. He kept on smoking.

Man also sometimes had white powder in a piece of tin foil that looked like the kind of sugar or cake flour that her grandma used to make yummy goodies. Kyrie had come across this once while at her grandma's house with her mother one day. They were in the bedroom, and the foil had fallen onto the bed from her mother's open bag. Kyrie was examining it further when her mother walked into the room.

"Kyrie, what are you doing? Did you take that out of my bag?"

"It was on the bed, Mommy. It fell out," Kyrie replied without looking up. She had opened the foil and was inspecting the fine white powder. Her mother gently removed the tin foil from Kyrie's hand and sat down on the bed next to her, holding the tin foil in her hand, staring down into the packet silently. Kyrie was not worried. She didn't know if she had done anything wrong, but her mother rarely got really angry, even when she was bad.

"Is that the flour that Daddy puts in his nose?" While Kyrie referred to her father as "Man" in her mind, she knew that she had to call him Daddy when talking to him or about him to her mother. Anything other than "Daddy" would not be good. She had tested that out.

"Can we put it in our noses, Mommy? Is it medicine to make the sniffles stop?" Man did a lot of sniffling, so she wondered if the white flour was medicine that helped his cold. She didn't have a cold, and neither did her mother, but perhaps the medicine also helped to keep the sniffles away. The question snapped her mother out of her silence. She turned to Kyrie, who was sitting crossed leg next to her. Her chin was resting in her palm as she stared at her mother expectedly, waiting for the answer.

58

"This is not flour, Kyrie, and you should never touch it again if you see it sitting around. And you should never, ever, put it in your nose."

"But what is it for then? Is it sugar? Is it yours or Daddy's? Can I taste it?"

Her mother exhaled hard. "Yes, it's Daddy's. I'm holding it for him, but it's not flour or sugar, and it's not sweet. Here."

Pam stuck her tongue out and quickly grazed her pinky finger over the tip of her tongue to wet it. She then stuck the wet pinky into the white powder and held it up in front of Kyrie. A light film of the powder was on her mother's pinky, just inches in front of Kyrie's face.

"I'm going to let you taste this, so you see it's not sugar and flour or anything good to eat, and you have to promise me never to bring it up. Never tell anyone about it, and never touch this if you ever see it again. Promise?"

"I promise, Mommy." Kyrie stuck out her tongue, and her mother grazed her pinky over it. The white powder was not good at all. It was bitter, and the tiny bit that went down her throat made her throat sting. She didn't like it at all.

"That's nasty, Mommy," Kyrie exclaimed with a frown. "I don't want to put that in my mouth or nose! Yuck!" She jumped down off the bed and left the room, having heard the front door open and shut. "Granddaddy's here!" She had lost interest.

Around the time Sire started walking, there was a lot of angry talk in their apartment. This angry talk was different because it was coming from her mother, who was rarely the angry talker. In addition to the angry talk, Pam was also crying a lot.

Kyrie heard her mother say, "How could you do this? You couldn't keep it in your pants while I was pregnant? You did this to me? You brought her here, to my house. I know you did!"

Kyrie didn't understand much of what this meant initially, but at some point, she figured out that there was a person, a lady, that Man had brought to their apartment, and her mother didn't like it. Over the next several months, Kyrie overheard plenty of similar conversations between her mother and Man.

One peculiar grey day, her mother laid out a nice outfit for Kyrie to wear and told her to get ready while she dressed Sire. The day was odd to Kyrie because her mother didn't get dressed.

"Why aren't you dressed, Mommy?"

"I'm not going anywhere," her mother replied, her voice high pitched and fake sounding. "You and your brother are going out with your dad."

"Without you?" Kyrie asked. She was alarmed; she couldn't recall any instances where they went out with Man and without her mother. "Where are we going, Mommy?" Pam didn't respond.

"Just get ready, Kyrie. Your dad will be back soon, and you need to be ready."

When they left the apartment, a friend of Man's was waiting outside and drove them to a strange house not far from where they lived. Man didn't introduce them, so Kyrie never learned his name.

"Wait here for a minute," Man said to Kyrie. He went into the house for several minutes while Kyrie sat in the back seat, pulling Sire into her lap to stop him from fidgeting to get out of the car as soon as the car stopped. Man returned and ushered them out of the car and around the side of the house into a side door. His friend did not get out of the car.

Kyrie held Sire's hand as they went into the house through the same side door that Man had entered previously. They entered into a very small room. Within it, another door was closed, which Kyrie imagined led to the rest of the house. The room was mostly bare, containing only two small bassinets and a small folding chair.

60

Kyrie glanced around, surprised that there was no adult in the room and that the bassinets were sitting there, alone. The room didn't even have any nursery room decorations. However, particularly strange to Kyrie, augmenting the already peculiar nature of the day, was that no one was tending to the small inhabitants of the bassinets. Kyrie wondered if someone had brought the bassinets into this lonely, uninviting space, especially for their visit. Kyrie stood awkwardly by the door, unsure as to what she was supposed to do. Man had picked Sire up and was holding him in his arms, standing over the bassinets that were side by side.

"Come over here, Kyrie," Man said gruffly. Kyrie walked over to the bassinets and peered in. A little baby was lying in each of them, both appearing to be little girls with symbolic pink satin headbands around their foreheads.

"Kyrie, these are your sisters. They are twins." Kyrie stared at the babies, confused. How could these babies be her sisters? And twins?

Man put Sire down and picked up one of the babies from the bassinet, holding her close to his chest. The other was sleeping, so he just rubbed her back with his free hand.

"Do you want to hold her?" he asked Kyrie.

"Um, ok," Kyrie replied quickly. She sat down in the metal folding chair and held her arms out so that Man could place the baby in her arms. She stared down at it. She was so confused. Her brain had transformed into a racetrack with questions speeding around like cars. She could barely think over the roar of the engines revving.

Was Man going to explain what had happened to bring them to this place? Who was caring for these two babies in this empty room, cold and unwelcome in its bareness, with no baby pictures on the walls and no baby things around? Why hadn't her mother told her she was growing two new babies in her tummy, and why didn't her mother's tummy get big and hard this time, like it had with Sire? Why were these babies here in this strange house and her mother back at their apartment, waiting for them to return? Would the babies be leaving with them now? Whose house was this, and where were the grown

61

people who lived here? Were they hiding? Why were the hidden people not watching over the babies? How would her mother have money to buy milk for two new babies when they didn't have enough for themselves now? These were the questions racing the track. She didn't ask them because her mother wasn't there, and she didn't dare pepper Man with them.

Man picked up the second baby after giving Kyrie the one he was initially holding. After a few minutes, he put the baby back down into the bassinet and then bent down to relieve Kyrie of the bundle she was holding. Sire was running around the room in a circle; he had no clue what was going on, nor did he seem to care. Kyrie peered into both bassinets to get another look. Why, if these were really her sisters, was their skin the color of butter when both Kyrie's and Sire's skin was like a Hershey's kiss. Kyrie continued to stare at the little babies and remained silent.

As she stared, she caught a tiny bracelet on the baby that she had been holding. She leaned in closer to get a good look at the inscription. "Copper," it read. She wondered if that was the baby's name and whether the other baby had an identical bracelet since they were twins. Man did not tell her their names, and she did not ask. However innocuous the queries were, she kept them to herself. While he seemed to be in a pleasant enough mood, Man's temperament was generally unpredictable. She would not risk her questions soliciting the ire that was often lying in wait.

They remained in the room for a short time longer. Kyrie kept thinking someone would appear, but that never happened. Eventually, Man escorted them back to the car where his friend sat waiting and then returned to the house through the same side door where he remained for just a few minutes more. He returned to the car accompanied only by a scowl and issued a perfunctory, "Let's go," and they were off; the enigmatic visit was over.

Sire, oblivious to it all, fell asleep as soon as the car pulled off. During the ride back to the apartment, Kyrie remained quiet, anxious to get back home and talk to her mother. Man offered no explanations.

The apartment was quiet when they arrived, void of the usually singing or music playing her mother generally had going on. Man deposited a sleeping Sire onto his bed, did not speak to her mother, and left abruptly with his friend, who he had told to wait for him. After the door closed behind him, Kyrie went into her mother's room.

She was lying on the bed, her back to the door, her body very still.

"Mommy, we're back. Mommy, are you awake?" Kyrie shook her several times, and after a few minutes, her mother replied, "Not now, Kyrie, I'm resting." She said that without opening her eyes, but Kyrie was leaning over her and noticed that her face was wet.

They never did talk about that day, and the events of that day were never repeated. Kyrie buried her questions in the depths of her young mind, in the tunnel she had begun to dig some time before. It was the tunnel where her curiosity, fears, resentments, hopes, and desires began to lay the tracks of her life.

CHAPTER 9

High Rise No Lie

"The Ghetto" - Donnie Hathaway

They left Queens one day to live in Manhattan. Kyrie didn't really have a sense of how much time had passed since they had returned from California, but she felt like they were not staying in any one place for a very long time. Sire was getting bigger and was walking very well. Kyrie no longer asked why they were leaving one place to live in another because the questions hung in the air like invisible cobwebs, never addressed as if they were not uttered. Instead, she became fastidious when conversations were going on around her, sometimes picking up enough details to construct her own ideas about what was going on. Recurring themes were money and the fact that there was not enough of it, so Man would tell her mother that she needed to do something different to make it. Kyrie noticed that Man didn't do anything except tell her mother what she needed to do, which made Kyrie angry.

Pam mostly sang. She sang background for recording artists, sang in groups, and did what she called gigs. She was always singing to make money because that's what she really loved to do. However, the money she earned from singing was often not enough, and Man was usually very loud when he told her mother that.

Kyrie also overheard that Queens had become too hot for Man. It took some time for Kyrie to figure out that "too hot" didn't mean the sun was hotter in Queens than it was in other places. The more she overheard, she began to understand that it meant that the police were coming around a lot more in the neighborhoods he was known to hang around in, asking about him. Kyrie didn't quite understand at that time why the police were looking for him, but she would hear Man tell her mother that the cops had visited his mother's house "again," questioning his whereabouts.

Kyrie's Uncle Will came to see them often. Uncle Will was Pam's younger brother and was a lot of fun. Kyrie loved when her Uncle Will came; he would bring her a toy and lift her up on his shoulders. He usually came to give Pam money when they needed it, which was often. Kyrie would hear her Uncle Will tell her mother about stuff happening that Man was involved in, but she didn't understand most of it, so she didn't usually remember it.

So, when Kyrie overheard that they were leaving Queens to live in Manhattan, specifically Harlem, she assumed it was because of Man. She just hoped that they wouldn't be going far away again. The emergency departure from California had left an unsettling impression on Kyrie, and she feared going through something like that again.

The move to Harlem came quickly, even though they didn't have a place of their own when they moved initially. Pam was waiting for something to come through for them in Harlem, so the plan was for them to stay with friends while they waited. Sharon and Jitterbug lived in a housing development called River Park Towers in the Bronx. Kyrie didn't know how long they stayed with Sharon and Jitterbug, nor did she remember much about them or their stay. She always remembered the building was a high rise, and the apartment they stayed in was on a really high floor. Being up high remained with her because of the night of the baby and the window. She also knew that she didn't like Jitterbug. He acted crazy.

There was only one bedroom in this apartment, so her mother put Kyrie and Sire to bed in the bedroom at night, and the adults would hang out in the living room until late into the night. At whatever point in the night when the adults were finished with the hangout time, her mother would move Kyrie and Sire to the pullout couch in the living room, where the four of them would sleep together.

One night, Kyrie was in the bedroom well after bedtime, lying with Sire beside her. She was not sleeping because she rarely slept when the grown-ups were hanging out. She was always nervous because frequently, a loud argument would occur. Man was usually the loudest voice in those verbal sparring matches. The loud yelling scared her.

On this particular night, Man and Pam were in the living room hanging out with Sharon, and there was mostly talking and laughter for most of the evening. Sharon and Jitterbug had a three-month-old baby sleeping in a crib in the bedroom where Kyrie was lying with Sire. Kyrie believed she had dozed off when a loud voice jarred her awake, and she sat straight up in the bed. It was Jitterbug's voice yelling, a voice that she had not heard before she drifted off.

"Where is my motha-fuckin son?" Jitterbug's speech was garbled, and his words slurred.

"What the hell is wrong with you, Jitterbug...coming in here with all that crazy talking shit this time of night. Keep your voice down. The kids are sleeping!" Sharon's voice was quiet and tinged with anxious energy.

"Don't tell me to keep my voice down in my own damn crib!"

Kyrie could hear him clearly, although the bedroom door was closed. He was louder than usual, and his voice sounded different. "Something is wrong with him," Kyrie whispered into the darkness.

"I know all about yo-your shit, Shhh-Sharon. I'ma hurt you, dammit. Where's my fuckin son? I heard you gonna leave me and take him somewhere. No, you not, godd-ddammit. I'll ff-ucking kill you first. Ya hear what I say?"

The slurring was coming closer. He was in the corridor leading to the bedroom now.

"Jitterbug, you are talking crazy. You've been smoking that shit, haven't you? I told you I'm not doing this anymore! We got a baby now. You said you were going to leave that shit alone. Jitterbug! Jitterbug, where are you going? Please, the kids are sleeping." Sharon's tone had transitioned to pleading. They were now right outside the bedroom door.

"Come on, man. Come on back in the living room and sit down. You want a beer?" That voice was Man's.

"No, I don't want no beer. Mind yo fucking business! You know you my main motha-fucka, but you in my crib. I wanna see my goddamn son right now."

There was a scuffle, and the bedroom door came crashing in with Jitterbug stumbling in right behind it. He was very tall, and his legs and arms seemed to be everywhere at once. As the door opened, Kyrie sat up and quickly pulled Sire into her arms.

"Please don't hurt me and my brother. Please don't hurt me and my brother." Kyrie was rocking from side to side, chanting the words over and over under her breath. She didn't realize that no one could hear her. She held Sire tight.

Jitterbug regained his balance with surprising agility. Before anyone else could get into the room, he grabbed his sleeping baby from the crib and took a couple of short strides to the window. Kyrie scuttled to the corner of the bed furthest from where he was standing, unable to tear her eyes from the scene unraveling. She continued to hold her brother tight. It didn't appear that Jitterbug even knew she was there. His focus was his newborn baby held in his arms and the adults standing and talking at him a few steps away.

"Y'all motherfuckers think I'm stupid! Y'all not taking my son from me!" He held the baby under one arm while he reached up to pull the window down from the top. Sharon was screaming and crying hysterically.

"Don't come near me," Jitterbug shouted. "I will drop him out this fuckin' window, I swear."

68

"Jitterbug! Stop it! Stop it! Oh Lord, please help me…please don't let him hurt my baby. Please!!! Bug!!!!!" Sharon screeched.

Having gotten the window open, Jitterbug took the baby with both hands and held him outside the window.

"I will drop him to the street before I let you take him from me. You fuckin with me bitch."

Jitterbug began swinging the baby's body from side to side outside the window. Sharon sunk to the floor, screaming hysterically, and began crawling towards Jitterbug and the open window. Sire was also crying in Kyrie's arms, and she held him tighter and buried her face. She felt her mother sink onto the bed with them and encircle them both in her arms. "It's going to be ok. Nobody is going to get hurt." Pam murmured the words softly.

Kyrie did not see what happened next since her eyes were buried in the top of Sire's head, fearing the worse. Somehow, Man had been able to distract Jitterbug enough to pull him and the baby down to the ground. It was over almost as quickly as it had begun.

Sharon grabbed the baby from Jitterbug's grasp once Man had him on the floor, and then Man wrestled Jitterbug and pinned his arms until he was subdued. Then it was over. No baby got dropped out of a high-rise window that night. Kyrie felt really relieved about that because it was really high up. That was no lie.

Sharon didn't put her baby back in the crib that night. Pam stayed with Kyrie and Sire until they fell asleep that night. They left Sharon and Jitterbug's apartment a few days later. Pam had worked out a new situation that would hold them over until an apartment in Harlem that she was on a list for came through.

Kyrie never told anyone about that night until she was an adult, not even when the nightmares about the baby, her, and Sire, being unceremoniously tossed out of a high-rise building began.

Kyrie was almost 8 years old.

CHAPTER 10

Harlem, Sweet Harlem

"Rapper's Delight" - The Sugar Hill Gang

Harlem was loud in a jamboree way. It was colorful and vibrant. Harlem had a monolithic black vibe like no other New York City community with its idiosyncratic cultural characteristics. Home of the 1930's Harlem Renaissance and labeled the jazz capital of the world, the neighborhood beginning immediately north of 110th street and Central Park West and running straight into Washington Heights was its own independent melting pot of the wide-ranging diaspora encompassing African-American, British West Indian, and Latino cultures. Beyond the structural construction of brick tenement buildings, city-operated housing projects, and historic brownstones, most streets offered a panoply of diverse choices that personified its inhabitants' essence and needs.

On Lenox Avenue, or Malcolm X Boulevard as it was renamed in 1987 but rarely referred to as such by Harlemites, one would find Sylvia's fine soul food dining, an African Methodist Church storefront, a table set up and run by a bow tie-wearing member of the Nation of Islam to sell the Nation of Islam publication and $3 bean pies, a West Indian restaurant, a liquor store, a Chinese restaurant and on 135th

Street, The Schomburg African American cultural museum directly across from Harlem Hospital. On Adam Clayton Powell Jr. Boulevard, also known as Seventh Avenue, Harlem boasted its very own Harlem State Office Building. Tucked in between Seventh Avenue and Lenox on 138th Street was the landmark Abyssinian Baptist Church, and just south of 125th and Seventh Avenue, there was J&J Records, a real black-owned community business.

On Eighth Avenue, also with its African American historical moniker, Frederick Douglas Boulevard, one would find several black-owned funeral parlors, and eventually, its own Magic Johnson AMC theatre would open in the nineties. St. Nicholas Avenue boasted a long-standing Popeyes Fried Chicken on the corner of 125th at the mouth of the D train entrance and at the foot of the historical City College area on 145th Street, a fish and chip spot known as no other than "The Little Lady's," only spacious enough for three people to order at a time. That lack of space resulted in a line which stretched to the corner daily until all of the savory deep-fried inventory was exhausted.

In its parallel but central existence was and still is the infamous 125th Street, the commercial spine of Harlem, and officially Martin Luther King Boulevard, home of the world's famous Apollo Theatre and Harlem's first Starbucks, marking the emergence of gentrification in the late 1990s. Furthest west on 125th, right before hitting the Hudson River, was the legendary but newly incarnated Cotton Club, opened in 1977 and dissimilar from its predecessor locations on 142nd and Lenox Avenue in the 1920s and midtown location from 1936-1940, which, while featuring the most popular black entertainers at the time, was a whites-only establishment for decades.

North of St. Nicholas Avenue on 145th Street through 155th Street, Convent and Amsterdam Avenue and some would include Edgecombe Avenue, was the area that was affectionately referred to as Sugar Hill. The name "Sugar Hill" was earned during the 1920s when the area became a favored destination for the African American elite and financially well off. A neighborhood lined with trees, distinctively stately row houses, and ornate brownstones, boasted famous inhabitants like U.S. Supreme Court Justice Thurgood Marshall, jazz artist Duke Ellington and others.

The sounds reverberating off the streets of Harlem were bold and uninhibited; African Americans unapologetically engaging in dialects rich with urban colloquialisms, and the multitude of varied Southern and West Indian accents, including Trinidadian, Bajan, Jamaican, and Haitian. Added to that mix were Latinas originating from Cuba, Dominican Republic, Puerto Rico, El Salvador, and Mexico, all speaking Spanish differently and some interspersing their dialects with English heavy with accents. Also, a key component was the hustle of the gypsy cabs, screeching to their next stop while verbally jarring with jaywalking pedestrians in their paths, sidewalk musicians bestowing their latest rendition of a well-known rhythm & blues selection for the hope of passerby's time, loose change, and superfluous bills while the brother a hundred feet away played jazz on his worn saxophone, his incentive the same. Harlem was not complete without the street hustler boisterously playing Three Card Monte on a folding card table, catching the unsophisticated and street naïve in his net.

This experience might have proven symphonic to some while cacophonous to others, depending on one's perspective. The myriad of colors, personified through the varying hues of brown skin and the eclectic range of styles and attire, was fascinating to behold. This panoply of qualities characterized the very essence of Harlem, its inhabitants plentiful, colorful, loud, and sassy. The vibrant culture, also expressed intrinsically through its politics and the arts, was poignant and compelling. This culture was insistent in its demand to be experienced by whoever disembarked from the various subway lines traversing between 110th and 165th street, as far east as Lenox Avenue and as far west as Riverside Drive.

The economic strength of Harlem experienced cyclical waves; at times, a dynamic central nervous system replete with black-owned businesses unreservedly supported by willing and able consumers, and in other times the preponderance of drugs and poverty overpowering the positive economic spend as crime waves and despair became pervasive. However, throughout it all, new transplants made Harlem their home, and many natives remained.

They were artists, writers, educators, dancers, musicians, civil service workers, government workers, drug users, drug dealers, corporate professionals, small business owners, homeless folks, doctors, lawyers, thugs, and some folks who were just down on their luck. They all coexisted in the same community. However, they experienced a varied quality of living epitomized by the dilapidated housing projects with crackheads and drug pushers lurking in the halls and urinating in the elevators and tenement buildings with five-floor walk-ups, juxtaposed to upscale high rise buildings with doormen and urine-free fresh-smelling elevators, stately brownstones, row-houses, and modest apartments perched above storefront businesses.

Kyrie loved Harlem. She couldn't quite articulate it as a child, but when she got older and traveled to other New York boroughs, communities, and out of the state, she knew just what set Harlem apart. Kyrie realized much later in life that this Harlem likely enticed Man, with his young 25-year-old wife in tow and their two young children, to escape and settle into Harlem, a microcosm of New York City. It was, in many ways, a diverse little city of brown folks within a bigger city of all kinds of diverse people. Years later, Kyrie would speculate about her parents and why they may have made the decisions they did, including leaving Jamaica, Queens, where all of their family support derived, to choose Harlem. Perhaps it had something to do with the ease of obscurity in Harlem, particularly when the person avoiding detection was of a brown hue.

Similarly, the comfort of an environment so racially homogenous to Man must have been welcoming because Kyrie's perception of him, given how often he spoke about "the white man," was that he resented all that was not black like him. All that had gone wrong in Man's life, he seemed to attribute to that mysterious "white man." *Where is this all-powerful white man, and why, if he was so important and all-powerful, didn't he ever show his face?* Regardless of the reasons that her parents chose this place to finally plant their roots, it was also this comfortable homogeny that made Kyrie feel like being in Harlem was just where she was supposed to be.

However, their quality of life did not prove to be that much better for them in Harlem; in fact, "down on their luck" might be how a more well-positioned observer would describe their family's lifestyle as they began their Harlem journey after leaving Sharon and Jitterbug's place.

Their next place of residence was in an apartment building on 117th Street and Seventh Avenue. Kyrie thought it was a nice building; she liked the shiny black and white ceramic tiles bordering the entryway door. The building was on the corner, and the apartment they stayed in was a short second-floor walk up.

Given its close proximity to the northern most entry point into Central Park, 110th Street, the location should've rendered it a find commensurate with a discovered treasure. However, despite the nice building and coveted location, Kyrie couldn't remember much else that was good or right about the apartment or their time there. What she remembered the most was the darkness and the unwelcome inhabitants that made themselves at home in the darkness.

"Mommy, why are we putting the milk outside on the windowsill?" She was sitting on a radiator that was close to the window, looking out. They were in the living room, where there was not much furniture. There was only a foldaway bed that she slept on at night. She preferred to sit on the radiator. Its iron curves had never emitted heat that she knew of since they had been there, so it seemed a suitable window seat, particularly since it was covered by a box-like encasement which was just the right size for her small frame. There was no running water in the apartment, so they were not able to flush the toilet. There was no electricity, so they had no lights and no refrigerator. They did not buy perishable food items except for the smallest container of milk sometimes – a quart-size container small enough that it would fit on the windowsill.

"To keep it cold, sweetie." Pam's tone was matter-of-fact as if storing milk on the windowsill was as common as donning a coat before braving winter's first blizzard.

"But why don't we put it in the refrigerator?"

Her mother sighed and then took a breath before responding.

"It doesn't work, Kyrie, just like the lights don't work. The refrigerator runs by electricity just like the lights. We don't have electricity right now, but the landlord is going to turn it on soon."

"Is he waiting for the big money you have coming in any day now? I heard you talking about it. Will he turn the water on too?"

"Yes, everything is going to be all right any day now. Don't you worry about it."

"I'm not worried, Mommy. I like Harlem. There are so many people here."

"Is that why you spend so much time sitting in the window? I always think you are daydreaming."

"I like looking out at the people. I like watching the kids going to school and then playing after school. There are always so many people on the sidewalks in Harlem, walking, standing around, sitting in front of buildings in folding chairs, even when it is cold outside. I watch the people just standing at the bus stop and wonder where they are going. I watch the people standing on the corners and wonder why they don't seem to be going anywhere. It is so different from Queens and California. I never saw people walking around on the sidewalks unless they were walking to get in a car."

"That's the difference between the city and the suburbs, honey."

Kyrie thought it was really cool. The people and their unknown lives intrigued her, and she imagined she knew them and their stories, names, where they were going, and what they had been doing before they passed under her window. She created stories about the strangers in her mind.

Kyrie created stories about her own life as well, but they were different. Inside her life and the apartment they were living in, she was always a superhero with special powers. During the day, the apartment was normal, even pleasant. It was a wide open space, sparsely furnished and illuminated only by the daylight streaming through the beautiful, oversized windows that overlooked Seventh Avenue. It was normal, that is, as long as they avoided the bathroom. Since using the bathroom was something they couldn't get around, the experience was quite vexatious.

The other aspect of unpleasantness was the rodent cohabitants that generally came out at night. Her parents became aware that they were in a shared living space after discovering that bread left on the kitchen counter would have a fairly large tunnel gnawed straight through the packaging if left out overnight. Man set traps and ventured into the kitchen at night when the rustle of their undesirable roommates disturbed the night's silence, invading whatever garbage was left. He confronted them with a large broom and killed the unwelcome visitors encroaching on their space until he found the hole that provided their entry and stuffed it with steel wool and broken glass. Still, even after evidence of the rat's inhabitance was gone, Kyrie avoided the kitchen altogether. She was petrified.

Despite the unfavorable aspects, the move to Harlem marked a point of happiness for Kyrie primarily because she was finally going to school. With the exception of the short stint at Usian Shule with Cousin Kadiri, her mother had always taught her at home. She loved to read, and she did her math sheets dutifully although she didn't like them very much. She wondered what other things she would learn in school. Kyrie was excited about the friends she was sure to make. As far as she could tell from her observations, the kids in the neighborhood they lived in now seemed to have a lot of fun.

"Jarel, where you been? We been looking for you." The high-pitched voice traveled through the living room window, which her mother left slightly ajar to allow fresh air into the apartment. Even with the bathroom door closed tight, there was still a rank odor in the apartment. Kyrie went over to the window ledge and propped herself up onto her elbows so she could peer out.

The girl had screamed across the street to the boy who must have been "Jarel," who was hitting a rubber ball against the building. A little boy who appeared to be a few years younger sat with his legs crossed on the concrete with his back against the building playing jacks. Kyrie assumed it was the girl's brother because she often saw them walking together to school.

"I was at my cousin's in the Bronx yesterday," Jarel replied, pausing to look for cars and then dashing across Seventh avenue. "What y'all doing?"

"Waiting for CJ and Kim to come outside so we can play tag. I'm calling you for my team – you know you run faster than CJ."

"Yeah, I know. I run faster than you, too."

"Whateva! You always gotta be bragging all the time. We gonna play for two rounds. Then we gonna play 'Hot, Peas & Butter.' Let's go knock on CJ's door and see what's taking them so long."

They walked across the street together, their animated conversation becoming less discernible as Kyrie watched their retreating backs. She had watched similar exchanges perched in the windowsill. She so wanted to be outside playing with them, bantering back and forth.

They played tag with a stoop assigned as base. They played Hot Peas & Butter, hiding insignificant objects underneath random cars parked along the street and behind old metal trash cans that teetered off-balance, sometimes leaning precariously against the sides of buildings on the block. Kyrie longed to learn their names and join their fun, but Man didn't allow her to go outside. School would be great. She just knew it.

Junior Academy was a private school in Brooklyn, and her mother had convinced Kyrie's grandparents that it would be the best thing for her. Kyrie figured that her grandparents were helping with the tuition because she heard her mother talking to her grandmother on the phone, and soon after, they had to go to Queens to pick up the check.

"Is Brooklyn far, Mommy?"

"It's a different borough from Manhattan, but it's not very far."

"Can't I just go to the school the kids around here go to? I could walk with them."

78

"No. The public school in this neighborhood is not good. I want you in an environment that will build upon the foundation I've given you. You are smart, Kyrie!"

"What do you mean, Mommy? The kids that go to school around here seem smart too."

"You'll like Junior Academy, Kyrie. You'll see. You even get to wear a special uniform. We are going to go buy it tomorrow."

But Kyrie's foray into her first organized school experience was not quite what she expected. For starters, despite her mother's assurances, Junior Academy was far away from Harlem, and she had to get up really early in the morning to be ready to board the school bus that came to pick her up. Unlike her homeschooling, which was not really structured in terms of when it started and ended every day, the bus was outside at 7:15 am, and it took over an hour to get to Brooklyn every morning.

Junior Academy gave Kyrie several tests when her mother applied for her to attend. The school administrators were very impressed with her test scores, and although she should have been placed in the third grade, after extensive reading comprehension and math competency tests, several interviews with various school administrators, and her mother's insistence, Junior Academy agreed to place Kyrie in a fourth grade class. Pam assured the headmaster that Kyrie could handle the work. So, Kyrie started in the fourth grade, wearing her plaid skirt, tights, yellow collared shirt, light blue vest, and navy cardigan, and a beautiful navy-blue wool coat with brass-colored buttons that her grandmother had taken her shopping for. She loved the coat; it had deep pockets perfect for her to jam her hands into to contain her overflowing excitement and enthusiasm. Going to a school where there would be friends to make would certainly be better than lessons in the apartment day after day with only her mother, Kyrie thought to herself.

Kyrie was 8 years old.

CHAPTER 11

School Blues

"Don't Stop the Music"
- Yarbrough & Peoples

"Who wants to tell us what connections can be drawn from what we've been discussing in class and the short story we just read?" Ms. Trillinger asked the class, her gaze scanning the room for willing participants. While a few hands shot up, Kyrie's did not, although she had plenty of thoughts about the story. She had enjoyed the short story so much she had read it three times. The rest of the class seemed to read a lot slower than she did.

"Kyrie, we haven't heard from you today. We've been talking a lot over the last couple of days about personal qualities and values. Did you recognize any themes in the story that exemplify a personal quality or value?" The class turned to her.

Kyrie hesitated, feeling more than a dozen pairs of eyes on her. The impromptu scrutiny felt strange and uncomfortable. The unwavering gazes made her body overheat, and she felt her armpits immediately moisten beneath her shirt and sweater vest. Ms. Trillinger smiled at her,

her eyes encouraging. It was her third day. Things were not going horribly, but they also were not great. Kyrie had been thinking this right before Ms. Trillinger had called her name.

Ms. Trillinger seemed really nice so far and was pretty. Kyrie could not stop staring at her freckles and her perfect strawberry blond ponytail, which hung down her to the nape of her neck and swung like a pendulum every time she turned her head. As for her classmates, they mostly stared at her, without saying even as much as "Hi."

At first, Kyrie had smiled whenever she saw caught a classmate staring, but when that didn't yield either a reciprocal smile or any other pleasantry, she had resorted to turning away and staring straight ahead. There was usually something interesting on the wall that she could fixate on when words escaped her or when the moment in time just didn't feel like a safe space to release them. The classroom didn't fall into that category, at least not at first. She enjoyed the learning environment, albeit quite different from the one that she was accustomed to. It was interesting to be a part of other kids' learning processes, and they a part of hers.

She swallowed hard and fixed her eyes on the pictures of Abraham Lincoln and Christopher Columbus taped to the wall above the blackboard directly above Ms. Trillinger's shoulder. To anyone looking at her, it appeared that she was staring directly at Ms. Trillinger when in fact, she wasn't looking at the teacher at all. Kyrie ignored the knot in her throat and breathed in deeply before parting her lips to speak.

"The story is about hard work and sticking together. But I think that the main character, Joey, learned that continuing to work hard after his mom died was really difficult to do because he was so sad. He had to block out his sadness and all the bad around him, and although he felt so alone, he focused on his commitment to his mom to look out for his younger brother and continue to do well. So I know we didn't talk about this one, but I think a personal value he learned was perseverance."

When she stopped talking, the room was so quiet Kyrie could hear nothing except what sounded like a roaring wind. After a few moments, she realized that the sound was coming from her, the air rushing through her lungs challenging the otherwise deafening silence in the room.

Ms. Trillinger, looking momentarily dumbfounded, regrouped quickly. "Yes, Kyrie. That is an excellent analysis of Joey's challenges and his growth in the story. Thank you, Kyrie."

The bell rang, signaling dismissal, and immediately the scraping of chairs, shuffling of bodies moving quickly to retrieve belongings from cubbies, and the resounding chatter of dozens of voices ringing with the excitement of the end of the school day replaced the silence. Kyrie gathered her things quickly, and as she walked past Ms. Trillinger's desk, the teacher stopped her.

"Kyrie, thank you again for sharing your thoughts about the story today. Had you read the story before today in class? I know you've been home-schooled up until starting here with us. Perhaps it was something that your mother came across and discussed with you?" Ms. Trillinger was staring at her, her eyes quizzical, awaiting her response.

"No. I never read it before today, although I did read it three times today while I waited for you to start the discussion." She glanced past the teacher into the hall to see how empty it was. She had no idea what would happen if the bus left without her. Her mother didn't have a car to come and get her from Brooklyn.

"You read the story three times? Today in class?"

"Yes, ma'am. I read fast."

"I see. Well then. And where did you come across the concept of perseverance? That's quite a big word for an eight-year-old. You are eight, right? Not nine like everyone else in the class, isn't that right?"

"Yes, I'm eight, but I read a lot. And I really like words, so my mom taught me to copy words and definitions from the dictionary. I started with the letters "S" and "P" first to make it interesting. *Simultaneous* was my favorite "s" word, but *perseverance* was my favorite "p" word. First, I learn how to spell my favorite words, and then I practice using them when I speak. I really have to go before the bus leaves me. See you tomorrow, bye!" She left the teacher standing there with her mouth agape.

Kyrie ran down the hall and out of the building to board the waiting school bus. She sat in the first empty seat close to the front. She knew from the previous days that everyone would already have a friend that they would have either saved a seat for or would be in the process of doing so, so she didn't bother walking down the bus aisle looking for a friendly face.

As she sat down, she heard a girl's voice from a row behind her whisper loudly, "That's the new girl from our class. Did you hear her today? She thinks she's a smarty pants, but who cares because she's black, skinny, and ugly." The girl's friend giggled.

Kyrie bit back the hot tears she felt creeping into the corners of her eyes. She started humming quietly. No one heard her because it was so loud on the bus, with everyone else chattering and having what seemed like a good time. She pulled out her homework and settled in for the long ride back to Harlem. She wouldn't worry about those girls, she thought. There would be plenty of girls to make friends with, she assured herself. It was still so early. The first week had not even come to an end.

But Kyrie did not make friends at Junior Academy, nor did she continue to shock Ms. Trillinger with her insight and advanced vocabulary for much longer. Kyrie's time at Junior Academy came to an end quite quickly. The tuition combined with the bussing was too expensive. They also moved to a new apartment further uptown, so her mother found a more convenient school choice. It turned out that Junior Academy wasn't so great anyway, so she wasn't very sad to find out that her stay there was short-lived.

"I found a new school for you!" her mother exclaimed excitedly.

"Really? Where is it, Mommy? What kind of school is it? Are there a lot of students going there?" The questions came faster than her mother could answer them.

"The Modern School is one of the first black-owned and operated private school in Harlem, New York. I've been looking into it for a while and actually filled out an application some time ago, but I wanted to surprise you. Mildred Johnson Edwards was a black woman who founded the school in 1934. When she first opened it, only people she knew were willing to send their kids, and she only had eight students enrolled. In a few years, she had two hundred students! It is a great school!"

That's exactly what she had said about Junior Academy. "Well, I just hope it's not far," Kyrie remarked, somewhat wryly.

"No, it's right on 152nd Street between Amsterdam and Broadway." Kyrie knew that was far to walk, but it was a short bus ride.

Kyrie was so ecstatic that she would still be going to school, so any school would do. She picked up her fourth-grade year at The Modern School somewhere in the middle of its ten-month trajectory but with the same zeal and promise commensurate with a child's first visit to an amusement park.

"How was your first day of school today, Kyrie?"

Pam had just come in from work and was sitting in the living room, rubbing her feet. She was working now what she called a "9-5" at an office downtown. They had moved to an apartment that they had been waiting for in a building on 127th Street between 5th and Lenox Avenue, two blocks north of the Apollo Theatre and four blocks north of the Mount Morris Park historical area. Man's sister, Aunt Grace, lived in the building with her husband Marvin, also known as "Truth," and Kyrie's little cousin, Daisha.

Kyrie was happy with the move for many obvious reasons given the condition the prior apartment had been in, but in addition to that, their new apartment was on the second floor, so they were spared a multi-floor walk-up. She also had her own room, and it had a door that she could close so she could finally keep Sire out. He annoyed her. There was so much old paint on the door jamb and on the door itself that it didn't close smoothly, with a click. However, if slammed hard enough, the very paint that prevented it from closing smoothly was thick enough to jam it pretty tight.

"School was good. I had a spelling and vocabulary test."

"Why did you even take the test, Kyrie? It's your first day. You didn't have the words prior to the test to study like everyone else. I'm sure your teacher didn't expect you to know them." Her mother was staring at her with a quizzical look on her face.

"She said that I didn't have to take it 'for real,' that I could just do it for practice so I would know what the tests were like for the next time. But I knew all the words, so I told her that she could count it for my first grade when I handed it in! And guess what, I think I did really well, maybe 100%. And the math we did was easy for me too; it was multiplication. I hope we do some harder stuff tomorrow. Oh, and Mommy, we take turns making morning announcements. I can't wait until it's my turn. The teacher said, you have to speak loudly and clearly, and I can do that!" The words came tumbling out like a waterfall clamoring over an unleashed dam. Kyrie paused, waited expectedly for her mom to say something.

"Of course you can do that, Ky. You can do whatever they put in front of you. I prepared you well." Her mother smiled slightly, not showing all of her teeth smile. Kyrie had come to realize that that smile, the "not really a real smile" smile, meant that something was wrong.

The rest of fourth grade slipped away seamlessly and without any fanfare. Kyrie didn't remember much about it except that tuition had to be paid to maintain her attendance which provoked conversations around her that were fraught with agitation. She imagined that her time at The Modern School would be short-lived, so she relished each day with an unwavering intensity.

When the school year came to a close, her mother informed her that she would be enrolling her in the fifth grade in the local public school. Kyrie's private school stint was over. No memorable relationships or experiences remained with her, but she did maintain the year she had gained on her peers. Kyrie entered 5th grade at the start of the following school year at nine years old, her mother armed with her records of having completed fourth grade with a report card and testing metrics that exemplified a stellar student, poised to one-up any public school administrator who dared to refute Kyrie's advanced grade placement.

Kyrie successfully started the fifth grade, joining a host of children that were all an entire year older. She had an acute awareness of that fact which gave her academic confidence that carried her through the next several years of elementary and junior high school. Unfortunately, that self-assurance did not translate into social assurance, and her ability and need to fit in became her primary challenge. Public school introduced a different element that she had not encountered in her prior abbreviated dips into the private school environment; close proximity to children from the neighborhood housing projects who wore an armor and a swagger that often belied their years. Kyrie had no clue what she was in for.

"So, ok, Mommy, listen. The morning announcements happen as soon as we get to our seats in the morning. Well, really after we stand and salute the flag and say the Pledge of Allegiance. Do you want to hear it, Mommy? The teacher gave me a paper with it. She said I should memorize it because everyone else knows it by memory…Mommy, what's wrong?" Kyrie stopped abruptly.

Pam was looking over her head. Kyrie felt his presence before the words began spilling from his mouth. The room felt different. She always felt uncomfortable when Man was around, and he had entered the apartment and was standing behind her in the doorway to the kitchen.

"What are you talking about? They got them saying the Pledge of Allegiance at this school? Saluting that bullshit ass flag? That's not happening, not in this house." Man walked over to the refrigerator, removed a forty-ounce bottle of malt liquor, and took a swig.

"Honey, I'm guessing it's the school policy. I'll go up to the school tomorrow and find out about it."

"No, you won't find out about it. You will go up there and let them know that my child is not saluting no damn American flag. What the fuck is wrong with you? Huh? You should know better. If you listened to the shit I try to teach you, you would've made our values clear in the beginning." Man took another swig from the forty-ounce and belched.

"Kyrie, go to your room and finish your homework. I'll come to look at it in a little while."

Kyrie turned and ran from the kitchen, passing a three-year-old Sire sitting on the floor in the living room playing with some pots. She rounded the corner of the hallway leading to her room but did not go in. She stood there, peering around the door jamb to get a glimpse of the scene unfolding. Man was angry. He had just gotten home, and he was already angry. It seemed to her that he was always angry. He was angry with the world.

"Baby," Pam began, her voice so quiet that Kyrie could barely make out what she was saying, "calm down. I didn't know the children recite the Pledge of Allegiance until Kyrie just told me. I will talk to the principal tomorrow and find out what the policy is."

"Calm down? Who the fuck are you talking to? What the fuck are you talking about? I don't give a fuck what the policy is. They call themselves a school in the black community. That flag represents a country committed to enslaving and discriminating against black people, so it certainly doesn't represent free black people!

"Our rights and freedom are not represented by that flag, and the motherfucker who wrote that bullshit song was a slave owner! You need to read a fucking book, Pam, so that you learn something before you want to be taking care of business that has to do with my mother-fucking kids. You need to learn some shit."

He was standing in Pam's face now, screaming. His last words were punctuated by jabs to her forehead with his index finger. He was so close to her mother's face that Kyrie wondered if she could feel his spit flying from his mouth. Kyrie turned and ran into her room and closed the door. She sat down on the floor with her back against the door and covered her ears with her hands. She didn't want to hear anymore. She needed music in her head and in her ears. She started singing about the music, not stopping. She sang about the music rocking her. She closed her eyes and sang quietly. It didn't block out the voices completely, neither Man's angry one nor her mother's pleading one, but she was able to focus on the song and not the screaming.

When Man was angry like this, the screaming went on for a really long time. She probably should've picked up Sire and brought him back to her room. *Oh well, he's just a baby. He doesn't understand what is going on anyway.* Just at that moment, she heard Man's voice scream something unintelligible and then a loud noise. Kyrie heard Sire begin to cry from the living room floor where he sat. She buried her head into her knees with her hands over her ears and continued to sing quietly. She wasn't going back out there until it was quiet. She wouldn't leave her room until Man was gone or sleep. And she didn't stop the music.

I pledge allegiance to the flag of the United States of America.

And to the Republic, for which it stands,

one nation, under God, indivisible, with liberty and justice for all.

Kyrie sat still in her seat, her head cast downward as her classmates stood all around her, their palms resting on their chests and their eyes trained reverently on the red, white, and blue stripes. She had felt their eyes on her first until the teacher sternly directed them to face forward. She felt the tears stinging as she struggled to keep them from falling. She was so angry with herself for opening her mouth to share with her mother that this practice took place. If she had just kept her mouth shut, Man wouldn't have overheard her, and she could have continued on her path to being normal, just like the other kids. Instead, now she had to sit there, humiliated.

The class went straight into song following the Pledge of Allegiance.

My country 'tis of thee, sweet land of liberty. Of thee, I sing.

Land where my fathers died, land of the pilgrim's pride!

From every mountainside, let freedom ring!

She didn't understand anything about why Man had gotten so angry when he had heard that she recited the Pledge of Allegiance with her class. She heard him talking about the "cracker who wrote it who didn't care about black people." She wondered how he knew that. Man did read a lot of books, so Kyrie assumed he had read it somewhere. During free time in class the next day, she went to the class Encyclopedia and discovered that Frances Bellamy wrote the Pledge of Allegiance in 1892. While he was a white man who wrote it, the information about him didn't say anything about him owning slaves.

She just didn't understand what the big deal was, and her mother had spoken to her teacher out of her earshot. All she knew was, Pam had told her to stay in her seat when the Pledge of Allegiance and "My Country 'Tis of Thee" were recited from now on. Her teacher had just looked at her and then averted her eyes when that PA system crackled after the bell, marking the time when the children would be addressed by the principal and asked to stand to salute the flag and begin the day. So Kyrie sat, the only child to be omitted from the daily school-wide practice. She sat humiliated, confused, and angry. She was certain that this new development would not help her make friends in her new school. No, not at all.

As the class concluded its rousing rendition of America, otherwise known as "My Country, 'Tis of Thee," they went immediately into "Lift Every Voice and Sing." Kyrie had looked that up as well and discovered that not only was it written by James Weldon Johnson, a Black man, it was commonly referred to as the "Black American National Anthem." She decided for herself that Man shouldn't have a problem with her participation in just singing that song. She also decided at that moment that it wasn't worth checking with her mother to make sure. From now on, what happened in school, stayed in school.

During recess, Kyrie was perched on the edge of the swing reading *The Lion, the Witch & the Wardrobe* by C.S. Lewis. She had read the series, but she really enjoyed re-reading the second book; it was one way of escaping the monotony and discomfort of her life. Dwayne Graver snatched her sweater that she had tied around her waist and started holding it out of her reach. She remembered his name because he had received one of the three highest grades on the vocabulary test her first week. She, however, had tied a girl named Yvette for the highest grade. Yvette had smiled at her warmly when the teacher called them up and announced that they were the highest scores. Dwayne had gotten just two points lower and was also called to the front of the class. He, however, had scowled at her.

"Hey, weirdo! New girl! Reading about how to take over the government?"

Kyrie kept her head down in her book for a few seconds, caught off guard initially and unsure of how to respond. Then she reached up to grab her sweater from his outstretched hand; he sneered at her and tossed it to another boy who was standing several feet away, laughing hysterically.

"Give me my sweater back!" Kyrie said, not quite loudly enough. She ran over to the cackling boy, only for him to throw the sweater back to Dwayne.

"Give me my sweater!" She was a little louder this time.

"Oh, I know why you can't salute the flag. You a booty scratchin' African. Don't she look like those African kids on the commercials when they beg for money? They don't salute the flag because they're not American. Yo, look at her stick legs. Yo, listen to this: She so skinny, she so Black, she an African booty scratch!"

Kyrie had stopped chasing the sweater toss before he got to the end of his chant. She stood there, staring at them, dumbfounded, as they held their stomachs laughing.

"Leave her alone! Y'all are so ignorant. Here Kyrie." Yvette had managed to grab the sweater mid-air.

"Oh, of course, Ms. Piggy. I mean, Yvette. Always minding somebody else's business."

"Whatever. You can't even spell 'business.' And call me Ms. Piggy again!" And with that, the two boys ran away laughing. Kyrie assumed they were off to find a more interesting target.

"Don't worry about them. They're stupid." Yvette handed Kyrie her sweater and sat down on the swing next to where Kyrie had been sitting.

"Thanks." She sat back down on the other swing, not really sure of what to say. "They don't seem to mess with you much."

Yvette put her hand on her hip. "Well, first of all, I've been in school with those fools since the first grade, and I'm smarter than all of them, so nothing they say bothers me. Second of all, they know I've got a bunch of older brothers that I threaten will kill them if I tell them to, so really, they're scared." Yvette said this with the gravity of an adult delivering an edict. Kyrie's eyes widened, and then Yvette burst into laughter. Kyrie realized she was kidding and joined her.

"Oh, the Narnia series! I love these books!" Yvette picked up Kyrie's book from off the ground.

"You do? Me too! My Aunt Michelle sent me all seven. She lives in Phoenix, Arizona, and she's a television producer. Anyway, I read all seven, but *The Lion, the Witch and the Wardrobe* is my favorite. I've read it like five times."

"Really? What's your favorite part?" Yvette asked.

"My favorite part is when they go into the wardrobe in their house and come out in Narnia."

"That's so funny. There are so many other exciting parts in that story. What about when they meet Aslan? What about the battles? It's interesting that your favorite part is the calmest part of the book." Yvette laughed, but it was a good-natured laugh that started way down in her belly. Kyrie knew that she wasn't laughing at her like most kids appeared to be doing when talking to her.

"I know. It is weird." She hesitated and then, not looking at Yvette, replied. "I just think it would be so amazing to enter a closet in my apartment where time would stop while I escape to another land where I am an important princess with powers and not afraid of anything." Kyrie's voice had dropped; her tone was wistful. Yvette was quiet for a few minutes, and they sat there on the swings, rocking ever so slightly, kicking at the ragged rubber mat beneath their feet.

"Girl, you know that is not happening in no apartment in Harlem unless you write it yourself!" They collapsed into giggles, holding their stomachs. The bell rang, signaling the end of recess and the day their friendship began.

At home that night, Kyrie said nothing about the day to her mother. She didn't breathe a word about the morning, nothing about recess and Dwayne Graver's mean chant, and nothing about her new friend.

In the following days after "Pledge of Allegiance" with only about half the eyes trained on her sitting quietly in her seat, Kyrie began to feel more at ease. On the fifth day after the exuberant rendition of "My Country 'Tis of Thee," Kyrie stood up promptly and joined in for the last song while Yvette sent an encouraging smile her way.

Lift every voice and sing
Till earth and heaven ring,
Ring with the harmonies of Liberty.
   Let our rejoicing rise
   High as the listening skies.
   Let it resound loud as the rolling sea.
Sing a song full of the faith that the dark past has taught us,
Sing a song full of the hope that the present has brought us,
Facing the rising sun of our new day begun.
Let us march on till victory is won!

CHAPTER 12

See-Saw

"Shining Star" - Earth, Wind & Fire

"Hey, Toothpick, where you going so fast?"

"Wait up, Toothie toothpick! With your teeth sticking out the front and your twigs for legs, how do you hold yourself up?"

Kyrie had read a story once about a little girl who was bullied. The little girl's grandmother told her that love was in everyone's heart, but you just had to search a little longer to find it with some people. Kyrie couldn't fathom how that could be true as she listened to the mean-spirited laughing that immediately followed the comments. It was an offense to her senses, akin to a bad choir following her with everyone singing off-key. In reality, there were only three boys.

Kyrie grimaced but didn't allow her stride to falter one bit. She also didn't turn her head to acknowledge that they were behind her or even talking to her. She had hoped that they had forgotten about her today, even if just this once. She had actually depended on it since she left the school grounds in record time after the dismissal bell rang. Her reasoning for rushing out of the school building and towards home was two-fold, although not at all triggered by a desire to begin her evening with her family. If her arrival at home was tardy, there was a strong possibility that Man would arrive at the apartment before her, and she would suffer for being a few minutes late.

Man had a job now, and she could not recall him leaving the house to go to a job any time before this. She had overheard him say that "his man" had hooked him up with a construction foreman who needed workers for a project and would pay him "under the table." Kyrie didn't know what that meant, but she imagined that anything that took Man out of the house every day and getting paid had to be a good thing. The way he said it suggested that something about it was wrong, but she didn't think it should matter that he had to crawl underneath a table to get paid. She hoped that Man having a job would be great for his general mood, but it didn't seem to change it much for the good as it applied to her. He still wore a scowl as his normal expression and still barked when he spoke to everyone in the house, except for Sire.

The second reason for her hurried departure from the school grounds was that she could not evade being picked on. At recess and after school, there were a group of boys led by the loud mouth of Dwayne Graver, who clearly derived pleasure from coming up with the most insulting remarks about her appearance that she had ever heard uttered about anyone. Today, it appeared that he and his cronies had diverted their attention from her hair and her overall face, the focal point from the previous week, to her teeth and legs. She did study herself in the mirror intently, and she knew that her legs were indeed very skinny. Kyrie was not surprised, nor did she really disagree with the comments, but they were very mean and made her feel bad. The jeering and laughter behind her got louder. She was walking as quickly as she could without breaking into a run, which would likely result in them chasing her like an animal being hunted. It didn't feel good.

Kyrie's walk from school was short. The apartment building where she lived was actually on the same street as the school, 127th Street. She lived between Fifth and Lenox Avenues, and Public School 154 was on 127th Street between Seventh and Eighth Avenue, so it was a mere two avenue walk. Usually, her insult-obsessed classmates would lose interest when she hit the corner of Seventh Avenue. She learned fairly quickly that ignoring them resulted in their attention waning, and they would usually turn off before she reached the corner of Seventh Avenue. Alternatively, shouting, "Leave me alone," repeatedly only seemed to transform them into honeybees released in a summer field of sunflowers.

Kyrie felt as dissimilar from a sunflower as one could be. Sunflowers were light, yellow, pretty. These bees buzzed ugly insults that she had begun to accept as true, or else why would they utter them. Toothpick. Blackie. "Blackie" was a reference to her skin color. Although she knew it wasn't black, it was actually brown. Her mother called it beautiful, but Kyrie had surmised that was because it was very close on the color palette to her own.

She had resorted to ignoring Dwayne Graver, his sidekicks, and most of the girls in her class, many of whom lived in St. Nicholas projects across the street from the school. The schoolwork was fairly simple since her mother had been teaching her Math and English & Language Arts for years at an accelerated pace. Science and Social Studies were new to her but easy to grasp since it was primarily terms, concepts, and facts that had to be memorized for tests. Weekly spelling and vocabulary tests were a joke since usually, the words were familiar to her and amongst a slew of words that she knew since age five or six. She and Yvette always scored 100% on the tests, sometimes 105% if an extra credit bonus question was thrown in.

Dwayne scored the same or just under most of the time, which likely added to his frustration with her. Both she and Yvette were called the "brainiacs" by many of their classmates. That is, when they weren't being called "Toothpick" and "Ms. Piggy." It was ironic that Kyrie and Yvette were physically opposite to each other but alike in so many ways. Kyrie liked being smart, so she welcomed sharing the "brainiac" label with Yvette, who had worn it graciously for years. The moniker really didn't bother her at all. What bothered her was the spiteful manner in which many of her new peers paid her attention, as if she had caused some grievous ills upon each of them in a prior life that they were seeking retribution for.

Kyrie continued to ignore them, and as she got closer to Lenox Avenue, she could tell their voices had ebbed. She didn't dare turn around. She knew that any indication from her that she was paying attention would mean a full-frontal attack. She wasn't really afraid of them. They never hit her or did anything to actually harm her.

Once when she was little, she was walking around barefoot and wound up with a splinter deep in her foot. It had hurt so much, and she remembered crying really hard. It took Pam hours of digging with a needle she sterilized over an open flame to extract what turned out to be a minuscule shard of wood. She remembered her mother's patience with her near surgical process and sharp chiding at Kyrie to stop crying and fidgeting so that she could successfully remove the splinter. Pam told her that if she was not still and the splinter was not removed, it would escape into her bloodstream, travel to her heart, and pierce it.

When the splinter was finally removed, Kyrie was appalled at how tiny the offending piece of wood was and how searing the pain had been despite its smallness. Dwayne and his sidekicks were like that splinter. The words and the people who voiced them were so small, they should have been insignificant to her. She knew that they didn't know anything about her and she shouldn't care what they said about her, but the words hurt terribly. She could not understand why they made her feel so bad. The hateful words were actually like dozens of splinters shot at her body from the cannons of insensitive mouths. When they were fired, they penetrated her mind and became embedded there, so deep that she thought about them often and often questioned herself as to whether their insults were true.

Was she ugly? Her skin certainly was dark, like they said. Her body was very skinny, not curvy like the bodies of many of the other girls in her fifth-grade class, although her breasts were starting to bud. She looked into the mirror a lot, trying to decide for herself. She just wanted the kids to like her, and she didn't want to feel the way she felt around them. Kyrie despised the way she felt around them, the mean words slicing tiny abrasions through her spirit. Much like the way Man's shouting and smacking her mother around made her feel. She thought that school would be safe, but she realized that there was nowhere she felt protected. Shelter was as elusive as the love she was groping for; both were far beyond her reach. Home and school were like playing on the see-saw in the playground; she wanted so bad for it to be as fun as it looked, but in actuality, there was no reprieve from the nauseous feeling whether she was on the way up or on the way down.

The apartment on 127th Street was certainly in a lot better condition than the last, primarily because they were living there with everything it was supposed to have, like lights and running water. It was in an old building, with five floors and no elevator, but they were lucky enough to be on the second floor in a street-facing apartment. That meant they enjoyed a short one flight up and had windows that provided a view of the street below, instead of the brick wall of the building next to it or a back alley and building behind it. Street-facing also meant light entered the apartment every day, which certainly made Kyrie happy. She loved sunlight. It made her smile when she awoke to it, even if the day beyond was bleak.

The apartment was railroad-style; the front door opened up into a long hallway stretching more than twenty feet with a narrow bathroom and kitchen situated along the hallway. The other rooms, which included a living room, sitting room, and two bedrooms, were set deep in the apartment just beyond the long hallway. Kyrie had her own room at the very end of the hallway directly opposite the front door. To the right, immediately before reaching Kyrie's bedroom, was the living room and behind the living room, separated by French doors, was a small parlor room that Pam and Man used for their bedroom. This room had another door that opened at the top, creating a pseudo window when used. Pam said it was an old laundry drop and had pushed their bed in front of it so that it wouldn't be used to go in and out, but sometimes Sire stood on their bed and pushed the window/door open to annoy Kyrie.

The third room was on the opposite side of the parlor bedroom used by her parents. That room remained a storage space for the duration of their time there, although she believed the plan was for it to be Sire's room when he was older. Kyrie was taking it all in. With the size of the apartment and the fact that there were working utilities and no visible rodents, this was a significant step up. In fact, in Kyrie's eyes, this was the highest quality living space they had since the California rental house, which she remembered only faintly. Even so, her mother said that the presence of a feline was a necessary preemptive measure to keep unwanted critters away, so Kyrie got a kitten that she could call her own.

When the kitten arrived, Kyrie loved her immediately. She was tiny, not much larger than Kyrie's hand when she first got her. The kitten had orange, black and white lines spread over her little body like lightning bolts and her paws were completely white. Kyrie carried her all over the house and would've taken her to school in her bag if she thought she could get away with it. She talked to it and stroked it until it purred so fervently that she could feel it reverberating through its small body. Kyrie decided to call her Tabby. She adored her. Likewise, after just a couple of weeks together, Tabby adored Kyrie. The kitten followed Kyrie everywhere she went in the house.

Man was working construction sporadically. Sometimes he would work for a week, sometimes only a few days at a time. Kyrie heard her mother tell her Uncle Will, "It's not consistent money, but it is better than nothing and good for him."

On the days that Man worked, he'd come home filthy, his clothes and the skin beneath them covered with dirt and hardened splashes of cement. It was that thick grime that only physical labor produces, leaving the residue of the construction site clinging to him. His routine was to come home to a scalding hot bath that he insisted be drawn for him an hour before he was due in. The water running through the pipes in the apartment didn't get extremely hot. To achieve Man's desired temperature in the bathtub, one was required to boil several pots of water and add them to the tepid tub water. When the process was complete, it would be so hot in the bathroom that steam covered the mirror and emanated from the room every time the door was opened.

After running the tub and adding the boiling water, Kyrie knew that she was supposed to close the door behind her to keep the heat in. However, one day, after filling the tub, she carelessly left the door wide open in her haste to return to her room. Tabby had followed her into the bathroom, and Sire was on her heels, as usual, the latter being a constant annoyance to her. She ran into her room and slammed her door.

Sire was fast on his little chubby toddler legs. She grinned. She had just made it past the threshold and slammed her door to keep him out. She sank back onto her bed to get back into her book. Seconds later, she remembered that she had left Tabby in the hallway and rose to get her. As she stood, she heard the piercing screeching of the kitten's desperate wails. Kyrie flung open her bedroom door and ran at breakneck speed back down the hallway in the direction of Tabby's cries. She reached the bathroom to find Sire standing in front of the tub, watching the little kitten flailing around in the scalding hot water.

"Kitty swimming," Sire remarked, pointing to the water, a proud grin on his face. The kitten was trying desperately to pull itself out of the tub, so Kyrie was able to scoop the suffering cat out without touching the water herself. The kitten's body was so hot she almost dropped her on the floor.

As she stood staring at Sire in disbelief, her mother walked in the front door. Taking in the scene, she immediately grabbed a towel and took the kitten from her, wrapping her gingerly. Kyrie could not even look at the animal, which was now barely moving in her mother's arms. Within the next several minutes, Man entered the apartment. When hearing what happened, he remarked, "Why the fuck did you leave the bathroom door open? You better be happy your brother didn't burn himself because your ass would be mine right now."

Kyrie said nothing. It was her fault. Sire didn't receive any blame. He was barely three years old. He didn't know better. If he got hurt when she was around, it was always her fault. This was no different. She remained quiet as the tears rolled down her face. There was nothing to say that would make this better.

They took Tabby to a veterinarian that day. The veterinarian treated the burns that covered the kitten's body, wrapped the animal in gauze, and put a cone on her head so that she could not interfere with the bandages. He taught Kyrie how to remove the bandages, apply the medicated cream every few days, and reapply the bandages. The vet also warned Kyrie that the kitten was burned so badly that it may not make a full recovery. When they returned to the apartment, Kyrie lined an unused shoebox with a towel and made it Tabby's bed. She cared for the animal dutifully for the next several days, but before the end of the first week, Kyrie awoke to find Tabby motionless. She leaned in to pick her up from her makeshift bed and pulled back immediately, crying out. The kitten's body was cold and hard. During the night, Tabby had been taken away, a chunk of orange, black, and white cement left in its place.

"Mommy, Mommy, something is wrong with Tabby!" Pam came into her room and peered into the shoe box. She prodded the kitten with her forefinger and then grimaced.

"I'm sorry, Kyrie. Tabby died during the night. She may have been dead before you even went to bed last night, judging by how hard she's gotten already."

Kyrie gasped. She had slept the night with the kitten at the foot of her bed. She began to cry softly and grabbed the box onto her lap, staring down at the unmoving mass of bandages and what was left of the patches of fur.

"Don't cry for Tabby, Kyrie. Death is nothing to cry about. This is not even her; her spirit is what you loved and still lives on. The body was burned on the outside and broken inside, and it's better that she let it go because she was in so much pain and discomfort. You know that, right?"

Kyrie sniffled and nodded her head. "I know, Mommy. I just don't understand why Sire would do this to her. He did this to Tabby, and he didn't even get in trouble. He didn't get yelled at. He didn't get a spanking. Y'all didn't even tell him he shouldn't have done it."

Pam's expression hardened. "Oh, Kyrie, grow up and get over it! Your brother is a baby, he loves you, and he loved the damn cat. He didn't know any better. Now get yourself together and find the top to the shoe box. We have to get that out of here before it starts stinking." She strode out of the room.

Kyrie located the box top underneath her bed and took one last look at the little kitten before she placed the top on the box for the last time. She carried it out of her room and sat it on the floor next to the front door of the apartment. As she turned away and slowly walked back to her room, she heard Man greet Sire, who was just waking up. "Good morning, my little son."

She closed the door to her room gently and threw herself onto her bed and sobbed quietly. She asked the room repeatedly as she cried, "Why, why, why?" She didn't understand why it was that no one could hear her. She didn't understand why no one seemed to care.

She vowed that day she would never call another pet her own.

Pam got another cat shortly thereafter. It was an adult cat. Kyrie ignored it. It was there for one purpose; to keep the mice away. She decided that she didn't like cats anyway.

"Kyrie! Kyrie!"

She closed her eyes momentarily and took a deep breath. *What now?* She had just finished cleaning the bathroom, which included changing the cat's litter box and scrubbing the toilet, both inside and around it. Cleaning the bathroom was her most dreaded chore, the toilet in particular. She didn't understand how so much urine could land outside the bowl and why it occurred to Man that she should be the one to clean it when her urine assuredly went into the toilet given that she sat on top of the toilet opening instead of standing in front of it. She had to hold her breath during the cleaning process because it repulsed her so much, but at almost 9 years old, there was no doubt that she could and would handle it without complaint, at least not outwardly. But she hated it. She had just finished and settled back into her library book, a new one from the Nancy Drew/Hardy Boys series. She had three of the series that she planned to devour that day.

"Kyrie! Get your ass in that kitchen and wash those dishes. Don't make me get up, and don't let me have to tell you again, dammit!" Man shouted this from his perch on the sofa.

She sighed and dragged herself from her bed where she had been curled. She knew better than to take her sweet time getting to the task at hand. All that would earn her was a backhand slap across her face. It was a Saturday, and although Man had been working construction off and on, he never worked on Saturdays, which meant that he was usually in the apartment, seemingly looking for chores to order her to do.

She glanced into the living room as she passed to go into the kitchen. He was sitting on the sofa with a Budweiser in his hand, watching television. She sneered and stuck her tongue out at him as she walked by. Sire was sitting on the floor playing with pots and pans that had been put in the living room for his entertainment. He giggled, having caught her stick out her tongue. She smiled as she walked into the kitchen. He was annoying but cute.

As she was finishing up the dishes, there was a soft knock on the apartment door. She opened it quickly, hoping Man hadn't heard it. Her friend Diamond was standing there with her older sister Kimmy. They lived on the fifth floor in an apartment with about six siblings and their mom. Kyrie thought they were a very interesting family because they all looked so different.

"Hey, Kyrie! whatcha doin'?"

"Hey, Diamond. Hey, Kimmy. Nothing, just washing the dishes. What are y'all doing?" Kyrie spoke softly. She didn't want Man to know she was at the door, or he would quickly come and embarrass her. Plus, if he heard her say "y'all," he'd have a problem with that. Neither he nor her mom allowed her to talk in any way that wasn't proper English.

"Fittin' to go outside. We got some new telephone wire from the Bell telephone man yesterday so we can play some good double dutch. You think ya' daddy will let you come out and play?" Diamond punctuated each word with a swing of the plastic bag in her hand that had the telephone wire in it. She was also popping her gum and as she spoke. Kyrie admired her because she always seemed so happy. Kyrie thought for a moment about asking to go outside. She had fun with Diamond and Kimmy whenever she went outside, but she didn't want to risk Man coming up with another chore for her to do because she asked. No, it wasn't worth it. Plus, Nancy Drew was waiting.

She was giggling at some ridiculous dance Diamond was now doing and thinking of an excuse of why she could not come outside when she heard Man's footsteps behind her.

"Who's at the door?" he asked gruffly as he strode purposefully towards the open door. He didn't wait for a reply as he brusquely moved Kyrie out of the doorway and replaced her with his large frame, filling the opening.

"Kyrie can't come outside." He slammed the door, turned around, and said to Kyrie sharply, "Don't open that fucking door anymore. Finish those dishes." He grabbed another Budweiser from the refrigerator. Kyrie returned to the kitchen to wipe down the counter, wondering why he never thought to survey her work before reiterating his directives. If he did, he might be compelled to give her a compliment, perhaps say a nice word. She wondered if he knew any nice words.

She had actually finished the mundane task in record time despite the pile of dishes and pans that had accumulated from a day of Man eating and not cleaning up after himself. Why, she asked no one in particular, was it impossible for him to scramble cheese and eggs and then immediately wash the pan before the residue hardened into the pan making it really difficult to clean? She sucked her teeth, making a loud, cheeky sound, then looked around quickly to ensure that he wasn't behind her. In any event, she scrubbed the countertop fervently in order to return to the sanctity of her room and her books.

Kyrie read a lot. For one, it was required of her. Man gave her assignments of books to read and write book reports to validate that she had actually read the books. She had no indication that he actually read the book reports she wrote, but it was mandatory, so she just did it. She really liked to read, but the books he gave her often didn't interest her at all. They were usually dense, usually relevant to African American history or a classic. Kyrie's worst memory of such an assignment was the requirement that she read *Frankenstein* by Mary Shelley while she was in the fifth grade. She didn't understand most of it, but she did get a bunch of new fancy additions for her word list from its pages.

Since her Aunt Michelle also sent her books from Arizona, and she went to the library every chance she could, she always had something she wanted to read, and it was her preferred pastime. It certainly attributed to her high achievement when she took the state English exam for the first time in her fifth-grade year; she tested at a ninth grade reading level. Her teacher, Ms. Jones, seemed very surprised. She asked her to stay during recess to talk to her the day the results came in and asked her a lot of questions. She said that given Kyrie had not been to school except for a few months of fourth grade, her reading comprehension and language arts skills testing four grades above her current level had to be a mistake. However, after Ms. Jones heard the list of books that Kyrie had read in the previous few months, she pursed her lips and said nothing more.

So Kyrie stayed in the apartment most of the time reading her books. Their pages harvested the dense fields of obscurity where she lost herself daily, diving through the brush and evading the thorns of the outside world around her that threatened to slash through her spirit. Through her books, she traveled the distance within her mind to all kinds of places, met a plethora of people, and achieved a special appreciation for experiences, fantasy, and most of all, words. She was never just sitting in the apartment, which is why she didn't mind not going out to play. Playing outside was fine, but not nearly as adventurous as what she experienced in her mind while reading.

Reading also deepened Kyrie's awareness of how much she liked the way words sounded rolling off her tongue, so much so that sometimes she would sit in her room and read out loud. She loved language and words, and since hearing them was entertaining to her, she became enamored with her speaking voice, although sometimes she stuttered. The stutter didn't happen all the time, so while she was sensitive about it, it didn't stop her from volunteering to read passages out loud in class, which her teacher seemed to appreciate given the widespread reluctance of her peers to do the same.

In the spring of fifth grade at P.S. 154, the announcement was made that the school would participate in a Storytelling Contest. Students were encouraged to memorize a storybook, speech, or fable. The challenge was memorizing the work and then reciting it with as much energy and flair as possible to convey the story without hand gestures or other bodily movements. Participants were judged based on their memorization of the work, voice clarity, enunciation, tone, volume, and compelling storytelling.

Ms. Jones announced that there would be a classroom round in one week, followed by a grade level round where the winner from each classroom would compete against winners from the other fifth grade classes in the school district. There would then be a school-wide competition where one winner from the school would move on to a district-wide competition. The winner of the district-wide competition would compete for the New York City title. Ms. Jones thought that Kyrie should certainly compete and kept her after class the day she passed around the sign-up sheet and saw that Kyrie's name was not on it.

"Yes, Ms. Jones, you wanted to see me?" Kyrie waited impatiently by Ms. Jones' desk as the teacher finished up with giving another student a missed homework assignment. She tugged on her cornrows. Her signature style was so tired. She had asked her mother if she could perm her hair so that she could wear it in curls like most of the other girls in her class, but her mother didn't believe in perms right now.

"Kyrie, I want to talk to you about the Storytelling Contest. I was surprised that you didn't sign up. Did you have questions about it?"

"Um, not really. I just don't think I would be good at that," Kyrie replied. She heard the jovial sounds of the schoolyard at dismissal time and wished that she was a part of that fun. Then she remembered that Yvette had left school early that day for a doctor's appointment, so really, there was no one else for her to laugh and joke with after school today. The other girls continued to ignore her except to make fun of her clothes, shoes, or hairstyle.

"What makes you say that, Kyrie? You have a nice speaking voice, and I believe, a talent for public speaking. This contest would be great for you."

Kyrie shook her head. "Thanks, Ms. Jones, but I don't think so."

"I'm going to insist that you tell me what you are apprehensive about. You read aloud in class whenever you have a chance."

Kyrie glanced at the clock above the classroom door. Ten minutes had already elapsed since dismissal. If she didn't get home soon, she would have a whipping waiting for her, just for being late, and an excuse that she was kept after school by the teacher would not help her to avoid it. Her mother was working, and Man's construction job had not come through for the last couple of weeks, so he was home with nothing to do but wait for Kyrie to get home from school and order her around. Ms. Jones's eyes followed Kyrie's to the clock.

"I will write you a note to give to your parents that I asked you to stay after school, will that be ok?"

"Yes, please, Ms. Jones. I'd appreciate that." Ms. Jones didn't appear willing to relinquish her hold on her, so she decided to just get to the point.

"Ms. Jones, I have a lot of chores to do at home, and I really don't think I have time to memorize an entire book by next week."

"But, Kyrie, from what I see from your reading log that you hand in weekly, you spend a considerable amount of time reading, so you clearly find time for that in between your chores, which is great. That can't be it."

Kyrie sighed and glanced at the clock again. Note or no note, she had to get out of this classroom.

"Sometimes, the words don't come out," she blurted. There, she had said it.

"What do you mean, Kyrie?"

"I stutter. It doesn't happen all the time, and since I'm not nervous reading in the classroom, I am usually fine. But standing in front of the room participating in a contest? That's different, and the words would probably get stuck. That's what happens sometimes. The words just get stuck."

Ms. Jones' expression was skeptical. "Well, now that you mention it, I have noticed that sometimes you hesitate before your speak. I may have even heard a slight touch of a stutter at some point. Still, it's not something you don't have completely under control, or you couldn't do what you do every day in class. You couldn't have this conversation that we are having right now without stuttering." Ms. Jones handed her the signup sheet and smiled warmly. "Just sign up and prepare for the classroom contest next week. See how it goes and take it from there. If you don't do well, it won't matter because you won't advance. If you do well but still decide to withdraw, I can certainly choose a runner-up to advance to the next round. Do we have a deal?"

Kyrie took the sheet and scribbled her name on it. If she didn't, Ms. Jones was obviously prepared to continue to hold her hostage.

Ms. Jones smiled and quickly wrote a note for her parents.

I'm sure your parents will be very proud that you volunteered to participate," she beamed.

"Thank you!" Kyrie grabbed the note and ran out of the classroom.

Kyrie chose a children's folktale that she adored called *Anansi the Spider: A Tale from the Ashanti* by Gerald McDermott. Kyrie had loved reading the book aloud since she had come across it in Usian Shule, when she was much younger. She memorized the story over the weekend and began reciting the story before reporting to school on the Monday morning after Ms. Jones had insisted on her participation. At that moment, Ms. Jones reminded Kyrie of her mother, except she was white. Pam was always so confident in Kyrie's ability to do something that she wasn't even sure of herself.

When the day of the classroom competition arrived, Kyrie was nervous but confident. There were several of her classmates competing. Ms. Walker, the school guidance counselor, joined as an additional judge along with Ms. Jones for the classroom round. The students had chosen numbers out of a box that morning to determine their order to present their selections to the class. Kyrie had picked the lowest number, so she would recite last out of four students. Initially, she was happy about that.

A girl named Dawn James recited a passage from *Charlotte's Web* by E.B. White. Dawn wore a red jumper dress and a crisp pair of white Nikes, which she had told everyone who would listen, were brand new. Kyrie watched Dawn carefully, thinking that given how nice Dawn looked, surely she'd do a good job. However, Dawn didn't get beyond the fifth line of her recitation before she was standing there with her mouth gaping open and no words coming out. Memorization was the bare minimum requirement for participation.

After several moments of waiting for her to recall her lines and continue, Ms. Jones politely asked Dawn to take her seat. Next up was Dashawn Williams. Dashawn didn't appear to have on anything new, which made Kyrie feel better about the fact that she certainly didn't have a new outfit today. Dashawn recited a passage from *Tales of a Fourth Grade Nothing* by Judy Blume in the most monotonous tone Kyrie had ever heard. Kyrie wondered if Ms. Jones or someone else had also forced him to participate.

The next person was another girl named Sherece Mathers. Sherece had long cornrow braids that hung down her back and had pretty multi-colored beads on the ends. Kyrie was always fascinated with Sherece's hairstyle for the week; she had a lot of hair, and it was always in a different style. Kyrie was fixated with the swinging of Sherece's braids until her voice floated over the classroom.

Sherece was reciting a poem by Langston Hughes entitled "Mother to Son." Her voice was melodic and strong, and she was very expressive. Kyrie knew that Sherece did a great job when she was done, and the class erupted in a smattering of applause. As Ms. Jones called Kyrie's name to come up, she had started to feel discouraged about her ability to do well.

When Kyrie reached the front of the classroom and turned around to face the class, she was immediately struck by how many classmates were staring back at her; the class just didn't seem as large when she was sitting amongst them. She inhaled deeply, seeking to elicit some strength from somewhere within her. She felt like they were just waiting for her to open her mouth and discover that no words were waiting to come out. She inhaled deeply again. "You can do this, Kyrie," she said to herself.

She had worn her favorite outfit, and while it wasn't new, her flare bottom jeans with the flowers embroidered along the pockets and hemline were really cute, notwithstanding the fact that they were handed down from her cousin. Her white peasant-style top went well with it. She caught Ms. Jones' eye and returned her encouraging smile. Then, fixing her gaze on a hole in the wall, just slightly above the desk of the student in the center last row, she parted her lips and began weaving the tale of Anansi and his seven sons, her voice modulating where appropriate and emoting like no other peer had done. Kyrie felt more encouraged with each page that she turned in her mind, the cadence of her delivery as passionate as if she had written the words herself.

Kyrie did not falter that day, easily winning the classroom round. She won the school-wide competition and beat a dozen other fifth graders from other elementary schools in the district-wide competition. However, she lost in the city-wide competition. The girl who defeated her had long jet-black pigtails tied neatly with yellow ribbons. However, her delivery was exceptional, so it didn't matter to Kyrie. The experience was a good one and taught her that her voice was a force and that people wanted to listen to her. It felt good, despite the loss.

Not long after the school year ended, Kyrie overheard her mother and Man talking about moving again. There was a newly renovated building that Pam had applied for before Man's sister, Aunt Grace, convinced the landlord to rent them the apartment they were currently in. The new apartment was the one Pam had been waiting for. They could move immediately. The apartment was closer to the junior high

111

school that Kyrie would be attending in the fall. In fact, Kyrie would be able to walk to school or take the city bus a couple of stops. Pam was really excited. It was a smaller apartment, but with the city subsidy, she would pay much less than the rent in their current apartment. The packing began.

The day the rented U-Haul was to be loaded, there was trouble. Aunt Grace and Uncle Truth were helping Man and Pam load the truck all day. Kyrie liked Uncle Truth. For reasons unknown to Kyrie, he was called Truth, but she figured that wasn't his real name. She was accustomed to folks being called names other than the ones their parents had given them at birth, although she didn't understand it and it had never been explained to her.

Uncle Truth was nice and quiet, very different from Man. Sometimes Man would get pissed off with Uncle Truth and start an argument, and Uncle Truth would generally not engage. Man probably thought Uncle Truth was a punk, as he was prone to calling any man who didn't argue back with him. Kyrie silently thought Uncle Truth was smart. *Who wanted to be arguing all of the time, especially with family and even more especially when they lived in the same building and had to see each other all of the time?*

On packing day, after the truck was loaded and locked up for the night, Uncle Truth had gone back to his and Aunt Grace's apartment, and Aunt Grace was hanging back talking to Pam in the hallway by the front door. After a few minutes, Man rushed past them without a word, grabbing the keys to the truck on the way out. Pam called after him, but he kept going, returning a few minutes later with an enraged look on his face.

"What's wrong, baby? Did something happen with the U-Haul?" Pam's tone was laced with a forced cheeriness. Her mother knew as Kyrie did, there was something up, and it was not good.

"Where the fuck is Truth?" Man was addressing Aunt Grace and ignoring Pam's question altogether.

"You know Truth went upstairs to have a beer and relax. He told you that a few minutes ago. What's wrong?" Aunt Grace was annoyed.

112

She was generally mild-mannered, and she didn't like Man yelling and cursing.

"Well, he needs to get the fuck back down here. My piece is not in the truck, and he's the only person who knew where it was. He's got some questions to answer, and I'm going to get them answered right the fuck now."

"Are you kidding me?" Aunt Grace was staring at Man with an incredulous look on her face. "You cannot be serious! Are you honestly suggesting that Truth took something from you? I know you have lost your mind now."

"If he didn't take it, where the fuck is it? Get him the fuck down here and let him speak for his damn self." Man was standing in his sister's face, poking his fingers in her direction as he was talking. Aunt Grace was several inches shorter than him, standing a little over five feet. Despite the size difference, she did not appear afraid of him. Kyrie was sitting on the living room floor playing with Sire when the ruckus started and at that moment, was transfixed, glued to the scene unfolding in front of her. She wanted to disappear but could not will her legs to stand.

"Baby, let's just calm down," Pam interjected, placing her hand on Man's arm, the one with the finger poking hand attached. "I'm sure there is an explanation for this. Maybe you didn't put it where you think." Pam's voice was steady. Man flung her hand off of him.

"You shut the fuck up! Don't fucking question me. I know what I did, and I know who was with me," he roared.

At that moment, Aunt Grace laughed wryly. "Just leave this alone, Pam. I'm done. My brother must be crazy. My husband breaks his back all day helping you move your shit, and you have the nerve to accuse him of stealing from you? And a gun? Why would he want or need your gun? Please! You need to get a grip!" Aunt Grace started for the door.

Whack! The backhand slap landed on the side of Aunt Grace's face before she could take two steps. The force of it sent her stumbling in the direction that she was turning. She grabbed her face and hastened to the door screaming obscenities toward Man, who was easily talking over her.

"Who the fuck do you think you are talking to? You better remember who the fuck I am! I am not your punk ass husband! Not a goddamn thing has changed just because you are married. I will still kick your ass. Now tell Truth I want my fucking piece, or I'll be putting my foot in his ass tonight."

Kyrie had not been able to will her legs to pull her up, but she had crawled into her room by this time, dragging Sire across the floor with her. She was hiding behind the door, peeking around at the horrible scene. By this time, Aunt Grace was in the hallway inconsolably crying and screaming at Man, but her words were mostly intelligible. Kyrie was only able to make out, "You call yourself my brother! What kind of brother hits his sister?" She also screamed, "I feel sorry for you," in the direction of her mother.

Eventually, Aunt Grace went upstairs to her apartment and Uncle Truth returned. He and Man argued that night, but Kyrie didn't hear the details because she hid underneath her bed with her new Sony Walkman that her Uncle Will had bought for her recently, reading a book until she fell asleep there. She overheard at some later point that the gun, otherwise referred to as a "piece," was eventually located.

As they drove away from the apartment building the next day, in the U-Haul truck that Uncle Truth and Aunt Grace had helped pack, from the apartment building that Aunt Grace had helped them get into, Kyrie solemnly stared out the window taking in the part of Harlem she had slowly been acquainting herself with. It was slipping away along with the family relationships that had just been eviscerated in the space of a few hours. Kyrie wondered if she would ever see her Aunt Grace and Uncle Truth again. She felt so badly about the whole situation and wished she could do something about it. She wished she could talk about how alone and powerless she felt, with someone, anyone. She didn't. She didn't know who would understand or care.

She turned from the window and back to the book she had escaped into the night before while hiding under the dusty bed. It was fantasy science fiction, and she enjoyed that genre more than anything. Within the worlds created by an author's imagination, the characters could do anything, be anything, and survive anything. Kyrie was enamored with the power those characters, vicariously by their puppet masters, had within their stories.

She gazed at the shining stars at night before she went to sleep and yearned for the power, deep and mysterious powers to control her existence and the bad around her. If she had powers, she would disappear from this existence, and then she would obliterate all the bad feelings. The see-saw would be fun, regardless of whether she was going up or down.

Kyrie was almost 9 years old.

CHAPTER 13

Power of Her

"Back Stabbers" - The O'Jays

The move uptown delivered Kyrie into a predominantly Hispanic environment. Where previously Kyrie had interacted mostly with other black folks, here there was a bodega on the corner of their block that Cubans ran. Kyrie went there frequently to pick up items that were needed for the family. The people working in the bodega and those that hung out inside and on the corner only spoke Spanish to each other. Kyrie loved the way the language sounded, although it was sometimes frustrating that she had no clue about the conversations around her.

The newly renovated building meant the apartment was in pristine condition when they moved in. Newer should have meant nicer, but Kyrie missed their old place, which made her feel more upscale and mysterious with its ornate crown moldings, French doors, and long hallways. Also, this apartment was much smaller.

There were only two bedrooms; her parents took the smaller one because Kyrie had to share the larger bedroom with Sire during the day. This meant that she could no longer keep him out, which did not sit well with Kyrie. He was cute, but she couldn't tolerate him around her all the time; she desperately wanted her own space. She found that solitude on the fire escape. There were no window shades in either of the two windows in her room, so her mother hung sheets with nails. Sometimes she would go out there, close the window behind her and pull the sheet. In the beginning, Sire wouldn't immediately think to look for her out there so she could steal some moments for herself. Beyond that, he was at her side.

Junior high school was promising initially. I.S. 195 in Manhattan boasted a program called S.T.A.R.S that segmented children who were high achieving academically and kept them together for the three years of sixth to eighth grade, exposing them to a uniform set of teachers focused specifically on the group and a higher degree of academic standards than the general population. Kyrie was proud to have been selected for this program and excited to start and meet new people.

The school also touted being a performing arts school so those not in S.T.A.R.S could choose various sub-schools to focus on, including Vocal Music and Instrumental. Kyrie loved to sing and felt she had some inherited vocal talent from Pam. She sang at home whenever she could, so she thought she would have enjoyed the Vocal Music sub-school, but S.T.A.R.S was identified for her, so she began with no complaints.

She was happy that she would be able to take Vocal Music as a class at some point. Yvette was attending the same school and program so she felt reassurance in that she would have at least one friend, which alleviated much of the trepidation that she generally carried into new environments. She soon learned that many of her other fifth-grade brethren were also attending I.S. 195, some of which also were also placed in the S.T.A.R.S program. While the work was different and the venue had changed, the peer composition was very similar.

They settled into the new apartment quickly. Man quickly identified the local number spot to play his numbers, various denominations of 50 cents and up on straight and number combinations. Any variation of that number would win him some money as long as he played it

118

straight in addition to combinations. If he hit the number, he'd win money.

Kyrie never understood how it worked, and since he lost daily and won infrequently, she began to wonder if it wouldn't make more sense to just save the dollars he took to the number spot instead of betting the money, particularly since he didn't have a job to support his habit. The sporadic construction work had dried up sometime before they left the old apartment, and it didn't appear that there was any other employment for him on the horizon.

Pam had started a new job and was working in an office downtown in the Times Square area. She still sang as much as she could, but she often said that the infrequency of singing gigs made singing "an insufficient income stream from which to feed four mouths." Then, soon after they moved to the smaller space, Pam shared that she was five months pregnant. Their family was growing to five. Kyrie was partially excited; she'd always thought that she would enjoy a sister, but then she wasn't thrilled about having one more person to do laundry for and clean up after.

And then there were the conversations about money or lack of money. At age 10, these conversations interested Kyrie; by age 13, they frustrated her, and by age 16, they incensed her. They were the same every week. On payday, her mother would cash her check before she came home from work. Within five minutes of having entered the apartment, Man would be calling out. This day was no different.

"Pam, let me get that money."

"Here you go. They took out a lot for taxes."

Man counted the money, put it in his pocket, and remarked brusquely. "You're going to have to figure something else out. This shit ain't enough to do much of nothing."

"Yes, I know. I've got a few things I'm working on. We're going be all right in just a minute." When Pam spoke of her ideas, or her next move, her voice was always full of promise. "Thinking positive is the only way to live, so I've got positivity drenched in enough optimism to fill a large body of water!" Kyrie heard her mother say that at least once a day.

Man always left the apartment shortly after collecting Pam's earnings from her. He would return after playing his evening numbers and with his entertainment for the evening. On a regular, non-payday, the drink of choice was Budweiser. Weed, sometimes referred to in their apartment as reefer, was around the apartment daily. Man would leave it on a magazine and roll his joints to smoke throughout the day. Kyrie didn't love it, but she could tolerate the smell of weed; it didn't make her nauseous like some of the other smells that often raided her senses.

On Pam's payday and the days immediately following, there would be brandy, sometimes cognac; Man's label of choice was Hennessy. Both delivered odors she despised. And frequently incorporated into Man's repertoire was the white powder. The white powder didn't have a smell unless Man put it into a cigarette and smoked it. She preferred for him to put it in his nose because then it was odorless. The smell of it burning made her sick to her stomach. Kyrie later learned that its name was cocaine, but fearful of its power, she referred to it only as "the white powder," "She," or "Her."

Kyrie never forgot when she had come across the white powder as a young child and Pam had placed a tiny bit on her tongue to prove to her that it was not sugar. Kyrie hadn't liked Her then, and she liked Her less now since Kyrie understood the white powder's strength. The white powder had powers, mind-altering powers, and the very presence of Her in the apartment infused Kyrie with intense fear.

She arrived lying innocently inside tin foil. Kyrie would watch Man unleash the white powder gingerly. After inspecting Her closely for a few moments, he would use a razor blade, chopping Her and moving Her around in a saucer until the small pebbles were granules so fine they were individually indiscernible. Kyrie would sometimes inspect Her when she was left unattended, as she wasn't always consumed in one sitting.

After dicing Her for several minutes, Man would then use a small piece of cardboard to get a pencil tip size portion onto the tip. Then he would raise the cardboard slowly and carefully to one nostril so as not to waste one morsel. While pressing the opposite nostril flat with his forefinger, he would snort the white powder quickly into his nose. That motion would immediately cause what appeared to be an involuntary but hard shake of his head, followed by a few sniffles in close succession. That would continue for a while until he had enough, all the while taking long sips of his brown liquor sitting in the glass beside him.

On the nights that the white powder reigned, Kyrie stayed out of the way, not venturing out of her room unless she had to use the bathroom. Kyrie had watched the scene unfold enough times to know that it was generally the same episode, although she was always scared that one day it would have a different ending. While indulging in Her, Man sat in the small dinette area, the only area of the apartment that provided a clear view of the apartment's front door. He'd sit there for hours tightly clutching a large butcher knife he would remove from the kitchen drawer early in the evening.

Man didn't really talk much during this time, so it was beneficial only in that Kyrie couldn't get in trouble for anything during her reign. He'd sit there for hours, watching the door and shooting furtive glances around him. Eventually, he would rise every few minutes, hugging the wall as he approached the door. He would bend down, getting so close to the doorknob that his ear likely grazed the cool metal, and listen, intently for several long minutes. The knife would be in his hand, held firmly as if he was poised to attack.

After a few minutes of crouching there, he would turn and slowly return to the chair, only to repeat the same conduct over and over, sometimes for hours. It was a scene that crippled Kyrie with fear for a long time. Kyrie had no idea what was going on. When she was little, she thought the white man that Man spoke about with such disdain was coming, and Man was waiting to kill him. As she got older, she realized that it was nothing more than the power of Her, the white powder, that made him act crazy. There was no one on the other side of the door.

Given Man's frequent bouts of anger even when sober, she had no confidence that he wouldn't decide one day that she, her mother, or Sire were the enemy, although they were on the right side of the door. What would stop him from stabbing them to death during a random night of Her reign? As the years accumulated, and he repeated the same scene but never actually did anything physically harmful, her feelings of fear transitioned into validation of her disgust of him, and she merely worked extra hard at being absent from his space when the white powder was in control for the night. In Kyrie's mind, She was queen, her power undeniably potent, yet Kyrie did not understand her purpose. Kyrie didn't understand why Man would put Her in his nose if it always made him believe imaginary forces that he had to defend against were outside the door.

But the issue that was really troubling Kyrie's ten-year-old mind was the money. They didn't have much, and Kyrie really didn't understand why Man didn't work. Her mother would just tell her that he couldn't. So Man sat on the couch all day, every day, while Pam went to work every day and then on payday, he demanded and fully expected her to turn over her pay to him, which she did with no argument. When food items and other necessities were needed, Pam would ask for money, and he would give it to her in increments. The way Kyrie saw it, Man primarily used the money to play his numbers and buy beer, weed, and the white powder whenever he felt like it.

Kyrie couldn't digest the seeds of disgust that grew within her, and with each bilious occurrence, they lingered in her gut and festered. They had no outlet. One day she tried to talk to her mother about it. Pam was noticeably pregnant and not indulging in alcohol intake with Man, nor did Kyrie ever observe her indulging in any of the drugs that Man seemed to enjoy so much.

"Mommy, why do you work all week and then give your pay to him?" She was talking quietly so Man could not hear her.

Pam shot her a sharp look. Kyrie prayed that she wouldn't begin speaking loudly where Man could hear. Her mother did that sometimes, appearing to Kyrie as if she intentionally sought to draw him into a conversation that had started between her and Kyrie, which

122

usually resulted in Man reprimanding Kyrie for something she had done or said.

"Because it really doesn't matter who holds the money, Kyrie. I work for our family. The money comes in for us to live on, and if it makes your father feel better to hold it, I'm fine with it, so you don't need to worry about it."

Kyrie did not say anything further, but she did continue to worry about it. She wanted so badly to ask her mother why she didn't feel scared when the white powder reigned and Man acted crazy with the butcher knife, but she decided it wasn't worth risking Man overhearing that query. She would surely get her butt whipped for minding grown-ups' business, as she had been long warned was not advisable. So she convinced herself to ignore it.

Ignoring the aspects of her life that were scary was the way she began to cope. Disregarding the events that unfolded around her that she didn't fully comprehend was the approach she began to take. Silence about the activities that Man engaged in was the required response. As she gained an overt awareness that agitation, not answers, would be elicited, she swallowed her questions. To compound matters, Pam gave birth to a little girl a few months later. They named her Kiyanna. She was cute, but Kyrie couldn't help but wonder how her mother was going to afford to feed her on her salary. After a few weeks, Kyrie realized that all the baby seemed to be good for was crying and eating. She began to ignore the baby because focusing on her presence gave Kyrie more angst than any pre-teen needed to be consumed with.

Silence became her solace, and her music and books her only dependable and consistent companion.

Junior high school suited Kyrie well academically. The work was not exceptionally challenging, and she was now accustomed to not being one of the popular girls. In addition to Yvette, by seventh grade, she made one other friend.

Mona Payne was new to both the school and the country. Mona's family had recently immigrated to the United States from Barbados. Mona was light brown and had almond-shaped eyes and long wavy dark brown hair that hung down her rear end. Her clothes were not particularly stylish, and given her "new" and immigrant status, she didn't immediately fit in. Mona was quiet with a kind demeanor. More importantly, she didn't act arrogant and conceited just because she had a bundle of coveted hair flowing down her back. She and Kyrie became friends fast. It also helped that she lived on the same street as Kyrie, one avenue over, so they could ride the bus home together. Having a buddy to travel with minimized the bullying from other kids.

It wasn't as bad as it had been. While Dwayne Graver had also transitioned to this school and remained in her class, he and his merry band of followers had either matured or lost interest in her because they barely paid her any mind. At this point, there was only unwelcome attention from a group of girls from the housing projects, with a specific interest in Kyrie paid by the most nondescript of the bunch, Rhonda Morrison.

Rhonda was very thin, not dissimilar in build from Kyrie but had a taunt wiry look about her face. Kyrie thought she favored a rat to a certain extent but would never say anything so mean out loud. Rhonda was fairly dark-skinned, a shade or two darker than Kyrie, which is why her taking to calling Kyrie "Blackie" was baffling to Kyrie. Rhonda would follow her to the bathroom, taunt her while she was in the stall, and get in her face at the sink while she washed her hands. Kyrie ignored her, which seemed to incense Rhonda further, and she began to threaten to beat her up after school.

After school, if Kyrie was with Mona, Rhonda would not bother her. If Mona was not in school or left early for some reason, Rhonda would follow Kyrie until she got to the bus stop, her friends in tow, laughing and bolstering her. Kyrie wasn't necessarily afraid of Rhonda, but she was afraid to fight. She had never feared that Dwayne Graver was going to actually hit her, so the taunting she received during her entire Fifth Grade year was merely embarrassing and annoying, yet it didn't scare her. Rhonda was different; she seemed to want to fight. Kyrie was so worried about it that she defied her commitment to not bring her school business home and blurted it out while talking to her mother one day.

"Rhonda Morrison won't leave me alone! I don't know what to do. She hates me for no reason! I haven't done anything to her!" Kyrie had planned on a calm delivery to not alarm her mother, but her exasperation took over as soon as she opened her mouth to speak.

"What do you mean, she won't leave you alone, Ky? What is she doing?" Pam's voice was tinged with concern.

"She follows me around. Sometimes, she knocks my food to the floor at lunch, acting like it's an accident, but everyone knows she does it on purpose because she's mean, and she tells everyone that she doesn't like me. She always acts like she has to use the bathroom whenever I go to the bathroom, and then when she gets to the bathroom, she teases me and says nasty things to me, calling me ugly. I try to ignore her, but the other day, she started saying she was going to beat me up if I didn't talk back." Kyrie's voice cracked on this last admission. She really didn't want to fight this girl. She didn't want to fight anyone.

"What do you do when she's picking on you?" Pam asked, her eyes tender with emotion. "And how long has this been going on? I will come up there tomorrow and straighten this shit out – get her mother's ass up to the school and let her know we will not tolerate this bullying."

Pam was pissed. Kyrie was now sniffling, holding back the tears. She wasn't sure if her mother coming to the school was the best way to handle it, but at that moment, she felt like anything was better than her having to fight Rhonda Morrison. Surely a fight would get her suspended. Plus, there was a rumor that Rhonda had slashed a girl in a fight in the projects.

"I just ignore her, and she usually gets angrier, but then she stops until the next day."

"Dammit, Ky, I wish you would have told me this before. I will go to your school first thing in the morning."

"Told you what?"

Man, as usual, moving with the stealthiness of a cat, had once again entered the room without either of them noticing. *He's always sneaking up on people.*

"Some little girl has been bullying Kyrie in school… threatening to beat her up. I'm going up to that school tomorrow to talk to the principal, and if he doesn't handle this, I will deal with the little bully myself." Pam was angry. Kyrie didn't recall seeing her that angry in a long while.

Man turned to Kyrie. "What? Some little bitch is messing with you, and you're here snitching to your mother about it? What the fuck are you doing while she's fucking with you?" He was speaking quietly, but Kyrie knew from his tone that he was mad.

"N-n-n-nothing," she stammered. "I usually just try to g-g-get away from her." Although it was Man and angry was his standard, she was taken aback by the tone. For once, she couldn't figure out what she had done wrong, and she wasn't sure where this was going.

"Oh hell no! Not in this house. I'm not raising no punks. If this little bitch is fucking with you, you better fight her. That's the only way she's going to leave you alone, and you gain respect in the street." He turned to Pam. "You're not going up to that school to protect her. She's going to have to learn how to fend for her damn self."

Pam's visage could not mask the shadow of uncertainty. "Honey, I don't think she should be fighting. Let me just go talk to the principal. I'm sure that…"

"No, dammit!" Man's fist smashed onto the table with alarming force. "Kyrie is going to handle this herself!"

He turned to Kyrie and bent down so that he was very close to her face. "Let me tell you something, little girl. In my house, you stand up for yourself. You're not ever going to get in trouble here for defending yourself, even if it means you have to fight! Now, if you come in here talking about somebody's fucking with you and you ran, that's when you're going to get your ass kicked, right here. You got that?" Man used his forefinger to poke her in the forehead, punctuating each word from the "get your ass kicked" part of the edict.

The finger poking was not exceptionally hard, but it seemed to make his words pierce her in a stabbing way. Pin-sized drops of spittle bounced onto her face as he spoke. She felt rage and fear simultaneously churning in her gut so violently she thought she would vomit or scream. She did neither. Self-control was best.

Kyrie nodded her head quickly to communicate an understanding of his message, swallowing hard to bite back the tears that she felt forming. She could see her mother out of the corner of her eye. Pam was no longer actively engaged in the conversation and had instead directed her attention to the dishes in the sink that she was cleaning intently. Kyrie was dumbfounded. Without thinking, she turned to her, silently begging her for support.

"Don't look for your mother to do a damn thing. Now get out of my face and don't come back in here with that punk shit again." Kyrie turned and quickly left the room.

That was one of the first times that her mother appeared willing to protect her but backed down and away. It was the first of many.

It didn't take long for Rhonda to strike again. Mona broke her leg and was out of school for several days, which meant that Kyrie had to walk to the bus stop after school solo. She went to the bathroom right before dismissal, and Rhonda followed. When she exited the stall, Rhonda was standing there, waiting.

"I want you to know that I'm going to kick your ass after school today, for real this time." Rhonda's voice was low, and she was standing so close to Kyrie's face that Kyrie could smell the remnants of that day's bologna sandwich lunch on her breath. *Why do people stand so close to me that I know all their food choices for the day?* Then she felt a drop of Rhonda's spittle bounce onto her; it landed in that small space right between her nose and her top lip.

127

Like the proverbial lightbulb being flicked on, she had enough. The rage rose within her so quickly it actually surprised her. Equally shocking was the power she felt. Kyrie examined the girl as if for the first time. Rhonda looked as insecure as Kyrie felt. At that moment, she felt capable of putting her hands around Rhonda's neck and squeezing the life out of her. This was not Man standing in front of her. Man, she could not beat. Rhonda, on the other hand, was not any larger than Kyrie. In fact, she was a bit scrawny. *I don't need to be afraid of this girl.* She felt a calming sensation. She stared at Rhonda's neck for a few moments and acknowledged that it was indeed a very frail neck. She smiled.

"Why are you smiling, ugly girl? Did you hear me promise to kick your ass today?" Rhonda's cronies were laughing behind her. Kyrie shook her head hard, summoning herself out of her momentary trance. She calmly wiped the spittle from her face and raised both of her hands, and shoved Rhonda out of her face with all of her strength. The force of the shove, along with the unexpectedness of it, landed Rhonda on her ass. Rhonda's friends gasped. Rhonda, stunned, was momentarily motionless, on the floor, resting in her disbelief. By the time she was attempting to pull herself up, Kyrie was standing over her. She addressed her calmly.

"I've been patient with you, waiting for you to find somebody else to mess with. Today, I'm done taking your shit. I've never done anything to you, but you want to fight – so let's go! I'll meet your ignorant ass in the yard after school. I've got your punching bag."

With that, Kyrie turned on her heel and left the bathroom. She returned to her desk and took a deep breath. She did not know what had happened in the bathroom, where that strength of mind had come from, but she was calm and no longer worried. She smiled to herself, realizing what she had done. *That was bad-ass!* Maybe Man was in her somewhere after all.

She had a momentary pause, thinking that Rhonda might emerge from the bathroom and go straight to the teacher to report Kyrie for shoving her, but she didn't concern herself with that for long. Man was right about something; kids from the hood didn't generally resolve their social battles through snitching. Instead, they handled their business themselves. True to form, Rhonda returned to her seat. Kyrie did not give her any attention and instead waited patiently for the bell to ring. However this was going to go, she had to be ready. Dealing with Rhonda was considerably better than dealing with Man's craziness.

After school, she hurried out and waited at the edge of the schoolyard. Rhonda took a while to come out, so most of the schoolyard had cleared. When she emerged from the school building, Rhonda was also alone. Kyrie was surprised. She had expected Rhonda to spread the word that she was going to fight Kyrie so that she would have a crowd of observers cheering her on. As she approached, Kyrie started walking toward her, talking loudly as she strode. Her voice was so loud that she didn't even recognize it as her own.

"Let's go, Rhonda. Why are you moving so slow? Let's see the ass-kicking you're supposed to be giving me!" As she got closer, she threw her book bag onto the ground and pulled her arm back, determined to swing first.

"WaitKyrielistenIthoughtyouweretalkingbout'mebehindmybackbu tVanessatoldmetodayitwasn'tyouafterallitwasTammyJosephsoIdon'tha venobeefwitchuyounomoreWedon'thavetofight." Rhonda delivered that soliloquy in a tumbling jumble of breathy words. "Unless you want to," she added with uncertainty.

"I don't want or need to fight you, but I certainly will to keep you out of my face." Kyrie looked at her incredulously. Rhonda's neck still appeared frail, her expression meek. She shook her head. She couldn't believe that she had let this joke of a girl bully her for weeks.

"You want to be friends?" Rhonda said with a small smile.

"Um, whatever." Kyrie rolled her eyes, picked up her bookbag, and for the second time that day, turned and walked away from Rhonda Morrison. As she made her way to the bus stop, she heard Rhonda yell. "See you tomorrow, Kyrie." She didn't respond. She was glad that Rhonda lived downtown and caught a different bus line home. She didn't want to be anywhere near that girl.

As she waited for the bus, she shook her head and thought about what had just transpired. The fear of Man disciplining her for not standing up for herself had incited her to do just that, and showing bravado and a readiness to brawl with her words was all it took to get Rhonda to back down. For once, she felt like Man's ire had paid off. He was right about something, but she wouldn't tell him that.

She had difficulty forgiving her mother, who had opted to forego standing up for her and failed to defend and protect her just because Man had told her not to.

Ironically, Rhonda spent the rest of the school year trying to be Kyrie's friend. Kyrie was civil enough to keep any problems at bay but had no interest in befriending her or any of her cronies.

After Mona broke her leg, she returned to school with crutches and a requirement to leave school 15 minutes early to avoid the crowds that would potentially jostle her leg in the hard cast. She was also allowed to choose a friend who lived close enough to her to leave school with her every day in order to help her with her books. Her choice was Kyrie. Kyrie felt special and was ecstatic when her parents agreed.

Kyrie and Mona had become close. They both loved to sing and were trying out for parts in the school production of The Wiz. Mona's voice was nice, but Kyrie knew that hers was the stronger voice. She enjoyed hanging out with her friend to help her practice various parts as they prepped for the auditions. Kyrie was nervous. The vocal teacher favored Mona; he said she looked the part for Dorothy with her long hair, and he would routinely take extra time with her in class. Kyrie knew she could sing every song from the production better than Mona. She prepared for and presented what she thought was a strong audition. A few days later, when the cast lists were posted, they ran to see them together before heading to the bus stop at dismissal.

"Do you see your name, Kyrie?"

Kyrie didn't answer. She was running her finger up and down the list as her eyes scanned. She felt her heart sink. Her name wasn't there. Mona's was.

"Oh my goodness! I was cast as Dorothy! I can't believe it." Mona turned to Kyrie. "I'm sorry, Ky. I just knew you would be cast as Dorothy! Your voice is amazing. You really rocked "Be A Lion" at the audition. It must be a mistake. Let's go talk to Mr. Barton." Mona was sincere.

It's ok, Mona. There will be other parts. He really likes you. And you will make a good Dorothy; you even have the pigtails." She smiled at her friend, who looked really sad. "I'll help you with the songs."

"Are you sure, Kyrie? I know how bad you wanted this. I can't believe that he didn't cast you for any part."

"It's fine. Let's go before we miss another bus." Kyrie linked arms with Mona, and they walked out of the building together. Inside, Kyrie was devastated. She had never felt jealous of Mona before that day, not jealous of her pretty hair or her perfect medium brown complexion, although they were together all of the time, and it was those attributes of Mona's that people commented on. Kyrie was just happy to have a friend who was nice and accepted her for her. But on the day that the audition results were posted, Kyrie battled jealousy for the first time because she felt deep down that her vocal talent should have earned her a role.

She swallowed her jealousy. She did not feel ill will towards Mona; Mona was her friend. She helped Mona practice, working with her after school on her notes and her range and then, cheered for her on production night, despite her heavy heart. She learned through that experience that when you are a true friend and have a true friend, you support them even when they achieve something that you wanted for yourself. You care about their happiness and care about the friendship. Home was a battlefield, so Kyrie decided she really needed her friends, of which she really didn't have many. Yvette and Mona were it. Keeping them was important to her.

131

At some point between seventh and eighth grade, Man began allowing her to spend time outside in the neighborhood. Their apartment building was located on a steep hill and nestled on the bottom of that hill, and across the busy Riverside Drive was a playground. She wasn't allowed to leave the stoop except to go to the playground, and most of the time, Sire had to be attached to her side. On the rare occasion that he wasn't with her, she would sneak behind the staircase with Mark Lorenz.

Mark lived around the corner and was the first boy that didn't pick on her. They started off just hanging out in the playground until his friend Chris, who lived in her building, told Kyrie that Mark liked her and wanted her to be his girlfriend. Mark was caramel complexion, skinny, and a little taller than Kyrie. His hair was cut short, and Kyrie thought he was cute enough, but he always did stupid things like ringing the bell to her apartment and running off.

When Chris told her that Mark liked her, she was happy. They progressed quickly from trading barbs at the playground to sneaking behind the staircase in her building. There, she would kiss a little and sometimes let him squeeze her breasts. However, when he asked her to let him stick his thing in her, she called him stupid, pushed him down, and ran into her apartment. He broke up with her the next day for another girl in the neighborhood. Their little romance had lasted all of three weeks.

The summer started, and she met a new girl who was in the neighborhood with her dad for the summer; her parents were separated and she lived with her mom down south. Bray was a few years older than Kyrie, 14, and she and Kyrie hit it off immediately. They had a love of reading in common and talked about books constantly.

Bray and Kyrie started hanging out together every day, usually in the playground at the bottom of Kyrie's block, and Kyrie thought for sure that Bray was destined to be her new best friend. It was great because she didn't see Yvette much over the summer because she lived down by 125th street, and Man rarely permitted Kyrie to leave the vicinity. Mona spent most of the summer in Barbados, and even when she was home, her mother was even more strict than Man. Mona hardly ever came outside.

Bray filled an immediate need; a girlfriend who lived around the corner, had a little freedom, and had things in common with her. They had a blast, laughing, playing cards on the stoop, and just being silly. Kyrie dreaded the end of the summer when Bray would return to her home state.

As the summer's end was approaching, both girls were sad, and after some begging, Man relented and agreed to let Bray sleep over. Kyrie told Bray they would sleep on the floor, and Bray agreed to bring her sleeping bag. After lights out, they lay on the floor laughing and giggling about the people in the neighborhood and Mark still trying to sweet talk Kyrie although everybody knew he was seeing some girl who lived on Amsterdam Avenue. Kyrie felt in that moment that she and Bray had more fun that summer than she had ever had.

"What is down south like?" Kyrie asked, yawning. It had to be 3 am, and she was finally feeling drowsy. Bray had hidden two Bartels & James wine coolers in her bag, which they had been sipping for hours. It was her first time drinking any kind of alcoholic beverage, so she attributed that to the cloudy feeling in her head.

"It's boring, compared to here." Bray sighed. She sat up on her elbow. "I don't have any friends back home that I like as much as you. I'm going to miss you, Ky. We have to write each other." Bray's voice was low. Kyrie could hardly hear her, but she attributed that to the fact that she was drifting off to sleep.

"Yeah, we should do that. We can write about the books we are reading, you can tell me about high school, and I will tell you about eighth grade." Kyrie felt her eyelids getting heavier. She yawned again. "I'm gonna miss you, too. We will definitely write. You first," she murmured, her eyes finally closed. She drifted off to sleep.

"Me first, huh? How much you gonna miss me, Ky? Let me show you how much I'm gonna miss you."

Within seconds Bray had pushed up Kyrie's gown, moved the crotch of her underwear aside while parting Kyrie's legs, and had her head firmly in between Kyrie's legs nuzzling Kyrie's vagina with her lips and tongue.

Kyrie's eyes shot open. She was frozen. She cried out, or she thought she did, but no sound came out. *What is happening?*

"Bray, what are you doing? Stop!" She was whispering because only God knew what would happen to both of them if they were caught. *If Man walked in here right now, what would happen?* Her mind was racing. Bray was moaning and holding Kyrie's thighs firmly with both of her hands, her mouth's pressure intensifying.

Kyrie realized at that moment how strong Bray was. Although she was only two years older than her, she had a stocky build and was probably about thirty pounds heavier than Kyrie. Kyrie tried to push Bray's head off of her, which just made Bray's movements intensify. Bray's hands were tightly fastened onto Kyrie's thighs, making moving difficult. Kyrie choked back a scream, and tried not to focus on what Bray was doing to her or what it felt like. All she knew for sure was that she felt sick to her stomach. *I'm not fighting her hard enough.* The moment that acknowledgment triggered in her brain, a wave of embarrassment, shame, and guilt overwhelmed her.

As if she was reading Kyrie's mind, Bray moaned a little louder and raised her head to look up at Kyrie. "You know you like this, Ky. Now, do me."

"No...Bray...Please... I don't want this. It's not right... somebody is going to come..." Her pleas were strangled and hoarse, delivered in the loudest whisper she dared. Kyrie struggled to lift herself from the floor as Bray firmly pushed her back down. As Kyrie fell back, Bray quickly hoisted herself upward, attempting to position her pelvic area above Kyrie's mouth. With her hand cupping the back of Kyrie's head, she forcefully pushed Kyrie's head towards her.

The perplexing feelings Kyrie reluctantly acknowledged when Bray's head was between her legs quickly turned to disgust as Bray's scent reached her nostrils. Kyrie gagged. She jerked her head to the side while using all of her strength to push Bray off of her.

Bray fell backward onto the floor next to her. Kyrie hastily pulled herself into a sitting position and tried to make out Bray's form in the dark. She couldn't see her, but she felt her on the floor next to her. Bray did not move, and she also didn't say anything.

Kyrie sat very still, her breathing shallow, her heart beating uncontrollably, and her mind racing. What would happen next? Would she have to fight Bray off of her right here in her bedroom? How would she explain that to her parents when they came into the room to investigate the racket? Kyrie started counting under her breath to calm herself, pondering her next move to keep Bray off of her without making any noise. Then it occurred to her, to flee.

Kyrie jumped up and went to the bathroom. Although she had not tasted Bray, she brushed her teeth for about 5 minutes in an attempt to rid her mind of the scent of her. When she was done, she brought her hand slowly between her legs and then snatched it away abruptly, sucking in air sharply. She was swollen down there. She grabbed her washcloth and wet it with the hottest water she could tolerate and rubbed vigorously to scrub away the memory of Bray's touch.

When she was sufficiently raw, she decided she was done. She glanced around the bathroom, taking in the cracked paint, the soiled walls, the dried, yellow-stained urine around the toilet. She glanced in the mirror and then quickly turned her head away. She had no desire to look at her reflection. She felt dirty, no different from the grime around her. She sat down on the closed toilet seat for some time, unsure of what to do.

After a while, she returned to the floor of her room to Bray's even breathing and knew that she was asleep. Feeling relieved, Kyrie lay awake for what felt like an eternity. She wasn't sure what she was supposed to do or what she was supposed to feel. She was so confused. She had trusted Bray. She thought they were friends. So many unanswered questions flowed through her mind. *What does this mean? Was this sex?*

She had heard that some girls had sex together, and she also heard that it wasn't right. She hadn't asked for it, certainly had not anticipated it, and had not conceded to Bray's attempts. *Had it felt good initially, before I realized what was actually happening? No! Absolutely not!* The thought made her stomach turn, but she wasn't sure if it was because Bray was her friend or because Bray was a girl. And when Bray demanded the reciprocal act from her, she had been thoroughly disgusted. *What Bray did to me was wrong, right? Is it my fault if I didn't willingly participate?*

Kyrie began to cry softly. *What did I do to make Bray think I wanted this?* Bray was supposed to be her friend. *Is Bray a lesbian? Is being a lesbian wrong?* She knew that her body had initially warmed and moistened to Bray's unsolicited touch. *Am I a lesbian?* There was the nausea again. *What's going to happen in the morning when we face each other?*

She had shared a lot with Bray over the summer, including the details of how she had let Mark kiss her and fondle her breasts. She had also told Bray that she liked how it made her feel to be touched but that she had no desire to let Mark stick his penis in her. *Did Bray assume that I wanted another girl to touch me down there with her mouth?* She reminded herself that although she wouldn't let Mark even touch her down there, she really liked him kissing her and feeling on her breasts. *Doesn't that mean I'm a normal girl?*

Kyrie cried harder. She lay in the dark and asked herself all of these questions, to which she had no answers. At some point, she drifted off to sleep. When she awoke late the next morning, she was relieved to find that Bray was gone.

"I guess your first sleepover was fun! You guys were up cackling into the night," Pam remarked cheerfully when Kyrie ventured tentatively out of her room. She was petrified about what had been overheard in the still of the night. "No surprise that you would sleep until after 1 pm this afternoon. Bray's dad was by to get her early; he said they had a lot of shopping to do before he got on the road to take her back down south in a few days. She said to tell you she would call you later."

Kyrie was quiet, only nodding in response. After brushing her teeth again and having some breakfast, she returned to her room and closed the door. She stayed in that room for the next week, leaving the house only to go to the store when forced. The nausea returned every time she thought about what Bray had done to her. She felt like a coward. She berated herself for all of the actions she should have taken but didn't. On the second day, she wrote a list.

Things to do to avenge Bray's backstabbing betrayal:

1. Go to Bray's apartment and demand an explanation.
2. Slip a note under her door telling her she was wrong to do that to her without her permission.
3. Go to the apartment, and when Bray opens the door, punch her in the face and walk away.
4. Something.
5. Anything.

But Kyrie did nothing but hide. As the days passed, she worked hard to push the memory as far away as she could, and she swore to herself to tell no one. Bray called a few times before she left New York. Each time, Kyrie pretended that she was busy and could not come to the phone. Her mother began to remark that they must have had an argument, to which Kyrie didn't respond.

On the day Bray was leaving, she called again, and Kyrie feigned sleep. Bray told Pam to give Kyrie her goodbyes wishes and promised that she would write. Then, Bray disappeared. For Kyrie, it was as if she never existed. She pushed both Bray's existence and the memory of what had occurred deep down into the tunnel in her mind. Kyrie never saw or heard from Bray again.

She did not speak of that night again, for decades. She also became more cautious of people she allowed to enter her space and call themselves friends, although she continued to long for connections. Eighth grade began, transpired, and ended with no further drama. After continuously surviving nights of the white powder's reign, Bray's betrayal, and Man's random wrath, she felt like she could handle anything. "I am the most powerful," she told herself. "I am a superhero," Kyrie repeated that until she started to believe it.

Kyrie was 12 years old.

CHAPTER 14

Whole Person

"Free" - Deniece Williams

Kyrie was particularly tired of hearing how proud she should be about her successful admission into the specialized high school system of New York City. This point was made repeatedly by her homeroom teacher, her French teacher, the school administrators, and her mother. Apparently, many students took the entrance exam annually, but few actually got in. "You are among the gifted and smart. What a great school and true testament to the value of a good public education, blah, blah, blah." She was sick of hearing it because it didn't matter to her. It was not her school choice.

"I don't like math or science," she complained to her mother the week that the acceptance letter arrived in the mail. "I want to go to LaGuardia, School of Performing Arts. I want to sing, and I can sing if I have the chance to study vocal technique and get better."

"This is a better school, Kyrie. Plus, you auditioned for LaGuardia. Remember, you didn't get in," Pam replied. Her voice was sympathetic. She had hugged a crying Kyrie the day she emerged from the audition, distraught because she knew she would not get in after her embarrassing display. She had a "nice, strong voice," they had said. However, she knew that the fact that she could not read music would be fatal to her audition.

They had handed her sheet music and asked her to sing several scales, represented in notes on the pages of the sheet music. She had responded, quite ignorantly, "I'm sorry, what would you like me to read? There are no words on this page." To that, the audition judges reminded her that she had checked off on her application that she could, in fact, read music. She apologized and looked at them with a dumbfounded stare; she hadn't understood the question to mean "music notes."

After a few moments of silence, she asked if she could sing what she had prepared for the audition, and they waved her on. She belted out the first verse of "The Greatest Love of All," which had been recently released by Whitney Houston. They stopped her after the first verse, smiled at her appreciatively, thanked her for coming in, and dismissed her.

She had cried all evening. She was disappointed in herself for not taking the music reading more seriously and angry with her mother for not preparing her adequately. Pam had been a singer her entire life, but she had no formal music reading skills either. Whatever her mother knew, she had picked up on her own over the years. So, although Kyrie was often told she had an amazing voice, she did not get in. The alternative was her local zone school, which was not very good academically, or the science, math, and engineering specialized high school that she had tested into, for which admission was highly coveted. The latter was what she was stuck with for the next four years. To comfort herself, she started writing music rhythms and singing every chance she got.

Traveling to Brooklyn for high school was a drag. She had to wake up at the crack of dawn and be on the subway platform by 6:35 am in order to get to school on time. It could take over an hour to get from 145th Street in Harlem to Dekalb Avenue in Brooklyn on the D train, especially since the subway arrival and departure from each station and delay-free travel time could not be depended on. However, Kyrie quickly realized that the considerable distance combined with the unreliability of the New York City transit system constituted the perfect opportunity for some unprecedented freedom. That freedom, however limited, was like sweet, whipped cream on an ice cream sundae for Kyrie.

Until that point, she had been allowed thirty minutes to travel home from school in junior high and not permitted to go further than the playground at the bottom of the block they lived on over the weekends. Brooklyn was a whole new world, and she could always use train delays as an excuse for tardy arrivals. Man told her that he had timed the ride door to door and that she'd better come straight home every day, but she was smart enough to know that he could not control the trains nor could he know for sure if they ran timely, so she took her chances. On one of those return commutes to Harlem in the winter of her freshman year, she met Shane.

It was after school and she was standing on the D train subway platform at the Dekalb Avenue station in Brooklyn, awaiting the Manhattan bound train. She was anxious for the train to arrive and settling into her book for the long ride from Brooklyn to Harlem. She was engrossed in *The Catcher in the Rye* by J.D. Salinger and really enjoyed the adventures of the main character, Holden Caulfield. She smiled as she thought about Holden, whom she wished she could hang out with. He seemed like a cool white boy.

She flung her shoulder-length box braids off of her neck. She had been getting her hair braided now that she was in high school, and everyone said it looked really cute on her. Box braids really paired well with her high-topped white Reebok Classics, tight jeans, and white Gap pocket tee. It was a real "Harlem look." Her Uncle Will had come through with her Christmas wish list, so at least she could dress decently for now. One could get beat up for un-cool attire.

Two teenage boys entered the platform in rambunctious fashion, announcing their presence before they came into view. Given the noise level, Kyrie was surprised to discover there were only two of them. Once they were standing within a few feet of her, she was further surprised to learn that the bulk of the noise was coming from only one of the boys, who was as loud as he was large in size. My god, Kyrie thought. He's got to be about 6'2" and well over 250 pounds. He was making some ridiculous joke, and the two boys were laughing like it was the funniest thing ever until they noticed her.

" Hey…what's up with you, shorty?" This came from the large dude.

"Nothing's up," Kyrie replied. She popped her gum and leaned over to glance into the tunnel to see if the train was coming. She thought she saw an approaching light. She stood up straight again and popped her gum again.

"Where are you coming from, shorty. You're a cutie," the large dude told Kyrie.

Kyrie caught a look out of the corner of her eye at the friend. She sighed softly. He was actually cute, but, of course, he was not even making any eye contact. Instead, he toed an invisible pebble on the ground in front of him. He had on green suede Bally shoes and a green leather jacket to match. *Nice.*

"School. I go to Tech. What about you two?" Kyrie asked nonchalantly, not looking directly at either one of them.

"Worrrrd? You go to Tech? We go to Tech too! Never seen you around, shorty. And I would have remembered you, looking like a smooth Hershey's chocolate kiss! I bet you're sweet too!" With that, they both started laughing as if that last line was the funniest joke ever told.

Kyrie smiled and responded merely with, "I'm a freshman…" as the train roared into the station.

They got on the train and found themselves in a car that was mostly empty. Kyrie sat down on one side of the car, and the two boys sat on the opposite side, facing her. She pulled her book out and opened it, attempting to discourage further conversation, but the big dude wasn't done.

"So, my name is Troy. This here is my boy Shane Meadows. He's kind of quiet." As if to validate that description, Troy laughed, and Shane smiled.

"Nice to meet you both. My name is Kyrie, Kyrie Graves." Given a head-on frontal view of them both, she could see that Troy was more than just tall; he was a bit overweight and had full facial hair, like a grown man. Shane looked younger. "What year are you in?" Kyrie asked, nodding at both of them.

"Well, I'm a senior a couple of times," Troy guffawed. "That's a long story. I'll tell you about it on our wedding day because you and I are definitely getting married." He smiled at her and laughed good-naturedly. "Shane is a junior."

She wondered why Shane didn't talk for himself. Kyrie took a minute to check him out while Troy continued to humor them with his ridiculousness. Shane Meadows had stark white straight teeth which revealed an enigmatic smile, flanked by one deep dimple on the left side. His smile was what Kyrie continued to notice about him, which was probably because all the time Troy was running his mouth, Shane just smiled. He had a slender build, was about six feet tall, and had smooth chocolate skin without a zit or blemish, which was rare for a teenage boy. His hair was jet black, cut into a Caesar that rippled with perfect waves that she imagined he brushed at least 50 times a day. *He is really cute.*

"Getting married? You just met me." She shot Shane an incredulous look. He grinned again. *Damn that dimple.*

"Well, I feel like I've known you forever. That gum you chewing sounds so good and juicy. Let me get a piece shorty." Troy, a.k.a. "big dude," was still talking.

"I don't have any more," Kyrie replied.

"Whatcha mean, you don't have any more? You got that juicy piece in your mouth," Troy joked.

Kyrie took the piece of gum out of her mouth and gestured towards Troy with it, jokingly offering it to him. She thought that might shut him up. To her surprise and complete horror, Troy reached over quickly, snatched the gum from her hand, and popped it promptly into his mouth.

"See, told you we were going to get married. Now it's sealed."

Kyrie stared for several seconds with her mouth gaping open as Troy chewed the gum from her mouth like it was the freshest piece ever.

"EWWWW! You are nasty! That is so gross." And then all three of them collapsed into laughter. They joked for the rest of the ride. Well, Troy made jokes while Shane and Kyrie laughed. It turned out they lived in the same neighborhood, so they were heading towards the same stop.

When the three of them were getting off at the 145th Street station, they said goodbye, and Kyrie turned to walk in the opposite direction. Within moments, she felt a tap on her shoulder and turned to find Shane's grinning face.

"Listen, don't pay Troy no mind. He was just messin' with you." He hesitated for a brief moment and then said, "So, you seem mad cool. Can I get your number?" Uncertainty tinged his tone.

"That wouldn't be a good idea; my pops is kind of strict. You can give me yours, and I'll see."

He took a fresh piece of gum from a full packet, popped it into his mouth, then scribbled his number on the empty wrapper and held it out to her.

"So you let your friend help himself to my germs and saliva when you had gum all along?"

"I was saving it for you," he said, that infectious grin reappearing. *So he was able to speak for himself.*

"I see." Kyrie smiled back at him. As she took the slip of paper from his hand, their fingertips brushed. She felt a tingling sensation run through her. She smiled all the way home.

Kyrie turned 14 in the spring of her freshman year and officially had a real boyfriend, and he was nothing like dumb Mark who would ring her bell and run. Shane was 16, much more mature, and he was super sweet. He never raised his voice, except when he was playing basketball in the neighborhood, which she would sometimes go to watch if she could spare some time when they got off the train in the afternoon. He was always concerned about how she was doing, whether she was happy or sad, and if the latter, he would kiss her gently and hold her in a tight embrace for as long as she wanted.

His mother, Ms. Mary Jean, didn't mind if Kyrie spent time in Shane's bedroom, and soon enough, she was skipping her last period class to leave school early with him since his school day ended a period earlier than hers. She would travel uptown with him and hang out in his room for an hour before she had to get home. They would listen to music on his record player that he had saved his money to buy. They talked; eventually, they kissed and touched each other. There was never more than that; she wasn't ready. Sometimes it would get really hard to stop, but whenever she said, "stop," he always stopped and held her, breathing softly and nuzzling her ear.

When the weather outside got warmer and the school year neared its end, they would sometimes go to Central Park and just lay on the grass; Shane would sit with his back against a tree and Kyrie with her body in between his legs, her back resting on his chest. More often than not, she would sing, and he would listen. Shane liked when she sang to him. Kyrie also talked a lot. Shane didn't talk much – but he listened.

For the first time, she shared with someone other than Malyka, the details of her home life. She shared how much she wanted to disappear from that space, away from Man and her mother. She was usually angry when she spoke of home, recounting some story about the evening before, about the drama that went on. Shane would listen, and at some point, he'd say something funny or so random that she would crack up laughing, and the anger would be forgotten. Being with Shane, wherever he was, soon became her most desired place to be. Shane was everything that home was not; low key, laid back, and easy to be with.

Freshman year ended, and her grades were satisfactory but not what was expected given her honor roll status throughout elementary and junior high school. The math and science classes were a struggle. Summer provided a warm relieving embrace.

She had recently discovered that the fire escape was more than her solace; it was her actual escape. She could slip out of her apartment undetected through the fire escape. Since Man kept late nights and when he was getting high, he was generally up through the night, she couldn't risk it on those nights. She referred to those nights as "lockdown" nights; she stayed put in her room. However, there were multiple nights during the week that he went into his bedroom and didn't come out for the balance of the night, especially since now Sire was older, and the living room sofa was his designated sleeping space at bedtime.

On those nights, Kyrie made sure the dishes were done, and the kitchen and bathroom were both tidy, so there would be absolutely no reason for Man to summon her. Then, as long as her mother was in the apartment and not at some gig or studio session that could have her coming in at some early morning hour, and Man had gone into his room and closed the door, she would ensure her room was ready for her clandestine departure. The first being the door blocker.

The day-to-day storage space for Kyrie's ten-speed bike was the roughly five-foot-long, three-foot-wide corridor inside her room and leading to the door. The bike leaned against the wall just behind the door. However, it often fell down when the door was closed, blocking the short, narrow corridor altogether and completely obstructing the door from opening from the outside. Anytime she planned to make an exit through the fire escape at night, Kyrie would lean the bike against the door in a way that if the door was opened, the bike would fall, blocking the entryway entirely and precluding entry into the room. More importantly, because of the narrowness of the passageway, the bike falling also wedged it in the space such that it could only be moved from the inside of the room.

Secondly, she would arrange blankets to appear as if a figure was lying there. The latter was unnecessary, she admitted to herself, and frankly, comical. No one could get into the room unless they entered through the window, and if by some miracle they did, the racket created by moving that bike while on the other side of the door should wake up the dead, so if the intruder, i.e., Man, did get in, he would certainly inspect the bed covers to determine if she were still breathing since she'd have to be dead to sleep through the noise that would be created breaking in. So, she'd be caught regardless and assured of her certain death by getting the shit beaten out of her when she returned.

Kyrie knew all this and thought about it a lot. However, she did it anyway. The preposterousness of the whole scene and the risk that she took was invigorating to her. The more she went down that fire escape, stayed out the entire night, and returned undetected, the more she did it. She felt powerful and in control for the first time in her life.

During the school year, she would go to Shane's house most of the time. They'd watch tv, engage in a fair amount of foreplay, and then she'd go home to get a couple of hours of sleep before she had to get up for school. But the summer was different. Since she had turned 14, she applied and received her working papers through school, and given her mother's low-income bracket, she was able to get a job with the summer youth program.

Her first summer job was with a Brooklyn Day Care Center, helping with the little kids. She would finally have her own money and not have to depend on her Uncle Will to drop by and grace her palm with one or two $20 bills. Besides that, she had earned a little money here and there, like when she accompanied her mother to her second job where she worked for a catering hall busting tables for weddings and other events.

The owner paid Kyrie $50 cash "off the books" to wash the dishes. That money was inconsistent, so she was excited about her summer earnings which would allow her to buy new sneakers and clothing items when school started and have money for when she snuck out at night.

She could go to the movies with Lisa and have money for their Times Square nights, where they would walk around, buy snacks, and take pictures for $5 in front of the backdrops lining 42nd Street. When she started making money, Man gave her yet another reason to dislike him.

"Kyrie, get in here." It was Friday, and she had cashed her first summer youth paycheck. She was excited about making a list of how much she was going to save and how much she was going to spend. She had just settled in the windowsill with her pad when Man summoned her from the living room. She couldn't imagine what he could want. She had done the dishes as soon as she got in from school, and while it was also her responsibility to take the family's laundry to the laundromat and wash and fold the clothes, she usually did that on Saturday mornings.

What do you want from me now? She put her money down and quickly went to the living room, where he was sitting in his usual spot, with a beer next to him and rolling a joint as he spoke.

"Yes?" She was sure to keep the annoyance she felt out of her tone.

"Didn't you tell your mother you were getting your first paycheck today?" Man asked her. He was not looking at her. Instead, he was focused on rolling his joint. His tongue came out to lick the ends of the Bamboo paper to seal the joint. She grimaced. That part disgusted her. *Let's get this conversation over before you light that up.* Although the smell of marijuana didn't usually bother her, she was not in the mood to smell it today.

"Yes, I did. I had to cash it at the check-cashing place in Brooklyn before I got on the train. That's why I was late if that's what you wanted to ask me..." Her voice trailed off.

"Let me see your pay stub." Kyrie stuck her hand into her back pocket and pulled out a crumpled pay stub and handed it to him. She wasn't sure where this was going, but she assumed she wasn't going to like it.

"Your check was $125. Bring me $25." *Is he kidding me right now?*

148

"Don't look at me like you are questioning me, dammit! You are one-fifth of this household. You will contribute one-fifth of every damn check you bring in here. Now go get my money before I take all of it."

Kyrie walked slowly back into her room and counted out $25.00. She was seething. She would not mind if that mandate had come from her mother. In fact, she had planned on asking her if there was anything she could do for her. But to hand money to Man?

Where is your one-fifth contribution? She wanted to ask him that. How did it make sense to him that she should provide one-fifth of her summer pay to him to play his numbers or buy beer and weed with? Kyrie wiped at the angry tears that were forming in her eyes. She did not understand his warped thinking.

Sometimes she wished she could express the thoughts running through her mind. *Can you explain how this makes sense to you because it doesn't make sense to me?* But that was wishful thinking. This was not *The Cosby Show*. There were no family meetings or discussions. Her opinion didn't matter. She had no say. Her mother had no say. Here, this was Man's world, and they just survived in it. One-fifth of a person, if that. She promised herself that one day, she'd rewrite her story and infuse it and her being with the power to be a whole person who could exercise her voice. She would create a different experience and narrative, one where she was free.

Kyrie was 14 years old.

CHAPTER 15

Feel Good

"I'll Take You There" - The Staple Sisters

Shane stopped returning her calls and coming to see her midway through the summer between freshman and sophomore year. She called his house several times a day for a week until she knew she was annoying his mother, who had said the last time she called, "I told Shane several times to call you back Kyrie, but he still ain't here." She decided that day to stop calling, after which time she cried for a few days. Then she accepted the reality that it probably did matter that she refused to go all the way with him, although he had assured her that he could wait.

He was cute and was turning 17 that summer, and she knew that there were plenty of girls willing to do what she wouldn't. It hurt that he hadn't just broken up with her. She thought about showing up at the basketball courts where he frequently played, but she didn't want to embarrass herself, so she decided against it. She would see him eventually. Eventually came the day he decided to wait outside the subway when she was on the way to her summer job in Brooklyn.

"What's up, Ky? You good?" Shane asked. He wasn't smiling like usual. In fact, he had a worried look on his face.

"I'm fine. What are you doing here? You do know you can't catch the train from outside the station." The sarcasm dripped like globs of melting ice cream from a mismanaged cone. She checked herself. Her intent was to be nonchalant, as if she had been way too busy to even notice that he had stopped calling and showing up. Sarcasm represented a modicum of care.

"Waiting for you, you know that." Then he smiled that smile that she loved.

"Well, what's up? I don't want to be late for work, and you know how the D train is." She waited.

"Yo, I'm saying Ky...I'm sorry I haven't been around and didn't call. I've just been busy. But I wanted to say I need to take a break for now. I've got a lot going on right now."

"Really, so you couldn't even call me or come by to tell me that you wanted to break up with me? We both know why you suddenly got busy. It's fine. I really have to go." She turned quickly so he wouldn't see the tears welling up in her eyes and began her descent down the subway staircase.

"Hey, Ky. I'm really sorry. I didn't call because I didn't want to upset you. I do care about you."

She was already at the bottom of the subway landing and didn't turn around or reply out loud. *I really care about you too.*

Lisa always had a cute guy she was dealing with, and that guy always had a friend. Kyrie didn't waste any time hooking up with another guy to hang with. In fact, she realized that summer that there was no shortage of guys to hook up with. She usually waited until one had enough of the kissing and heavy petting and realized that she would not actually have sex before moving on to the next unassuming suitor.

Lying in a boy's arms, being caressed and kissed, made her feel so good that she convinced herself that she was being loved. It just wasn't good enough for her to have sex; the thought of going that far scared her. She wasn't purposefully being a tease and was unaware of the term until it came out of the mouth of one guy in the litany of those that followed her courtship with Shane.

Case didn't go to her school but skipping out on her afternoon classes provided her with hours that she could do what she pleased and usually found a place to hang. She only dealt with guys who had parents who actually had jobs, which meant their residences were parent-free during the day. Case lived and attended school in Queens, so she traveled to hang with him. He was short and muscular for 16. He played football and lifted weights frequently, probably to make up for his short stature. His skin was deep chocolate and smooth, her favorite characteristic.

While kissing was usually really satisfying for Kyrie, she didn't particularly enjoy kissing Case because his tongue was abnormally thick and felt heavy in her mouth. But he could do amazing things with that tongue, so she indulged the kissing so that he would eventually move on. On this day, she was lying beneath him with her eyes closed, feeling his erection pressing against her thigh as his hands and tongue worked magic on her breasts and nipples. She was caressing his muscular back when suddenly he stopped.

"Kyrie, what's up with you?" He was sitting up on his elbow, staring down at her.

"What do you mean? What's wrong?" she answered, confused. He had just murmured in her ear seconds before about how much he loved her breasts, which, he had told her multiple times since he had started seeing her, were the largest breasts he had ever seen on such a "slim thang." She was "sexy," he told her. She knew her breasts invited considerable attention, and she was very proud of them as they were amply sized and still ripening.

"Don't I make you feel good?" She asked him, a flirtatious grin on her face. She knew she did.

"Yes, you do. And from how much you are usually moaning when I'm taking care of these," he paused to plant kisses on each of her exposed breasts, "it seems like to me, I'm making you feel good too. But I can't keep doing this without the real thing, girl, I mean damn! You've been hanging with me for like two months, coming here and getting me all hot for you for hours. What are we waiting for? Come on, let me really take care of you."

He pressed down onto her, so she could feel his erection. His voice had a bit of a hard edge to it that she had never heard before. It was making her a little nervous. Her mind raced quickly. He was a lot stronger than she was, and they were in his apartment alone. She needed to handle this right because she didn't want to do anything more than what they had been doing. She just wasn't ready. His lips covered her mouth in a long kiss. When he came up for air, she spoke quickly.

"I'm sorry, Case. I'm not ready, but I promise next time." Then, she did something she had never done before. "Let me take care of that for you." She grabbed his penis gently and began to stroke it while she kissed him on his neck and caressed his muscular chest and biceps. She stroked him slowly at first and then faster until he released.

As she watched him reach his climax, she was in wonder about the power in her to make a man feel so good. She could alleviate anger, assuage impatience, and elicit true pleasure. It was the best feeling. When he was done, he lay silently watching her fix her clothing, now rushing to get to the subway to get back to Harlem at the appropriate time since the last bell would be ringing at school any moment now. The timing of that last bell signaled her departure from wherever she was in lieu of school.

"You are lucky you are so fine and so sweet, but you know what else you are, don'tcha?" he said this to her with a smirk.

"What else am I?" she whispered, leaning down to plant another kiss on his lips.

"A dick tease."

Kyrie stood up, her expression changing. "What's that's supposed to mean?" But she could figure it out. She wasn't stupid unless, of course, you wanted her to do a 10th grade math problem. She didn't wait for him to answer her. She sucked her teeth and grabbed her book bag off the floor.

"Don't call me that. I made you feel good regardless, and I promised you next time. I need to use the bathroom so I can wash my hands before I leave."

"You know where it is. By the way, you're also lucky that I'm a nice guy. You might get yo' self hemmed up doing something you claim you don't wanna do messing with some other dude like this. But, yeah, aiight. Next time. I'm gonna hold you to that. Hold up when you finish in the bathroom. I'm gonna walk you to the train. I don't want none of these dudes around here trying to holla at you."

The kiss she gave him across the turnstile as her train was pulling in was the last one for him. She didn't respond to his calls to her house anymore and ignored his number popping up on the pager her Uncle Will had bought her. She didn't plan to see Case again, which was easy since he lived and attended school in Queens. After what had happened, she didn't feel safe with him. She had made a promise to him of "next time" that she had no intention of keeping. She also knew he was right and appreciated the warning. She needed to be more careful. *So maybe I am a dick tease.* She didn't care. She didn't need to go all the way to feel good, and she didn't need the drama that she was certain came along with having actual sex. Plus, she had heard that going all the way hurt. She didn't welcome pain. She got enough of that at home.

Sophomore year began, and as it related to its academic purpose, it was no longer going well for Kyrie. Chemistry was impossible for her to understand, as was Algebra II, and then there was the Machine Shop class where she had to build things, and she had absolutely no idea what was going on in there. Her brain just did not seem to comprehend these concepts, and she felt stupid sitting in the classes with everyone around her, seemingly getting it.

155

When she told her Mother she just didn't understand what was going on in class, her response was, "You need to study more, Kyrie." Feeling inadequate, she started skipping the classes that she couldn't handle. That meant she had to intercept the truancy cards that the school sent home weekly to notify parents that their child had not been in class for a particular period. To accomplish that, she had to pick the mailbox lock. That interception was not always successful if Man checked the mailbox before she got in, so she could count on some whacks from Man if he was not high as a kite on the days she failed to intercept the cards.

It was a gamble on all sides but feeling good was worth it. She decided that feeling like a dummy in school did not make her feel good. In contrast, her intimacies with boys made her feel amazing, powerful, and in control. She opted for the boys, although it meant more pain at home. It was unlikely that pain at home could be avoided anyway.

As far as Kyrie was concerned, she was flourishing socially. No one was threatening to beat her up, so that was a plus. While Yvette and Mona had also been accepted to and attended the same school as Kyrie, they both now had different interests, like attending class and school clubs. Mona had fit in well with the cheerleading/football player crowd. Yvette was doing a myriad of things, including being smart, so they had grown apart. Kyrie met Malyka during her second semester of freshman year, and they had become close and fast friends, although both Malyka and Lisa rarely cut class with Kyrie. While both Malyka and Lisa always had boyfriends and certainly did their fair share of hanging, they generally did it outside of school hours.

Boys became the center of her world, with no exceptions. If she wasn't hooking up with a boy, she was in the cafeteria playing cards where she could meet more boys. In the spring of sophomore year, she met Sterling.

Sterling was a Junior, a transfer student, and when they met in the hallway, she liked him immediately. He was light brown in complexion, which was different from her usual penchant for milky brown or dark chocolate tones. Slim. Funny. Smart. Really nice lips. Great kisser. They immediately became an item. Sterling had been going out with this high yellow girl who was fairly shapely before he noticed Kyrie, so that made her feel good, having been told often by her male peers that she was "cute for a brown skin girl." Sterling never said that. He told Kyrie that she was fine, very sexy, and smart. Period.

Kyrie liked talking to him, and he liked talking to her. With Sterling, there was an attraction that was much more than a desire for him to touch and kiss her, which, if she were honest, was the focus with most other boys. Sterling's lips on hers were warm and scintillating, so that was just a plus, and their conversation was about something. She hadn't felt this way about another boy since Shane, although there were more boys in the interim period than she cared to admit. As for Shane, she saw him all the time since school started. He was seeing some girl in school that he was always walking down the halls hugged up with. Kyrie ignored him. He was a senior, so he would be out of her sight soon.

It was all about Sterling for most of Kyrie's sophomore year. He was respectful and patient. While Kyrie spent time with him in his parent's apartment when they were both supposed to be in school, he never pressured her to do any more than she was comfortable doing, and he made her feel so very good. They talked a lot. He had a sharp wit and, at times, would piss her off, but it was never enough to make her question their relationship. However, before the end of her sophomore year, she found out he was seeing some other girl in school behind her back. That concluded their relationship; Kyrie did not believe in sharing.

Before her Sophomore year ended, she hooked up with David. David was light-skinned, had deep chocolate eyes and a slender build, and was equally respectful, which she realized was a prerequisite for her. He was really cute, but he barely kissed her on the lips, and when he did, there was no tongue. David would come to visit her and sit on her front stoop talking for hours. She liked him, but he never invited her to his apartment to kiss and see how far he could get, and in that way, David was different from all the rest. Kyrie lost interest quickly, and they broke up.

Instead of enrolling in summer school between sophomore and junior year to make up the classes she had failed, Kyrie decided to enroll in night school the following school year. At this point, she could tell her mother and Man basically whatever she wanted to about her academics; her mother would not opt to take a day off of work to actually come to Brooklyn to talk to a guidance counselor, and Man didn't get up from the couch for any longer than it took to either, play his numbers up the street, purchase alcohol, weed or the white powder, or smack the shit out of Kyrie for a truancy card, bad grade or late arrival, so she could basically tell them what she wanted to and plan her time to best suit her.

Kyrie wanted to have her summer days free to work. She got a job at a fresh-made donut shop in the South Street Seaport during the days and snuck out every night to hang with her friends. Lisa was always good for a party when she wasn't hanging out with her boyfriend, and Kyrie had met a new friend at the donut shop, Tasha, who was a few years older and funny as hell. With freedom came the opportunity to meet more boys. She had a great time, but her pattern didn't change. Hang out, talk, kiss, grope, move on. She moved on when the boy became demanding for sex. She was searching for something in these trysts with boys, but she didn't realize it then. All she knew was, it made her feel good to make them feel good.

And then Shane resurfaced.

Kyrie was 15 years old.

CHAPTER 16

Back for Her

"Second Time Around" – Shalimar

Shane resurfaced on a rainy day in May when Kyrie had planned to stay indoors. May was spring and her birthday month, so she felt strongly that it should be sunny with flowers growing, even in the midst of the concrete streets and brick buildings that surrounded her. Surely there was dark earnest earth flanked by green somewhere in Harlem, she thought. However, when it was 50 degrees, grey, rainy, and wet, it did not feel like May nor look like flowers should be growing. Absent sunny spring-like conditions which lifted her mood and spirit and made her happy, she stayed in.

It was a Saturday, and Kyrie had written out a plan for her day. First, she planned to finally write some lyrics to a song for which the melody had been floating around in her head for a while. She had been putting it off because she was feeling down about her grades, her crappy home-life, and her non-existent social life, except for her clandestine night time excursions. Thinking about making music was the only thing that excited her.

Her plan for the day included two books she wanted to read. The second thing on her agenda was mapping out how she would make up the classes she would need to graduate on time. She had convinced herself that if she developed a plan to fix her life, it would alleviate the sadness she was constantly feeling. Kyrie was surrounded by nerds, albeit cool nerds. Many of them were her friends, and they were exactly like she was supposed to be at this point; students worrying about what colleges to apply to and what the future had to offer. While that was most of her peers' reality, that couldn't be her primary focus because, at the current moment, she wasn't even sure she'd be able to graduate from high school, much less get into college.

She really had to get her life together. She was only 15, but it felt like she had lived much longer. Since she was a year ahead of herself from being skipped, she would be a Junior the following school year, which was very close to graduation to have the low number of credits she possessed. Not graduating would mean that she would not have the ability to go to college, which seemed to be her only way out of this place.

Kyrie also didn't know if she could get into any college because her grades were so bad, nor did she know how she would finance college since her family had nothing. One thing at a time, she thought. Maybe that's where financial aid would come in. Pam would figure it out. One thing Kyrie knew for sure, her mother was really good at getting folks to give her money. She had been able to get Kyrie's grandparents and her Uncle Will to do it for as long as Kyrie could remember.

The end of the school year was approaching, and senior prom had been the week before. Kyrie had lamented because she and Shane weren't together, and she hadn't had the opportunity to attend the prom until she heard he didn't even go, so it didn't matter. Kyrie was looking forward to the summer. She was going to commit to a fresh start in September, regardless of whatever craziness was going on in her home space. Her mother had also finally agreed to let her lay some vocals in the studio she had been recording in lately and encouraged Kyrie to place writing some music lyrics and melodies higher on her priority list. She really wanted to get a record deal, so the college plan was her plan B.

The intercom bell buzzed, and Man yelled at her to go see who it was. Since their apartment was on the first floor of the apartment building, she opened the apartment door and looked out to the apartment building's foyer. Shane's lanky form was in the vestibule, leaning against the wall with his hands in his pockets like he had the entire day to languish there. Kyrie buzzed the intercom, and he opened the door and stuck his head in.

"Hey, Ky." He called down the hall. "Can you come outside for a few minutes?"

She motioned to him to give her five minutes and then closed the door. She stood there for a few seconds, her breathing quickening. *What could he want?* They had barely spoken in months. She walked back through the apartment to her room to grab a hoodie, step into her sweatpants, and put on sneakers. As she passed the living room a second time, she remarked to Man in the best nonchalant tone that she could muster, "It's my friend. I'll be on the stoop." She didn't wait for consent or a reply and darted out of the door.

She preferred that he not know it was Shane. Man had made a lot of negative remarks during the six months she had been seeing Shane the first time. While there had been several other boys in the last two years, Shane was the boy that Man had seen most often, the boy she had spent the most time with. Shane had consistently sat in the playground on the corner with Kyrie and Sire because that was still the only place she was allowed to go when she wasn't going to a place of employment. So, Shane was the reference point when Man forbid her from having a boyfriend. Fortunately, that mandate was about a month shy of Shane and Kyrie breaking up, so as far as Kyrie was concerned, it was a moot point. She had worked harder to keep all other suitors out of Man's sight. Anyway, it was not likely that he would come out and check to see who the friend was, so a quick conversation absent Man-generated drama was possible.

"What's up?" she asked him, stepping into the vestibule. She shoved her hands into her pockets so that he wouldn't see that they were trembling. She didn't know why she was so nervous. He had come to see her. She sat down on the steps. He sat down next to her.

"I wanted to see you. How've you been? I mean, how's everything with your pops?"

"Same. He's still bugging. I'm still trying to stay out of his way."

"I hear that." He paused. "Let me know if you want me to have a talk with him." They both cracked up laughing, instantly dispelling the tense awkwardness. It had been a joke between them. Shane would fight anybody in the street if they pushed him, but they both knew that he was not saying a damn thing to Man. "Your pops – that dude is crazy! I'm not messing with him, ever!" Shane would say. Shane's personality was a direct contradiction to Man's personality. Shane was as mild-mannered, kind, and laid back as Man was loud, angry, and aggressive.

He smiled at her. Kyrie chuckled again, envisioning Shane getting in Man's face.

"So, really, Shane…you didn't walk over here randomly to find out how I'm doing. You could have asked me that in school, that is, if you could unhook yourself from your flavor of the month for long enough. What do you really want?"

"First of all, I'm not seeing her anymore. I came to see you because I needed to know….that dude Sterling has been telling people you let him…that he…." His voice trailed off. He had a look on his face that was not familiar to her.

"Let him, what? What did he tell you? Tell me!"

"Did you have sex with him?" Shane blurted out.

"No! Why would you think that? And why is it any of your business if I did? You've got a lot of nerve, Shane. You came here questioning me after you just disappeared without an explanation. No goodbye, nice knowing you, nothing! You treated me like a discarded candy wrapper, and we both know why! I told you I wasn't ready, and you got tired of waiting." She stood up. She was so angry she wanted to hit him.

162

"I know, Ky, and I'm really sorry. I was confused, I guess. But I really care about you. I really do, Ky. I knew I did all along, but it really made me think about how much when that dude said that he had...Damn! I can't even say that shit! That's how mad it makes me."

Kyrie was surprised and flattered. "Really, just thinking about him and I together makes you that mad? Wow." She sat back down on the steps next to him. "I'm not going to lie to you, Shane. I really cared about Sterling, and I came close a few times. But he's lying if he said we did. I've never done that with anybody. But it's really sweet that it bothered you unless, of course, you were just mad that you didn't get it first."

Shane turned her face to his and gently caressed her cheek., "So, you were saving yourself for me?" He punctuated his question with a soft kiss on her lips. Before his lips moved off of hers, he nibbled softly on her bottom lip while staring deep into her eyes.

"Maybe I was," she murmured.

Kyrie knew then she had gotten him back. She decided that day that she wasn't going to lose him again. She also decided she would do what she needed to do, to keep him.

Shane's reconciliation visit that day was an extremely effective mood lifter. After he left, she worked out her class makeup plan. She would do it through night school, which gave her a lot of options for classes and available times. She'd have to confirm the planned schedule with her guidance counselor, but it looked like she could get all the classes made up in order to graduate on time. While she would need to attend summer school for one additional class post-graduation in order to actually earn her diploma, she was thrilled.

The other thing she did was complete her first song; she called it "Show Me the Way."

Verse 1:

You're everything in my mind

My thoughts constantly – are of you boy

And what you do to me

I've been trying hard – trying so hard

To concentrate on some other things

Something has changed, got me in a disarray

I hope you feel the same

Chorus: What do I do – What do I say

I need some help

Show me the way!

Don't want to leave – Don't want to stay

Ah – ah – oooohh… Show me the Way!

Kyrie was 15 years old.

PART II

BIRTH

Birth: [berTH] NOUN.

1. The emergence of a new individual from the body of its parent; the start of life as a physically separate being.

"She forced herself out, a birth premature in term but ready to be relinquished from the unstable diseased womb that had developed but not protected her."

CHAPTER 17

Escape

"And the Beat Goes On" - The Whispers

He didn't come looking for her. There were no news reports, nor did any of her friends call her to report that he had been by their apartments harassing them for information about Kyrie's whereabouts. There was only silence. Then again, Man had never taken any interest in her friends to know where they lived. Kyrie had called Ariana to check in, who said that neither her mom nor dad had even knocked on her door, and that was just a few feet away.

He did have an idea of where Shane lived, and since it was literally two avenues from her parent's apartment, she thought for sure Man would have shown up there the very next day. She was certain that he would threaten Shane with bodily harm in an attempt to get him to reveal her whereabouts. However, Shane had not seen him. So, after several days, she called her mother at her job to test the waters.

"Hi Mommy."

"Kyrie! Where are you? Your father and I have been worried sick."

Really? You could've fooled me.

"I'm fine. I'm staying with a friend. How are you doing, Mommy?"

"I'm too blessed to be stressed, Kyrie, but you need to come home."

Kyrie took a deep breath. "I do need to come to the apartment to get the rest of my things, but I'm not coming back there to live, Mommy. Ever."

Her mother didn't miss a beat.

"Of course you are coming home, Kyrie. What are you talking about? Where else would you live? You are only 17."

"Mommy, I'm not dealing with the craziness from Man anymore. Really, I can't understand why you do because he treats you worse. I'll be 18 in eight months, and I'm done with all of that starting right now." She stopped abruptly. She knew she had gone overboard with her mother.

Her mother's voice hardened. "I don't know what you are talking about. Your father loves you more than anything. He just wants the best for you, and right now, that's for you to come home. And once again, you are 17. You're not even allowed to live on your own. It's against the law."

"Mommy, actually, it's the screaming, cursing, and smacking me in my face whenever he wants that is against the law." Kyrie sighed. This was the furthest a conversation with her Mother about Man's treatment had ever gone. She swallowed hard and added, "You were pregnant with me when you were 16, figuring out how to handle your not-so-great decisions. Don't you think I can handle just me?"

The question sat there, heavy in the air, its facetiousness weighing it down like a steel anchor. Kyrie figured her mother would leave it right there, and she did for several moments. The silence intensified the air between them. Kyrie took a deep breath and mentally searched for the right words to minimize the tension and refocus the conversation on her goal. When her mother responded, this time, her tone was chilly and abrupt.

"I seem to recall you finding yourself in the same predicament this time last year, so I'm not the only one with problems with good decision making."

Ow! Touché.

"Mommy, what does that have to do with anything right now?"

"It has to do with you thinking you are grown and ready to make adult decisions when months ago you were crying to me about having gotten pregnant. It has a lot to do with everything right now."

Kyrie's thoughts reluctantly returned to how scared she had been the previous year when she had gotten pregnant by Shane at 16, barely a year after relinquishing her virginity to him. She had been sloppy with her birth control pills, and she paid an early price. As soon as she suspected it, she had gone to Planned Parenthood, conveniently located near her school in downtown Brooklyn. After confirming the pregnancy, she made an appointment, and Shane promptly came up with the money for the abortion. He did not disagree with the decision. Neither one of them was ready to be parents.

It was a horrible experience. Sitting in the clinic, waiting to be called with Malyka supporting her on one side and Shane on the other, she tried really hard not to look at the other girls in the room. The shame of her irresponsibility was evident in her downcast eyes and the slump of her shoulders. The gripping fear she felt later as she lay on the gurney in the cold and impersonal operating room was incomparable to any fear she had experienced before.

Lying there, Kyrie thought about the twenty teenage patrons she had counted in the waiting room that day, silently begging to remain children despite the adult acts they had engaged in that brought them to this frigid, lonely space. Then, even as she drifted off to sleep from the anesthesia, she believed she read the judgment in the doctor's eyes, looking down on her. She didn't care.

Kyrie had awoken post procedure, saddened about the ordeal but intensely relieved about the absence of the growing life within her body. She was 16 at the time. Her life was shit. No way was she going to further complicate it by becoming a mother. No way. She was deeply grateful that she had the choice and had the means and will to exercise choice. She never once regretted the decision.

She had only told her mother because a few days after the abortion, she found herself doubled over in pain in the middle of the school cafeteria. She immediately assumed that something had gone wrong with the procedure and that she was surely dying. She went to the payphone in the cafeteria and called her mother, sobbing. She told her everything through her painful sobs, including the fact that she was certain she was dying from complications from the abortion.

Pam had left work immediately that day and took Kyrie to the doctor, who diagnosed her with a severe bladder infection, prescribed antibiotics, and sent them on their way. Death crisis averted. Her mother had been really good about the abortion then. Pam had shared her own experiences with Kyrie and told her if she was going to be having sex, she needed to be more careful. Most importantly, her mother had sworn that she would not tell Man. Until this conversation, it had not been brought up again. It was the one time in Kyrie's life that she felt like her mom had really been there for her.

"Yes, I made a mistake and then made a decision to ensure that mistake would not permanently alter the course of my life. I also executed that decision before you knew anything about it. If you ask me, I'd say it was an example of quick decision-making in a time of crisis which I think was very mature of me. I could've been crippled with fear and emotions and done nothing, and then where would I be right now?"

Her mother was silent. Kyrie decided it was a good time to end this torturous conversation. She didn't need her mother to agree with her decision to leave. She just needed her to let her know if a quick visit would be safe.

"Look, Mommy, I just need to know if I can come and get the rest of my stuff without any problems. Can you talk to Man, please? I'll call you back later to see what he says. If there is going to be a problem, I will just do without it and deal with what I have until I can buy some new clothes. Ok? Love you."

She hung up abruptly without waiting for a reply, needing to avoid hearing her mother's empty words. It wouldn't matter what Kyrie said to her. She knew her mom well enough to know that she would not relent. She just wished that she would acknowledge Kyrie's feelings. She wished that she would own the truth.

Kyrie was truly puzzled by the reaction, or lack thereof, from Man. She had been gone for almost seven days now, mixing and matching the clothing items that she had taken from her room the night she left and peppering in borrowed items from Candisse. She had since received her first paycheck and purchased a few things to hold her over, but she wanted her belongings. She had insisted on giving Ms. Jackson a little money each month to help with food. She needed to save every penny she earned beyond that so that she would have enough as soon as possible for a security deposit and one month's rent.

Perusing the newspaper for apartments had been a rude awakening about the realities of rent in the real world. Everything was so expensive. She wanted to live in Manhattan, but she had also started looking in the Bronx, where the rents were markedly cheaper. She was a little worried about managing rent and associated expenses on her own, but Shane had said he would move in with her, so that would help. She wasn't sure that was the right decision, living with her boyfriend before she was even 18, but he treated her well, and she loved him. Shane had never once yelled at her or hit her; he was actually a sweetheart. Not that she would ever let anyone yell at her or hit her ever again. Hell no, she wasn't having that.

Kyrie called her mother again the next day.

"Hi Mommy."

"Kyrie! I'm so glad to hear from you, baby. Are you at work?" Her mother's mood was pleasant and unaffected. It was as if they had not exchanged difficult words a mere twenty-four hours prior. It was

171

fascinating to Kyrie how her mother could bounce back and forth. It was certainly a skill that Kyrie knew she didn't possess.

"Yes, Mommy. I'm at work. So what did he say?"

"Your father? What do you think he said? He loves you and wants to see you, of course! He's not mad anymore, Kyrie. He just wants you to come home so he can tell you himself. I think you will be happy when you hear what he has to say."

Kyrie grimaced on the other end of the phone. *I doubt it.* But she kept her pessimism to herself.

"Ok, I'm coming tomorrow when I get off of work."

"That's great, honey," her mom replied eagerly. "I'll tell your dad you'll be home tomorrow. See you then, baby." This time Kyrie heard the click and dial tone before she could respond. She stared into the phone, her mouth open. Her mother's naïveté was always an enigma to her. Was she serious? Did she really think that she would come back there to stay?

She had several doubts about going back there in the first place, but she figured that since she had taken the plunge and actually left, it wasn't likely that he would tie her up and hold her against her will. He might get angry and hit her, but at this point, she had a lot more confidence considering he hadn't even come looking for her. Even if it got unruly, as long as he didn't kill her, she would eventually leave there again, and this time it would be with her things.

Actually, she no longer believed that he would kill her. Breathing the fresh air of freedom combined with the omission of an ongoing physical threat on her life had cleared her mind. Killing her by drowning as he had promised or by any other method would certainly land him back in prison, which she didn't think he would risk. Yes, she would take the chance of going back.

The next day, Kyrie left work promptly at 5:00 pm and traveled uptown. She didn't have classes on Fridays, so she had the evening free. She timed her visit strategically. Her mother would just be getting home as well, and while Pam got paid on Fridays and would be handing her money over to Man as required, he would not have had time by 6:00 pm to go out and buy his liquor and whatever else he planned on indulging in for a Friday night. There was a high probability that he would still be sober when she arrived, which may or may not be good for her, but she had to take her chances. Kyrie laughed to herself as she thought this through.

Look at me! I barely made it through algebra and failed just about every state math regents exam, and now I'm doing statistics in my head!

Her mood shifted as she got off the subway. She couldn't lie to herself; she was scared. She entered the McDonalds on the corner of 145th and Broadway and sat in a window seat, her gaze fixed on the exit to the uptown bound #1 train until she saw her mother appear. She gave Pam 15 minutes lead time so she would be in the apartment before Kyrie arrived. Although her mother had never before done or said anything to help her when Man was on a rampage, she still felt better with Pam there.

Kyrie had decided in recent years that Man's smacks and whacks weren't really seriously detrimental to anything else besides her spirit and soul and that if he ever tried to hurt her really badly, her mother would certainly step in. As she walked the two short blocks and her legs brought her closer to the uncertainty waiting for her in the apartment, her resolve weakened. Her feeble attempts at self-inflicted sarcasm had calmed her only momentarily, but now, as she neared the apartment building, her bravado disintegrated, and her breathing became increasingly shallow.

You can do this, Kyrie. She did have a backup plan if things went awry. She had called her friend Ariana who lived next door the night before. As she walked, she recounted their conversation, which was reassuring.

"Hey, girl. What's up? You and Laray doing ok?"

"We are good, Ky. How are you?"

"I'm great. It's awesome crashing with a friend with four outfits to recycle. You should try it," Kyrie said wryly.

Ariana chuckled softly at Kyrie's sarcasm. "I really can't believe your crazy ass daddy hasn't fixed his knuckles to knock on my door. He probably knows I wouldn't tell him shit. I ain't scared of his crazy black Kojack wanna be ass."

It was Kyrie's turn to chuckle. Ariana always made her laugh. She admired her spirit. She said stuff like that all the time when talking about Man and looked him straight in the eye when she greeted him too, even though Ariana knew that Man didn't care for her.

"Good Morning, Man. How are you today?" Ariana would say with boldness in her tone. Kyrie really believed that Ariana would go toe to toe with him if he ever stepped to her the wrong way. She was 5'11" and broad-shouldered. Kyrie might put some money on Ariana.

"I'm coming there tomorrow to get my stuff. It will be early evening, probably before 6:00 pm because I'm coming straight from work. What time do you plan on getting up?" Ariana worked nights at a law firm, so she usually slept during the day.

"You're coming to get your stuff? Are you crazy?" Ariana was smacking on a fried chicken wing on the other end of the phone. "You know Man might decide to kick your back in for old times' sake. If I were you, I would buy some new clothes and keep it moving. Just let me know if you need me to spot you some money. Hold on..."

"Laray, go get in the bathtub, girl. You know it's time for bed. Don't try to be slick because I'm on the phone. That girl thinks she is so slick, just like her daddy. Anyway, Ky, what time did you say you were coming again?"

"Around 6. My mom said he's calmed down and wants to talk to me. I'm hoping it will be quick. Will you be up by then?"

"Girl, you know I usually get up by 3 to get some dinner cooked before I get Laray from Sweety." Sweety was Ariana's older sister who lived in an apartment on the 5th floor of their apartment building. "Just tell me what you need, girl. I got your back."

Ky sighed, not wanting to get emotional at work. Ariana was a ride-or-die girlfriend.

"I really just need you to be home. I will leave the apartment door cracked when I go in. If you could just hover around in the hallway, maybe listen in. If you hear anything going down, I may need you to call the cops. Just in case. I really don't want to go there, and hopefully, it won't come to that, but he did threaten to kill me on more than one occasion if I left." Kyrie's voice broke.

"I got you, Ky. Of course. I mean, I'm sure it will be fine. I know CooCoo did say that he was going to throw you in the Hudson River if you ever left, but really, that would make him insane. Don't worry. I'll be in my apartment and looking out for you around 6. Tap twice on my door as you are going in."

Ky smiled. Ariana frequently interchanged Man's name for "CooCoo." "CooCoo, code name for Crazy," Ariana would add. It always made her smile.

So, as she entered the building, she felt some assurances that everything would be ok. If Man started to get out of control, she would just tell him that Ariana was prepared to call the cops. Kyrie had a feeling that Man knew that Ariana was not afraid of him and would not hesitate to act, so that would hopefully keep him from doing anything stupid.

Kyrie felt certain that Man did not want to tangle with the cops or risk going back to prison, so the threat alone should keep him calm. She took a deep breath as she approached the apartment door, hoping to suck in whatever bravado was hovering in the air and swap it out with the intense fear that had settled around her heart.

She tapped twice on Ariana's door as promised and heard Ariana on the other side. "I'm here," Ariana said quietly through the door.

Kyrie turned away from Ariana's door and entered her parent's apartment, leaving the door ajar. She paused at the tiny kitchen just off the front door where the dishes were, as usual, piled over the rim of the sink, haphazardly perched, and waiting patiently for her to enter and wash them. Not anymore, she smirked to herself. She took the few short steps to pass the living room area. Man was seated on the sofa, in front of the television with the day's newspaper spread around him, as usual.

"Hello, Kyrie," Man greeted her but didn't turn his head from the television.

"Hi. I just came to get some of my things. I spoke to Mommy."

"Yes, she told me." He didn't appear that he was going to get up, so Kyrie just stood there, momentarily frozen. Where was her mother anyway?

"Um, ok. So I will just do that now. It shouldn't take me long." She willed the ice that had settled around her legs to melt so that they could carry her the short steps into her bedroom. *My former bedroom.*

When she entered the bedroom, Sire was sitting on the floor playing with a handheld electronic game she had never seen before.

"Hey, little man. What's up?"

Sire jumped up into her arms, and she hugged him tightly, going down to sit on the floor with him as she tightened the embrace. He was a real pain in the neck, but she loved his scrawny ass.

"You're back, Ky! Mommy told me you were coming back today. That's great! Where were you? Look at my Nintendo Game Boy! Uncle Will was here yesterday, and he brought it for me." Sire was talking a mile a minute, as usual.

She loosened her grip and pulled him away from her to look at him. He was 11, but he seemed so young to her. She was doing so much and had seen so much by 11. To her, Sire didn't act like he was a day over 8.

"I'm not really back. I just came to get some things." She averted her eyes from his and stood up.

176

"What do you mean, you're not really back? You're standing right here!" She bent down and tickled him in response, and he fell out of her grasp, onto the floor, his body writhing with giggles.

"Stop, stop, I'm going to pee on myself," Sire choked out breathlessly. She persisted her torment for a few seconds more and then got up. She started pulling her clothes from the crates in the closet and throwing them into a large duffle bag she had borrowed from Candisse.

"I mean, I'm back today silly – but not to stay. I came to get my things."

"Vrooom, Vrooom…Get out of the way, you sucka! I'm gonna run you over and win the race, dude." His fingers were tapping furiously on the Game Boy buttons, his eyes fixated on the screen. "Get your things for what? Vroom, Vroom…Vroooooomm!" The race happening on the small screen was clearly his primary focus. Kyrie was thankful he was distracted.

"I'm not going to be living here anymore, little man."

Kyrie was moving quickly while she talked. She had already cleared the crates in the closet. She looked around the room to see what else she needed. There was no bureau; actually, there were no furniture items to speak of. There was a bed frame but no headboard and the mattress that she hadn't been able to sleep on for years.

Shane had lent her his record player some time ago. She had set it up in the windowsill, which was wide enough to double as a small table, and she usually lined whatever library books she was reading beside it. The room was void of accessories and character; it told a colorless narrative of the young girl who had merely resided within it. She wouldn't miss it.

"You are not living here anymore? Where will you live then?"

Kyrie realized the sounds of the soft tapping on Game Boy keys and the electronic sounds emanating from the game had been replaced by a voice laden with confusion. Kyrie sighed. Her back was to him, but she could hear him sniffling. She had not anticipated or planned for this. Why is he crying? She asked herself. She barely spoke to him; she tolerated his presence when she was forced to.

"I'm staying with my friend for now. But soon, I'm going to get my own place, and when I do, I will come to get you all the time. You can spend the night whenever you want, ok?" Kyrie said this without turning to face him.

She would not look at him because she didn't want to deal with the emotion she heard in his voice. *He is so damn sensitive! Such a baby! Why is he making this hard for me?* She finished tossing the clothing into the bag, not taking the time to fold anything, so the bag was sure to be awkward to carry. She got on her knees to reach into the back of the closet.

Hidden underneath all of Shane's albums she had accumulated over the prior two years were her old binders with Malyka's letters in them. She tossed them in the bag. This was one of the main reasons she needed to come here today, to get these letters. They contained Malyka's thoughts, happenings in her life, and reactions to things that Kyrie would have shared in her own letters. It was content that no one else should ever read. This bag was going to be really heavy, she thought. She was going to need to take a taxi back to the Bronx to Candisse's.

"But I don't want you to live in your own apartment. I want you to live here." Sire was officially sobbing now. She had to speed this up.

"You don't have to leave."

Man was standing in the doorway of the room. Kyrie stood up abruptly, momentarily startled. She did not immediately turn around to face him. His words had been delivered in a low, solemn tone. Its tenor was unfamiliar to her, its intent an enigma to her ears. Was this a trick? Regardless, she wasn't interested in figuring it out.

Kyrie bent down, grabbed the bag, and threw it around her body before she turned. She had everything she needed. Shane would have to get his record player and pile of albums that he had lent her some

178

other time. There was no way she could carry that stuff anyway. I need to get out of here, she thought. She didn't know where this was going, and prolonging her visit was not her desire. She was committed to making a quick exit.

"Actually, I do. Things will be better if I'm not here." *Better for me and for you since you won't have to bother your heavy hand with the task of knocking it upside my head. Yeah, that hand could use some rest.*

"Your mother doesn't want you living someplace else. It's not right for you to be living outside this house at 17. Just stay until you are 18. Things will be different. You won't have to wash the dishes anymore."

Kyrie stared at him in disbelief. She had never heard this in his voice. It almost sounded like remorse, although he had not uttered the words "I'm sorry." *Well, this is unexpected.* Where was the screaming and cursing that she was accustomed to? Where was the "Man in charge of everything and everybody. Do what I say, or I will spray spittle on you as I berate you and promise to kick your teeth in?" Was he kidding her?

"Your mother doesn't want you living someplace else," he had said.

Since when had my mother's wishes ever taken priority in this space? And promising that she would be relieved of her dishwashing duties? That was so hysterical that she almost laughed in his face. *Does he think that washing dishes was what this was about? And who was going to wash them? Sire?* Sire, as his name suggested, was treated like the little prince; he did nothing in the house; he had zero responsibilities. "My little son," Man referred to him often.

What about piling the laundry into the cart and traipsing to the laundromat every other week to spend my entire Saturday washing and folding the laundry for the family of five while Man literally did nothing? What about cleaning the nasty bathroom with the stench of urine around the toilet every week while my mother worked and Man literally did nothing? What about babysitting Sire and Kiyanna with any free time I have? Did he forget about those jobs which were hers alone to be carried out without even a "thank you" in return? *What about my freedom? What about my voice? What about the screaming, cursing in my face, the ungrateful, inconsiderate little bitch that I am...the smacking me around while instilling in me the belief that most of the time I was an ingrate and*

179

had done plenty to warrant the treatment? She deserved it, he would say often. *Maybe I did.* She wasn't even sure anymore.

All of these thoughts and questions raced through her mind, confronting her aggressively like she was the lone contestant on a game show. *Family Feud.* She really liked watching Family Feud, although Richard Dawson was corny, and there was rarely a black family. She often wondered why there was rarely a black family. Was it because black families weren't worth membership in the 100 people surveys? Were their guesses about the most frequent Thanksgiving foods one finds on the dinner table or the habits that husbands or wives find most irritating about their mothers-in-law, unworthy of being heard by America?

Despite that pet peeve, Kyrie still liked to watch it. This would be *Speed Family Feud,* and she had no family members to help. "Kyrie, you have 30 seconds on the clock, top 10 answers on the board. Here's your question: Name the things that you won't get your assed kicked for not doing properly, eagerly, or timely when you are gone and who will replace you as the target?"

There was the churning deep down in the bowels of her guts. Her eyes wandered to a spot on the wall behind his head. Was the roach around, cornered still? Oh right. It was gone, nowhere to be found. Not so stupid roach, given its absence. Like she was about to be. Absent from here. While she was physically here in this moment, she was actually already gone from this place. In that same moment, it occurred to her that life here would go on, like the beat in that song.

Despite the thoughts speeding through her head, Kyrie said nothing because there really was nothing to say. She bent down and kissed Sire on the forehead. Her mother was standing behind Man in the hallway right outside the room. She supposed Kiyanna was sleeping. She brushed quickly past Man, pausing only slightly as she passed her mother to brush her lips across her wet cheek.

Kyrie felt a certain irony in her mother's tears and, quite frankly, her very presence in the hallway at that moment. The tears irritated her. She could remember countless days and nights of being the target of Man's wrath where her mother failed to find herself either behind him or in his path to block his blows. Today of all days, she was there, shedding tears.

As Kyrie walked purposefully through the small apartment and out the front door this time, she was sanguine about her own prospects. However, she didn't feel any optimism about her mother. Kyrie knew then that she would remain at Man's side forever. The beat would go on and on and on. Everlasting.

"Thanks for letting me get my stuff," she remarked over her shoulder. "I'll tell Shane to stop by one day this week to get his record player and records. That's all that's left in there."

Man didn't respond to her. Instead, he addressed Pam. "Fuck it. Let her go. She's got a little bullshit temp job, and she thinks she can take care of herself. That job won't last, and she'll be back when she sees that shit out there is not easy. Shit, she got it easy in here." Man's remarks were gruff and matter of fact.

Kyrie kept walking. She did not react to his remarks and did not look back. Kyrie closed the apartment gently behind her. Ariana was in the hallway, putting her fifth garbage bag in twenty minutes down the incinerator that was a few feet from both apartment doors. She grabbed Kyrie and hugged her tightly and whispered in her ear.

"Thank God! I have put everything imaginable in my apartment down that incinerator!" And then, in a more serious tone, she said, "You are going to be all right, girl. You've got this!"

Kyrie hugged her back briefly and then, without any words, walked briskly out of the building and up to the avenue, struggling under the weight of the heavy duffle bag while she hailed a gypsy cab. She didn't release the air from her lungs until she was in a cab. Settling in for the ride to the Bronx, she closed her eyes and let the tears fall. She assumed they were tears of elation, but she wasn't completely sure. Her feelings were all jumbled up. "Who knew, escape would be this easy," she said in her head, or so she thought.

"What'd you say, gal? You ok?" the cab driver asked, his thick Jamaican accent dragging the last syllable as he peered at her curiously through his rear-view mirror.

"Um, nothing…yeah, I'm fine. Just talking to myself."

"Humph," he replied. His look, knowing and judgmental, in a comforting way. "Well, you know what de say. Don't worry, be happy. Nah-ting is as bad as it seems."

"Not as of today," she muttered under her breath. She closed her eyes and put her headphones on to discourage any further conversation. It was done. There was no time for self-pity or fear. She needed to focus on what was ahead. Whatever that might be.

Kyrie was 17 years old.

CHAPTER 18

A New Day

"New Attitude" - Patti LaBelle

There were several instances in Kyrie's life in which she lived in apartments lacking warmth. In some places, it was just non-existent in cold weather months. Heat was the exception, not the norm. As an adolescent, Kyrie had become accustomed to wrapping herself in the warmest blanket she could find with several books and retreating to whatever solitude space she could hide in. She wouldn't move unless Man summoned her to complete some household chores.

Kyrie spent her weekends in somewhat clandestine spaces as days morphed into nights and nights into the wee hours of the next day where she would somnolently drift off to sleep, only to start the next day again when dawn arrived, and she had only a repeat of the prior day's activities to look forward to. Even with the discomfort of a cold apartment, it was the only time she felt the satisfaction of true warmth growing up, as she wrapped in her blanket and traveled out of her reality into the fantasy existences of the characters in her books. She entered the characters' lives through the words on the pages. That same feeling of warmth and comfort enveloped her senses whenever she entered Ms. Jackson's house.

It was a semi-detached row house, similar to a Harlem brownstone. The entrance opened into a vestibule that hosted a staircase leading to an upstairs apartment. Before the stairs and to the left, another doorway led to where Candisse and her mom resided. The welcoming aromas of whatever Ms. Jackson was cooking consumed the entranceway, beckoning all who happened by to follow its path to the kitchen. Kyrie was no exception, and Ms. Jackson made it clear from the very first time she met her that she looked malnourished and, therefore, she needed to eat.

Kyrie was not malnourished, but she was thin, and Ms. Jackson decided that she needed some meat on her bones, as she put it. Ms. Jackson was sarcastic with a quick wit. She doled out sassy remarks with a tongue that was sharp to those that she didn't care for, but for those she loved, underneath her bite was really no more than a loving nuzzle. Kyrie adored her immediately, and Ms. Jackson treated Kyrie like she was family. Ms. Jackson worked nights in a hospital but would generally cook a hearty meal even when she worked, so there was always good food to come home to.

Candisse introduced Kyrie to Manhattan club life, which Kyrie didn't love, but indulged Candisse by accompanying her because Candisse loved it. Although the music was loud and the crowds overwhelming to Kyrie, she went without complaint at the beginning of their hang-out period, danced until she tired and then found a place to sit until Candisse was ready to go home. Kyrie and Candisse spent time hanging out on the weekends, generally confiding in each other and commiserating about their boyfriend drama. They sometimes argued over nonsense and then didn't speak for days, only to swallow their petty annoyances to resume hanging out and confiding some more.

Kyrie maintained her job and spent time with Shane, who Ms. Jackson also liked a lot, probably because he was also thin, so there was cause to feed him plenty. Ms. Jackson did not berate Kyrie for her comings and goings, she didn't curse at her, and she didn't hit her. For Kyrie, she had gained a sister in Candisse and a pseudo-mom in Ms. Jackson. For the first time, she felt like she was home, without a physical blanket wrapped tight and novel resting on her thigh. This blanket was a family unit that kept her warm and protected continuously. She felt safer than she ever had.

Even though Kyrie was very comfortable living with Candisse and Ms. Jackson, she was working towards saving for rent and the security deposit for her own place. She had promised Ms. Jackson when she moved in that she would only be there for six months, and while Ms. Jackson told her that she could stay for as long as she needed, it was very important to her that she kept her word. Shane was also saving his money since they had agreed to move in together.

It was hard to believe that she was at the point of sharing a living space with Shane when she had been sneaking out at night during the summer to be with him just a few months prior. She had been cutting school to spend the day with him not long ago. Kyrie marveled at the gall she had possessed to gallivant in and out of Shane's building in the middle of the day, a mere two blocks away from where her father had sat watching television and going out during the day to play his afternoon numbers at the number spot.

The adrenaline which had traversed through her body as she exited the subway mere blocks away from her parent's apartment at a time of day when she was clearly supposed to be sitting in a classroom in another borough had been almost electrifying. She had never been caught, hence the reason that her body was still assisted by the active use of all four limbs. And now, mere months later, she had empowered herself to make an independent decision to live with the very boy that she had been forbidden many times from spending time with. Kyrie wondered what Man would think about that. Well, it really doesn't matter what he thinks, does it, she thought to herself.

Kyrie felt like life was finally on an upswing. She wanted so badly to feel good, but for some reason, happiness eluded her. She didn't know what she felt or why. Practically and logically speaking, she was finally free, but most days, she woke up sweating, her heartbeat like a snare drum in her ears, her mind befuddled about where she was. The moisture collected in tiny swirls in her armpits and underneath her breasts, making her thin cotton night shirt stick to her skin uncomfortably.

When she oriented herself to her surroundings, she was sitting upright and shivering in the twin-size bed in the small front room in Ms. Jackson's house. The room faced the street, so she stared out, and the next feeling to overcome her was nausea. It took some time before she admitted to herself that awakening into bewilderment and discomfort was severe anxiety, but she didn't know exactly what she was anxious about. It was evident that Man was not coming for her. His threats of bodily harm and death by drowning in the Hudson River as a consequence of any departure had been left behind in the stale air of her parent's apartment and seemingly evaporated in the night along with her presence there. His words had shown themselves to be idle, meritless threats. Still, when she sat upright abruptly in the early morning hours in the small room that looked out onto the Bronx street, Man was walking down the middle of the road toward the house with a scowl on his face, his bald head gleaming illuminated by the streetlamp's glow, his arms hanging taut at his side, and his hands balled into tight fists. Kyrie's throat would tighten, and her breathing would quicken, only to realize that there was no one there. He wasn't coming for her.

Eventually, she acknowledged that no one was coming for her. "There is nothing to be afraid of," Kyrie told herself and pushed the feeling down, along with the confusion about why Man didn't come for her. She didn't voice those feelings to anyone. Kyrie was both scared and sad about the reality that although she had voluntarily left a living condition that was not good for her, in her self-motivated departure, she was also abandoned. That realization confused her. She momentarily pondered talking about it to someone but decided that no one would understand. She couldn't understand it herself, and she didn't want to give it energy, so she continued her pattern of pushing the fear, sadness, and confusion deep into the recesses of her existence along with every other unwelcome feeling that had preceded it.

I should feel strong. She had done what she never thought she had the courage to do. She decided that her discomfort must be derived from the fact that so much of her status was temporary. She was unsettled. She loved Ms. Jackson, but her living space at Candisse's was temporary.

186

Candisse was temperamental, and while they had grown really close, sometimes Candisse would stop talking to her for days and weeks, and Kyrie would not be able to reach her even though they shared the same living space. Kyrie didn't believe it had anything to do with her; it was who Candisse was, so Kyrie tried to accept it. However, it was hard living in her house in those periods of silence and moodiness. For that reason and a desire for true independence, Kyrie longed to move. She needed to feel as though she was forging her own way.

Shane worked a part-time job, went to college at night, and sometimes spent too much time with the wrong crowd. The latter concerned her, but she was grateful that he remained committed to her and was saving towards their rent and security deposit. Shane had her back, even when no one else did.

The job at the insurance company was interesting but far from challenging. She worked for two managers of the group plan division, and her day-to-day tasks were simple; answering the phones and taking messages. Occasionally one of them would require a short memorandum typed. She was happy that didn't often happen because her typing skills were lacking, and she didn't want them to have any reason to be displeased with her.

They really liked her telephone mannerisms. They received calls from customers at times who had complaints about their insurance policies, and she was adept at calming callers down, getting to the crux of their issues, and then directing the call to the correct person within the department. The person who was permanently in the job was on maternity leave for six months, so it was her goal to find a permanent role within the Company before the woman returned and evicted her from the very easy job. The pay was good, and it was on the east side of Manhattan, walking distance from Baruch College, where she was enrolled in evening classes in pursuit of her bachelor's degree.

Around the time the temp assignment was nearing its end, she came in one morning to one of the managers waiting for her by her desk.

"Good morning Kyrie. Come into my office and talk to me for a few minutes after you get settled, please." She nodded quickly. She took off her jacket, hung it up on the coat rack behind her desk, and put her bag in the desk drawer. Kyrie paused to glance in the mirror she kept on her desk and refreshed her lip gloss. She was stalling, not sure what this was about. The woman she was filling in for wasn't scheduled to come back for a couple of weeks. She had been watching the internal job listings but hadn't seen anything come up that she was qualified for. She prayed she wasn't getting fired. She needed a little more time.

Ray McMahon and Earvin Jones were the two managers she worked for. Ray was white, and Earvin was black. The pair was comical to her because while their physical characteristics were very different, they were very similar. Earvin was tall and thin, and Ray was short and broad; they wore similar crew cut haircuts, similar suits, and they even seemed to wear similar nondescript ties most days. The primary difference between the two of them was their races. Earvin was generally the one who gave her direction. She wondered if Ray thought Earvin was better suited to talk to her because she and Earvin were both black. Did he think that only Earvin could speak "black talk?" Every time that thought crossed her mind, it would crack her up. She envisioned walking into Earvin's office then saying, "So, wassup G?" It was that thought that triggered a bright smile that morning as she strode in.

"So, Earvin… you wanted to talk with me?"

"Yes, Kyrie. Have a seat." Kyrie sat in the chair closest to his desk and asked him how his weekend was. Small talk conversation. She was good at it. After a couple of minutes of chit-chat, he jumped right to the issue.

"So, Kyrie. How would you like to work here permanently?"

She responded immediately. "I'd love to. Is there an open opportunity? I've been paying attention to the internal job postings, but I haven't seen anything that would be a good fit for me."

"The opportunity is here in this group continuing to work for us. Shirley is not returning after all. She's apparently quite enamored with motherhood and has decided to stay home with her baby indefinitely. So if you want it, the job is yours. We are quite pleased with your performance so far and think you would be a great addition to the team.

"In fact, since Ray and I don't require an abundance of administrative support, we think you can handle primarily covering the complaint line full-time. You are great with customers on the phones. Of course, Human Resources will need you to complete some paperwork and pre-employment testing, but after that, you can consider yourself an official member of the team."

Kyrie was stunned. This was too good to be true. A permanent job with a big corporation like this one, without even trying? This was a company that offered benefits like tuition reimbursement. "Thank you so much, Earvin! I really appreciate the opportunity."

That role was short-lived. While Kyrie excelled at the customer service responsibilities and Earvin and Ray told her often that she was doing a great job, she was bored after just a couple of months. The company policy was that one had to be in a position for a minimum of six months before applying for other positions via the job posting program, so once she had passed the six-month mark, she began looking for other opportunities within the company.

Before her first year elapsed, she applied for a junior position within a departmental Human Resources group. The application and interview process was quick. Kyrie was a confident and articulate speaker. Most people she encountered in her new work environment failed to effectively mask their surprise when she opened her mouth to speak. White folks seemed particularly intrigued.

Kyrie was also quite adept at selling her attributes, which she knew came from listening to her mother tell anyone who would listen, what she had done, how good she was at doing whatever she claimed to have done, and the noteworthy people she knew as a result of all that she had done. It appeared to her that her mother engendered feelings of trust in those that listened to her. Kyrie had studied that quality her entire life and sought to mimic that confidence in her own style, minus the boastful fringes. It was intrinsic to who her mother was, and it impressed her immensely. Alternatively, Kyrie had a really hard time

189

understanding how this was the same person who demonstrated little to no challenge, much like a defenseless cowering child, when faced with Man's abrasive and authoritative affronts and slaps across her face.

Before the end of her first full year with the company, Kyrie had joined a new department as a Human Resources Associate Trainee. She was the most junior member on the team and had a lot to learn, but she was ecstatic about the opportunity, and the pay was even better. "I'm on my way," she became accustomed to saying to herself. Her mother had said for as long as she could remember, "Your words are power. If you say it, you will believe it, and you can achieve it." She realized that it was all about her new attitude; she could bring herself to believe just about anything.

CHAPTER 19

New Home

"Spread My Wings" - Troop

The apartment search was intentionally limited to the Bronx. While Queens was familiar and where her grandparents were, she knew that her grandmother would not approve of her living with Shane. Although she had no intention of asking for approval for her next steps, she also had no interest in ongoing scrutiny. Her grandmother's watchful eye was laden with judgment and criticism, which was doled out without a filter.

Kyrie was also certain that if she lived within the same borough, the close proximity would encourage impromptu visits from her grandparents so, Queens was not an option. While her grandmother had some limited insight into the life that Kyrie had left, she had never really spoken about the particulars of what went on in her household. Her grandmother would not accept that anything was bad enough for Kyrie to move in with a boy at her age and would be critical.

"What do you mean you are moving out to an apartment. A young girl shouldn't be living on her own! Just come live here with me and your granddaddy." These were her grandmother's words delivered scornfully into the phone when Kyrie informed her that she was looking for an apartment with Shane. She just listened to her and said nothing.

Living with Shane represented the closest thing she could get to being on her own. She needed to make her own decisions and live by her own rules, and Shane would not interfere with that. Queens was also a two-fare transportation zone from Manhattan, which was not the goal. She knew nothing about Brooklyn or Staten Island; those boroughs were as foreign to her as Queens was commonplace, although she had attended high school in Brooklyn for four years. Manhattan rent was more expensive than every other borough in New York, so the Bronx was it.

The apartment she found was not far from Ms. Jackson and Candisse's place. It was a one-bedroom attic apartment in a private house, and the landlord was asking only $650 for the monthly rent. The street was a long and continuous one, lined on both sides with deficiently maintained tenements. The light blue three-story house with a porch sat imperiously at the top of a very steep hill. The house peered downward in somewhat condescension, and its uniqueness validated its stature. The siding juxtaposed to the brick apartment building structures on the urban Bronx street rendered it superior to all of the other structures around it. It was a very steep hill to climb daily, but Kyrie and Shane quickly grew accustomed to it. Shane dubbed their final destination at the top of the hill, heaven.

When she thought about it in later years, the analogy had more meaning for Kyrie than she imagined he had intended. She had initially thought she wanted to be as far away from her parents as possible, and this part of the Bronx was relatively close to where her parents and siblings lived in Manhattan. However, there was something about the water that separated them and the bridge that connected the Bronx to 155th street in Harlem that gave Kyrie enough of a sense of distance. Space. Cover. She couldn't remember Man saying anything about going to the Bronx when she was growing up. It had also been almost six months since she left. Neither he nor her mother had come to Ms. Jackson's house, not even once. He had not come for her.

She was turning 18 in a few short weeks, and she was reassured by the fact that Man would have no further claim on her legally once that birthday passed. She told herself that she should stop worrying. She told herself that she was not concerned because she was grown, or at least she would be in a few short weeks. Still, her stomach was always twisting in knots, and often times her breath was shallow for no reason. Her worrying was incessant. Only being with Shane made her feel safe. With Shane, she was not only safe but free.

Kyrie saved every paycheck she could, minus bare necessities. Shane also gave her money to hold. They were both determined; Shane was attending college part-time and working part-time. Kyrie was working full time and going to school full time in the evenings. Failure was not an option. She would not go back, and she would not resort to living in the streets. The money they pooled funded two months' rent and one month of security, plus money for cheap furniture.

"Inexpensive," an older woman, Debbie, that she had befriended in her evening program chided her. "Don't call anything 'cheap' because it signifies low class. You can purchase items that are not necessarily low class and just do so inexpensively."

Kyrie had laughed in response and said, "Ok, that's semantics; they mean the same thing," but she started saying "inexpensive" and found that it did roll off her tongue differently. It did not leave the same lingering taste of low class on her pallet. She began to identify the neighborhood furniture stores on 125th Street in Harlem and Fordham Road in the Bronx as the cheap stuff. She distinguished Seamans as the store that sold inexpensive but tasteful items and opted for the latter. It was likely similar quality, but her mental process validated her immature consumer decisions, and she furnished their quaint one-bedroom apartment in the first several months in honey-toned wood grain-trimmed sectionals, and matching tones for the small kitchenette and queen-sized bedroom suite. A fully furnished apartment was not something she had ever experienced; a bedroom suite complete with a bed, headboard, bureau, and dresser had not been placed high on the priority list during her upbringing. Neither had intact mattresses void of escaping wire springs.

Kyrie didn't really care about the quality of the furniture. Anything was far better than what she was accustomed to. She had spent the last several years sleeping on old blankets piled together to create a makeshift pallet on the floor. Her mattress, which had probably been given to her mom by someone or purchased second hand, had worn thin, and once the springs started poking through, it became a hazard to sleep on. Since no new mattress was forthcoming, the pallet was a welcomed alternative to being unintentionally assaulted by mattress springs while she slept.

At first, her pallet was fun. Her mind would lend itself to creating the images of the firm earth of the forest within her own pretend fantasy land. Her forest was not unlike the forest in Narnia, the mystical land from her favorite childhood series, *The Chronicles of Narnia* by C.S. Lewis. She made a tent around her with some sheets and created stories that revolved around some new characters that she developed and inserted into the story that was already written.

In *The Lion, the Witch, and the Wardrobe*, the young characters traveled through the magical wardrobe in the sprawling mansion they were visiting and arrived in Narnia. It was truly fantasy rebirthing new fantasy because there were no black characters in the real story, so she became an extra 'adopted' sibling to the four white children well before white celebrities had made adopting little black children trendy and before transplants to a gentrified Harlem made living in close proximity to white folks, commonplace. Kyrie made the need to sleep on the floor magical and gained a whole extension of her family. For a time during her adolescence, she looked forward to going to sleep at night because her mind would take her to a myriad of places until something happened that changed that.

It was a night that she was in the midst of her dreams, likely slaying some mythical creatures on 148th Street and Broadway, when she was awakened by a wet feeling underneath her. She moaned softly, clamoring to her feet groggily, silently praying she hadn't wet herself. "I am getting too old for this," she berated herself underneath her breath. Her panties didn't feel wet, so she couldn't understand why her gown was sticking to her on one side. Her fingers groped the wall as she stumbled through the dark, feeling her way into the bathroom where the light was on, the sudden illumination basking her body with harsh light. The lightbulb wattage was high for such a small room, she thought.

She grabbed gently at both sides of her thin cotton gown, her eyes cast downward, half expecting to see the crimson markings representing the beginning of young womanhood her mother promised her was forthcoming. But her first period was not there. As her gaze traveled the length of her body, she observed that most of the wetness was perspiration, its moistness fresh and absent the pungency of bodily excretions that had rested on the skin for some time. However, there was one area in particular that felt significantly wetter, and as she examined herself, she realized that there was something stuck there. She bent her body downward, squinting as she brought her face closer to the offending section of the gown by her midsection, and realized that the wetness was concentrated in one spot. Its source was a small mass of grey fur complete with a tail, smashed and stuck to her thin gown and her skin beneath it.

It. Was. On. Her. Stuck to her, affixed by the residue of its mucky insides that had been squashed out of its tiny body when she apparently rolled over onto it as it likely scurried around her body while she slept, crushing it to death as she resettled in her slumber on her mystical pallet. The screams that ensued around her were immediate and continuous, mixed with cries of "Mommy, Mommy, get it off of me!" The sound reverberated in her ears as she heard her mother's footsteps quickly approaching her, and she realized the screams were coming from deep within her.

In the seconds it took for her mother to reach her, she was screaming and crying uncontrollably and unable to stop shaking. Kyrie stood in the shower for a really long time that night, the hot water unable to truly wash away the feeling of the mouse's bloody insides stuck to her skin. She remembered the feeling always, every time she heard of or saw a rodent or even evidence of one. No, she didn't care how inexpensive the furniture was as long as it kept her off of the floor with the mice and the roaches. Also, she had not seen any evidence of mice or roaches in her new apartment, and that needed to remain the case; those uninvited guests were a deal-breaker for her.

Shane and Kyrie moved into their new apartment in March, and she turned 18 two months later. By the summer, the small one-bedroom apartment was fully furnished with nice, *inexpensive* furniture. Neither her mother nor Man had ventured to the Bronx to see where or how she was living. She didn't acknowledge out loud how much that bothered her. She told herself that she should be happy because she was free; however, happiness still eluded her. She didn't know why and decided that it was part of her reality.

PART III

AWAKENING

ADJECTIVE: [a-wa-ken\ing]

1. Coming into existence or awareness; Merriam-Webster

"She thought that she had been through it all, and then she experienced an awakening that was life-changing."

CHAPTER 20

To Lead or Not to Lead

"Free Your Mind" - En Vogue

"Wow. This is so cool! You must be making a lot of money at your fancy job, spending all this loot on Christmas." Sire held the leather jacket up in front of the mirror.

"I'm really not, but I'm doing ok," Kyrie laughed. "Well, stop standing there grinning like the Joker. Try it on!" Kyrie shoved him playfully, unable to stop grinning herself.

She watched him pull each arm into the jacket. She had to look up at him now when he was standing in front of her, and that in itself amazed her. Her little brother was so impressionable, although he was not so little anymore. She studied him through the mirror. The several inches he had on her was accompanied by broad shoulders and a deep voice. His sharp chiseled features complimented his dark skin, and he had started growing dreadlocks, which looked good on him. Yes, her baby brother was growing up.

She looked around her apartment and tried to take in her surroundings through his eyes. After two years, she and Shane had moved from the attic apartment to a one-bedroom down the street in a newly renovated building, where they had lived for the last several years. This apartment was all new, and their wood grain furniture looked great in it. It was Christmas time, and while she hadn't purchased a tree, she had put up some Christmas decorations to make it festive. She loved this holiday. Its representation of the birth of Jesus Christ, the colors, and the festivities marked with gifts brought her joy. The freedom to believe in a greater power was new and especially comforting to her. Also, gifts made her feel good, both the giving and the receiving.

"It seems like you're rich to me. You sure know how to do it up! I mean, what do you even know about this bullshit holiday when we never celebrated any of them." Sire modeled the jacket in the mirror. It really did look good on him.

"I pick up things quickly," she retorted, a bit more sharply than she intended. She didn't want to think about it, but he was right. Man had forbidden anyone even mentioning Christmas, Easter, or any other holiday that was related to Christianity, any other organized religion, and anything commercialized in mainstream culture. "Do you have a problem with it?" Her tone was playful, but she was serious. She and Sire usually disagreed about one primary topic; her feelings about Man.

"What's wrong with not celebrating these bullshit holidays anyway?" Sire remarked nonchalantly. He walked into the kitchenette, still wearing the new jacket, opened the refrigerator, and removed a carton of orange juice. As he raised the carton to his mouth to take a swig, she reached him in two steps and smacked his hand. "Get a glass boy, what's your problem? This is not your childhood abode!"

"Well, all right, Webster!" He grinned at her. "This is not your childhood abode," he repeated, mimicking her tone. "What's your problem anyway?"

"My problem is that you don't see anything wrong with the fact that your father felt it against his morals to raise us knowing and loving God because he felt that Christianity was a form of shackles for black folks or something like that. We weren't allowed to participate in

200

harmless Easter egg hunting or celebrate the rising of Jesus Christ because, why? Who knows! He never explained it.

"Your father talks about these holidays with the same resentment he talks about Fourth of July. And while I can understand the contradiction of black people celebrating Independence Day in a country that enslaved black people and then subjected us to institutionalized, systemic racism for centuries, I am unclear about how it is an affront to black people to believe in God and celebrate the birth of Jesus Christ." She stopped to take a breath. Sire had turned on the television set and was flicking through the channels.

"Yeah, well, whatever. You are really bent out of shape about this stupidness. You want to celebrate Christmas and go to church all of a sudden, that's fine with me. Thanks for the jacket, I'll take it! But I'm not going to church. I might catch the Holy Ghost, and they don't have a cure for that yet." She looked at him and shook her head as he laughed hysterically at his own joke.

"Whatever. You can take these gifts home with you for your non-celebrating parents and Kiyanna. I bought Mommy a new winter coat and a sweater for your father. I don't want to hear Mommy's mouth if I don't send anything for Man. I bought some cute outfits and toys for Kiyanna."

"That's cool. Why don't you come home with me, Kyrie? I know Daddy wants to see you. And why don't you chill, for God's sake, with the 'Man' and 'your father.' He is your father last I checked, and he loves you. I know he was a little harsh, but he's never done anything to you to deserve all that attitude."

She sighed. She loved him so much, but his blind acceptance of Man irritated her endlessly. "I'm fine with sending the gifts with you. Now let's talk about you. It's your last year of high school. Are you going to graduate on time? And I still don't understand why you won't just apply to Cornell University. That summer program you got into last summer was amazing, and you even said you really liked it up there. Don't you remember how much that advisor loved you? He said that if you applied, he would give you a recommendation and talk to

201

admissions to give you a leg up even though your grades are not the best. What are you going to do?"

"Yeah, it was cool up there, but I don't know. I wouldn't have even gone to that program if you hadn't done practically all the paperwork for me to get in. I'm just not into all of that. I don't think that college shit is for me." Sire averted his eyes while he started rummaging through his jeans pocket for something.

"What do you mean? You think living the way you see Mommy living, struggling to provide for your family, or your friends hanging out on the corners, is the way to live? Is that for you? What about being able to provide for yourself, is that not for you?" Kyrie felt herself getting angry. She needed to calm down.

"Ky – stop tripping on me. You're fucking up my buzz before I even get it." He had found the joint he was looking for in his pocket and pulled a Bic lighter out of his back pocket to light it. "Seriously, if you like Cornell so much, why don't you quit that college downtown you are going to and go there yourself? Maybe you could finish faster because it's taking you forever…what is this, like your sixth year? I hope you're going to have a double degree all this time you're spending." He started laughing at his own joke again as he put the joint between his lips and lit the lighter.

Kyrie slapped at the lighter in his hand. "Uh uh. You know you can't smoke that in here. You must be kidding me!"

Sire frowned at her. "Fine, I'll wait and smoke it with Daddy when I get home."

"What? You mean to tell me he lets you smoke with him?" She shook her head in disgust.

"Fix your face and act like we grew up in the same house. Didn't your mother tell you that weed is good for the body? It comes from Mother Earth! Mommy is the healthiest person we know, and she smokes weed, so how could it be bad for you? And anyway, I know Shane smokes weed, so why are you bugging on me?"

"Well, regardless of what you 'think' Shane does, he doesn't smoke that shit in here, and neither will you! And for the record, Shane is grown, in college part-time and working, so you can refrain from commenting on what he does in an apartment where he pays rent."

"Whatever. Damn! Calm down, Ky! You need to take a drag of this yourself, you're so uptight!" Sire chuckled at his latest remark, grabbed the remote and started flipping through the channels.

She sighed. This was going nowhere. What was she doing wrong? She spent time with Sire whenever she could. She talked to him about making good decisions and doing the right thing. She wanted so badly for him to do well, make something of himself. Still, he screwed up in school and spent his time running around with his many girlfriends from his current Washington Heights school, the third high school for him since he had flunked out of two prior. Then, there was his penchant for smoking weed, which seemed to be becoming his favorite pastime.

Kyrie was plagued with the guilt of having left him and felt as though it was her obligation to get him out of her parent's apartment before it was too late. She wanted so bad to make things right for him, ensure his success in life. As she sat there watching television with him, laughing at Rudy Huxtable's antics in the near-perfect Huxtable household, she grimaced. These reruns were funny, but the show depressed her. Did black families like this actually exist, and if so, why couldn't it be hers? She glanced at her brother, cracking up. It dawned on her that attempting to rescue someone who doesn't believe that they are in peril was like walking uphill on icy terrain with roller skates on. Damn near impossible.

Bryan Miller, Vice President of Operations for the department that Kyrie job posted into five years prior, had been impressed with Kyrie immediately.

"Where are you from?" he had asked her in the first days of her starting in the job.

"I'm not sure what you mean, but I was born in Queens, raised in Harlem, USA." She got a kick out of saying that. She knew that Harlem was not an actual city in New York, but it sounded cool.

"Really? You don't have a New York accent," Bryan had replied, an expression of confusion on his face.

Kyrie knew that was code for "I'm not accustomed to hearing young black girls speak with such poise and diction." She was used to that reaction from white people. It didn't offend her. She appreciated being the wrinkle in their media promulgated stereotype of black youth.

"And you are currently pursuing your bachelor's degree, is that right?"

"Yes, in Communications."

"That's great, Kyrie. Well, welcome aboard. I think you are going to do well in this group."

Doing well turned out to be an understatement for Kyrie. Kyrie worked hard, learned fast, and quickly developed strong relationships with the director of the group, an older African-American man, Ben Reardon, and the manager, Barbara O'Reilly. They both mentored her closely and within three years she had been promoted twice, much to the chagrin of the older woman who had trained her when she first came into the group. Kyrie could understand the annoyance; Mildred had worked in the group for over 10 years, and in a quarter of that time, Kyrie had been promoted to the level directly beneath her.

Then there was another woman in the group, Jody, who had been hired into the group after Kyrie. Both women were seasoned professionals; Mildred was in her 50's and Jody in her early 30's. Since Kyrie was a mere 22 years of age with an undergraduate degree in progress, she was sure that both women felt they were far superior to her. The condescension was evident in the way they interacted with her in the office. So when Barbara, the manager of the group, decided to resign to attend business school full-time, no one was more surprised than Kyrie with the decision that came from Bryan.

"I'm going to promote you to Manager, Kyrie. I think you are the right person to lead the team." Bryan was sitting behind his big desk, signing stacks of papers, barely glancing at her as he spoke. His focus elsewhere was a good thing, so he was spared the frontal view of Kyrie's tonsils since her mouth gaped open for several moments.

The words spilled out in a torrent. "What do you mean, lead the team? Promote me over Mildred? She's been here forever. And what about Jody? She has been working in this field for over seven years. I'm aware that I handle several things and lead some major initiatives, but do you really think that's a good idea? Both Mildred and Jody have so much more work experience than I do. They are not going to listen to me." She stopped talking. Bryan was staring at her, a small smile on his face.

"Listen to me, Kyrie. I want you to run this unit. Ben agrees; we know that you can do it, so why don't you tell me what your hesitation is, other than you believe the others will resent your promotion over them."

"Well, that's just it, Bryan. I am concerned about the continued team cohesiveness. While we may not be friends here, we work well together, so as a result, we are effective. I'm just not sure that they will take direction from me. Moreover, why do you believe I'm experienced enough to be a manager? It's really about garnering the respect that I need to be effective in carrying out our initiatives. Look at what happened just yesterday in the strategic operations meeting with Mike O'Leary!" Mike O'Leary was the head of Corporate Security and one of the executives Kyrie's Human Resources team serviced. "Seriously, he tried to run over me when he realized I was leading the meeting in Barbara's absence. I had to quickly but respectfully put him in his place. Look, Bryan, I am truly honored by your faith in me, but I know it's not going to go over well, and I don't want to be promoted to the detriment of our departmental goals."

"Do you hear yourself, Kyrie? With zero preparation, you just gave me a well-oiled, substantially supported, and articulated presentation about why I shouldn't promote you. That passion, vision, and delivery is why I have no doubt that you are the best person for this job. What you don't see, Kyrie, is that your presence and your voice commands respect as soon as you walk into a room.

"In addition, your style engenders teamwork amongst your peers and others. You are an inherent leader, and I plan to continue grooming you to eventually own it. In fact, you've been leading this team since you got here, and you don't even realize it. Why do you think the other people on this team are apprehensive about you, albeit much older than you? I've heard from Barbara how Mildred attempts to order you around to do tasks you've already done. Mildred feels threatened. And about the meeting yesterday with Mike O'Leary, I heard all about his antics."

"You did? Well, I'm not surprised if he complained about me..."

"He didn't complain, at least not to me. In fact, he's probably embarrassed that he made an ass of himself. No, I heard from more than one of the Directors that were in the room, and from what I heard, you handled yourself and him quite impressively and maintained the utmost professionalism."

"Oh, well, thank you."

Kyrie was silent for a moment. She wasn't sure if she should say what was on her mind. Bryan had been good to her, but he was still a white man, and she couldn't help but hear Man in her head talking about how the 'devils' could not be trusted. As if Bryan could read her mind, he said, "What is it Kyrie, is there something else? You can trust me."

She took a deep breath. "Well, truthfully, I really don't think that Mike O'Leary likes me. He is really condescending in meetings and generally ignores my emails. I've learned that if I need to get his investment on an issue, I ask Barbara to send the email. I'm not sure what his problem is, but it is that kind of disregard that I am talking about. I don't want to become a bottleneck because someone like him, a really important stakeholder, is throwing up obstacles." She was staring at Bryan hard, hoping to read his reaction as she was talking. He sat back in his chair and stared back at her, his gaze thoughtful.

206

"Kyrie, I'm going to say something that I'm sure I shouldn't be saying, but I'm going to say it anyway. You're a gem, a gem with three life conditions that walk with you everywhere you go that you can view as either a burden or an asset. I see them as assets, and that is the way I hope you see them. However, they form a basis of how people see you and then how some people will judge you and consequently treat you because they have presuppositions about how the *who* that looks like you is supposed to present. Although it's not right, it is what it is. Do you know what I am saying?"

"I think so, Bryan, but I'd like to hear you out," Kyrie said quietly. Bryan had her attention.

"You need to be aware of how those three life conditions impact the way some people see you; one is that you are black, one is that you are a woman, and the other is that, at least for the time being, you are usually the youngest person in the room." He chuckled. "Now, your youthfulness will not be the case forever, meaning you will not always be one of the youngest in the room. For now, you have to deal with all three.

"As a result of those diverse aspects which comprise who you are, some people have biases, and biases play out in the way the folks that possess them treat you. Although I have worked with Mike O'Leary for many years, I don't know him extremely well, but I would venture to say that he is completely unsophisticated in dealing with someone of your race, gender, and relative youth, in positions of authority. It is also very likely, given the way he interacts with you, that he is quite uncomfortable with the reality of someone that looks like you giving him direction or advice. All that means is that he has to learn. It's not an excuse, but it is a reality." He looked at her expectantly, waiting for her to say something.

"In other words, what you are saying is that Mike O'Leary is a racist," Kyrie said. Bryan's look of alarm at her directness caused Kyrie to laugh out loud. "Well, I figured that. For what it's worth, I grew up in a household where pointing out racist conduct unleashed by white people was common, so I am pretty adept at identifying it. But thank you for putting it in those terms. No one has ever actually pointed out the glaring impact to me while it was happening to me." *Particularly no one white and blue-eyed like you.*

Bryan smiled. "Kyrie, regardless of how you label it, all you need to know is, this decision will be communicated widely under my signature, and I will have your back on every decision that you make, both within the group and outside the department. You will do fine. And I forgot the best part. It comes with a $25,000 increase in your annual salary."

"Well, in that case, you'll have no further argument from me." They both chuckled at her abrupt about-face.

"I'm glad to hear that. Anyone who hasn't appreciated dealing with you for the wrong reasons will have to figure out how to grow or just get out of your way."

Kyrie did do fine. In fact, after two years managing that group, Bryan moved her to another part of his organization overseeing two completely different functions simultaneously. When she began to question his decision to put her over not one but two teams in a functional area that she had no background in, he stopped her immediately with, "Kyrie, how many times do I have to tell you, leadership is second nature for you. I know what I'm doing."

She was starting to accept the reality that Bryan pushed onto her, but believing her worth proved to be more of a challenge.

Kyrie was 24 years old.

CHAPTER 21

What Love Feels Like

"Weak" - SWV

"So then, Bryan basically said that Mike O'Leary was a racist, although not in those words. I was floored! I have never heard a white person call another white person a racist! Very cool. Bryan has done so much for me that I cannot even believe that he is promoting me – again! I mean, I know Barbara is leaving, and she thinks really highly of me, so she is pulling for me. Can you believe she told me that I'm the only choice? Baby, are you listening to me or what?" Shane was kissing Kyrie's neck as she talked. She giggled.

"I'm listening, I'm listening..." Shane mumbled, his hands beginning to move up her body.

"Oh really? Well, I really want to talk about something else since I have your attention. We've lived together for almost five years. We handle this sharing a life thing pretty well. You love me. I love you. What are we doing? Where is this going?"

"Where do you want it to go?" He continued kissing her neck. "You know you are sexy as hell in the morning, don't you?"

Kyrie giggled. "Cut it out. We need to get up." But her protests were halfhearted. While the apartment was a mess and mess irritated her, it was Saturday, and they were languishing in bed. Their apartment was the go-to spot for Friday and Saturday night since they were among the few of their friends who had their own place. Kyrie much preferred being home with Shane and their friends than going out. It was a fun life, they were comfortable, but Kyrie was ready for the next step.

Shane was always there for her, dependable. She loved him, but given that she had never been in a real relationship with anyone else, her mind wandered when they argued over dumb issues. What would it be like to be with someone else? That question crossed her mind occasionally. It occurred to her that if he wasn't ready to talk about marriage, perhaps she needed to move on. There were other men out there. Sterling, for one. After some years had passed, she and Sterling had spoken, and she forgave him for lying about her sleeping with him, and they had stayed in touch over the years. Out of all of the guys that she had known, Sterling was the only guy other than Shane that she ever had real feelings for.

"Shane, you're not answering me." But her words were feeble. She was losing herself to his lips and fingertips. He was touching her in the places that he knew would quiet her mind. This was his power to obliterate her thoughts and all her intentions to dialogue. It was just like him to shut down talking with the alternative of lovemaking. She couldn't quite articulate what happened. He was very adept at making her feel good, sexy, and loved, just as he was skilled at listening to her. Talking, however, was not his forte. Since feeling good was her favorite pastime, they were usually quickly on the same page. *This has to be what real love feels like.*

"I'm wondering what's next for us, Shane." Several weeks had passed since the first time she had brought it up. Between her work and school schedule contrasting with Shane's work and school schedule, they rarely saw each other during the week. It was a Saturday again, and they were having breakfast and had been deciding whether they were going to go hang out at the South Street Seaport that afternoon when Kyrie abruptly changed the subject. This restlessness with the status quo was starting to eat at her, and Shane didn't seem to notice.

"Whatever we want to be next for us." Shane shoved a forkful of pancakes in his mouth and continued reading the newspaper.

"Well, we've been living together for five years. We love each other. I'm just not sure that I want to continue living together indefinitely without being married. That just doesn't seem to make sense. I mean, if we want to be together, and we share a life and space, doesn't it make sense to take the next step and get married?"

She held her breath. She really didn't know what he was going to say. She just knew that she wanted to talk about it and not continue to live with no direction and no plan, and he never brought up planning for what was next. She needed a plan – for everything, including her life.

"Come here, Ky."

Kyrie got up and walked around the table, and Shane pulled her down into his lap so that she was straddling him, their faces inches from each other.

"You know I love you, I'm here, and I'm not going anywhere. You should also know I would be happy to marry you, so I just don't think there is much to talk about. Figure out when you want to do it and plan it." Her face broke into a smile. He groaned and started kissing her lightly, in between phrases. "And you know I love your smile; it makes me want to do all kinds of things with that beautiful face and sexy lips of yours."

She smiled wider. He really did have a way of making her feel like she was the sexiest woman on earth, and it felt so right. She wrapped her arms around his neck and leaned into him, kissing him, long and hard. They didn't leave the apartment that day after all. Instead, they enjoyed each other, over and over and over again. It had been almost eight years since they met on the subway platform, and it never felt old.

Kyrie started wedding planning the next day. She was certain of his love for her. He wanted her to be happy, and she loved him. She decided that was all a girl could ask for.

CHAPTER 22

It Is Because It Is

"My Prerogative" - Bobby Brown

The planning culminated into a wedding just shy of two years later in a quaint town in Sleepy Hollow, New York. As the careful preparations for the nuptials brought the date closer to fruition, the conversations with her mother had become increasingly awkward, and Kyrie artfully ignored the proverbial elephant that planted itself in every space they found themselves in together. Three weeks before the wedding, Kyrie decided she wouldn't avoid it anymore if her mother brought it up, which she did. They were in a dress shop in lower Manhattan doing the final fitting for her mother's dress.

"Kyrie, when are you planning on talking to your father? He's been waiting for you to tell him what he needs to do." Her mother was admiring her reflection in the mirror. She looked very young, but that was because she was very young. That was the benefit of having been a teenage mom, and she kept herself in great shape. Her "mother of the bride" gown looked very good on her.

"Needs to do about what?" Kyrie responded listlessly.

She was sitting in the private dressing room on the bench while her mother tried on her dress. She began digging in her bag for an emery board to address a chip in her nail that had been annoying her all day. Prior to her mother's question, she had been enjoying this day alone with Pam. The two of them rarely spent time together because her mother rarely pulled herself away from her husband and his need to be catered to. Kyrie sucked her teeth. This nail was a mess. "Do you think we have time to get a manicure before we go to the hall? It's almost 2:00 now, and the catering hall appointment is at 4:30."

"Kyrie, don't change the subject! You haven't called your father to give him any details about the ceremony. How is he supposed to know where to stand after he walks you down the aisle? You should've had a wedding rehearsal so everyone would know what they need to do. Isn't that what people do now?" Her mother was looking at her expectedly in the mirror. Kyrie did not raise her head immediately, focusing instead on the back-and-forth motion of the emery board, creating a new smooth edge where the chip had just been. She took a deep breath and dragged her attention from her nail.

"Mommy, I am not calling him to tell him anything because there is nothing for him to do except to show up if he chooses. I will be walking down the aisle by myself."

Pam frowned.

"What? That's nonsense. Of course, your father will walk you down the aisle on your wedding day! Why wouldn't he? You sound ridiculous."

"Mommy, he's not walking me down the aisle for several reasons. Do you actually need for me to go down the list, right now?" Pam turned from the mirror, crossed her arms, and looked at Kyrie in the eye as if daring her to continue.

"Fine. For starters, if you haven't noticed, our relationship is non-existent. He hasn't ventured to say more than ten words to me since I picked up my things seven years ago and said I would not be back. Second, the underlying premise of the father walking the daughter down the aisle is to symbolically "give her away" at the altar. That tradition epitomizes a principle of ownership and control that I don't subscribe to, particularly as it applies to this father-daughter relationship. Third, it was me, Kyrie, who empowered myself to enter into the relationship that I'm in, to love the man I am marrying, who you might recall, Man forbid me from seeing until I relieved him of the ability to forbid it any longer. So no, he will not be walking me down the aisle, nor will he be giving me away. I reject that premise. Can't you just be satisfied that I don't have a problem with him being present?"

Her mother stared at her in silence for what felt like several minutes. Her expression had turned cold. Pam was angry. Kyrie knew that. Kyrie also knew her words hurt her mother deeply, which was why she had avoided the conversation for so long.

Kyrie shifted uncomfortably in her seat as she felt the guilt rise from the depths of her gut and into her throat. She loved her mom and hated to hurt her, but she knew that it would make her feel worse to swallow the resentment and discomfort that would eat her alive if she submitted to the pressure to ask Man to walk her down the aisle and give her away. While everyone would expect it, and the omission would be discussed, the idea was preposterous to her. It was her prerogative to make her own decisions about her wedding. When Pam finally opened her mouth to speak, it was in a low and controlled voice, but her anger was undeniable.

"Kyrie Graves, you need to grow up and stop harboring this bullshit anger that you have. It is toxic and unproductive. Your father loves you, is happy for you, and has done the best that he can for you. You have a lot of nerve thinking that you can just deny him the honor of walking his daughter down the aisle." Pam's expression seemed to dare Kyrie to even respond.

"I'm sorry you feel that way. The thing is, I don't owe him anything. I'm not denying him an opportunity to be in attendance for my wedding day. That's going to have to be enough." Kyrie picked up her bag from the bench and turned to leave the dressing room. "I'm going to take care of the final payment and let the attendant know you will be back next week to pick up the dress, and then I'll be outside, Mommy."

Several minutes later, Pam emerged from the dressing room, and they walked to the garage together where Kyrie's car was parked. The silence was oppressive. When Kyrie pulled the car out and began driving towards the west side highway, her mother remarked cheerfully, "Drop me off at my apartment, please. I'm not going to go with you to the hall; your dad needs me to come home to help him with something."

"Sure, Mommy. No problem." The plan had been for them to go to Sleepy Hollow together for Kyrie to confirm the final details of the wedding day, but now their day together was over. Kyrie hoped that the conversation was over as well; she knew that her mother was pissed, so she didn't bother to try to convince her to understand her point of view. This was not something they would agree on because her mother had no interest in considering, much less accepting Kyrie's feelings. Pam would continue to defend and make excuses for Man as she always had. But Kyrie remained staunch in her position. It would be as it was.

Neither Kyrie nor Shane claimed a house of worship of their own, so they chose the church based on the town's aesthetics and the proximity to the reception hall they selected for their wedding reception of just under one hundred guests. The church was a small stone structure nestled at the top of a valley that overlooked the Hudson River, offering a breathtaking view for its guests. The day they chose was blessed with nature's splendid hues of blues, greens, and sun rays of gold as if they ordered it that way.

Her wedding party was just as special to Kyrie. Her attendants were the women who had been her support network over the years. They flanked her in platinum gowns befitting of royalty. Malyka, her long-time "sister in drama" and the calming presence in her life. Lisa, her laugh partner, always able to make her happy with her antics. Tasha, her uptown "ride or die" girlfriend. Ariana, her big sister next door. Pauline, her trusted confidante. Candisse, who had provided her refuge when she needed it and would show up for her in a moment's notice, provided Candisse was in the mood to answer her calls. Lastly, her cousin Mika.

Kyrie and Mika shared a love/hate complicated relationship over the years. Kyrie knew that while she loved Mika, she made her maid of honor out of obligation to the family relationship. It was what was expected of her. Kyrie's internal commitment was to ensure that everyone who would expect to be a special part of her day would not be disappointed. Except for Man. She felt no obligation to him.

While Kyrie heard from her mother that he was hurt by her decision, he never sought to talk to Kyrie about the wedding or the distance and tension between them. Kyrie expected his silence; she attributed it to his prideful ego and navigated as if it and her decision were of no primary concern for her. However, it pained her just as much as his failure to ever come for her when she left years before.

White orchids adorned the altar and were delicately strewn within the white satin bows tied to the ends of each pew. When the church doors opened on that gorgeous September day, Kyrie stood tall with the sun shooting beams of glory onto her face. She did not admit it then, not even to herself, but years later, she acknowledged that the walk down the aisle was one of the hardest things she had ever done. Her legs felt like someone had bound her ankles together with iron shackles.

As she walked, she momentarily acknowledged that it would have been nice to have someone at her side, supporting her. *But that's not my reality*, she surmised. As her feet propelled her down the aisle to join her husband-to-be, she was saddened by the reality of her decisions over the prior years but had no regrets. Each step became more definitive than the last, and when she reached the altar and gazed up into Shane's eyes, his enigmatic and infectious smile spread across his face and tugged hard on her heart. She had walked alone to join the first man that had ever supported her unconditionally. Yes, that was about right.

Kyrie was 25 years old.

"Well, Kyrie, your home pregnancy test was accurate. The urine test we gave you here was positive, and my examination suggests the gestational age is about six weeks." The doctor stood up from the stool she was sitting on during her examination, removing her latex gloves as she rose. She smiled widely at Kyrie. "Congratulations! You can get dressed and come into my office when you are ready, so I can answer any questions you may have. Grab your husband from the waiting room before you come in."

Kyrie nodded quickly but said nothing as the doctor left the examination room. She lay motionless for several moments as the news began to sink in. Pregnant. She didn't know what to say, what to think, or how to feel. She imagined she was supposed to be thrilled. She and Shane had been married for almost three years, and everyone was always asking when they would have a baby. She had always refrained from giving any definitive response to these inquiries. She had not even agreed with Shane that she even wanted children. The concept was scary, and this pregnancy resulted from a temporary lapse in judgment where she had decided to give her body a break from the many years of birth control pills.

She shook herself out of the trance she was in and started to pull her clothes back on. Her mind was spinning. She certainly did have questions. How could she be a good parent when she didn't know anything about babies? How could she be sure that she would be a good mommy? How would she continue to pursue all the life goals that had begun to form in her head with a baby to take care of? And the most important questions that plagued her; what would prevent her from treating this living creature badly? Would it love her even if she didn't always have the answers? What about when she made mistakes? She brushed tears away. *I have to be able to do this.*

She thought about the abortion she had in her junior year of high school. Her first mistake, and afterward, she made sure she visited Planned Parenthood every six months to get her birth control pills replenished and never again missed the daily dosage. Her life would've been very different had she made a different decision then, and she had no regrets. But she didn't feel that she could go through that again. She took a deep breath, dressed quickly, and left the examination room to summon Shane from the waiting area. When she motioned to him, he stood up quickly and walked towards her. His eyes never left hers, and when he reached her, she nodded, and he immediately gathered her in his arms.

"So, we are really having a baby! Wow!" He squeezed her tightly and laughed. "This is amazing! Damn, I love you so much, girl!"

Despite Shane's excitement, Kyrie didn't speak unless asked a direct question during the rest of the doctor's appointment. She needed time to process. Fear ensnarled her like a vise and immobilized her tongue, motor skills, and thoughts. Sure, they had been married for three years, and things were going fine. She was even on the verge of graduating, finally enrolled in her last 13 credits, which would complete her BA degree after attending school in the evenings for over eight years. Kyrie had taken several semesters off throughout her time in college, having moved quickly both laterally and vertically within her job.

She had taken ownership over deciding when it was important to pull back from her academic workload and focus on the job as needed. As a result, she was probably the youngest manager of a multi-division organization in the company, albeit she did not have a four-year degree actually completed under her belt. That was about to change. She was graduating in June, and by the doctor's calculation, would be about seven months pregnant when graduation rolled around.

Shane had also graduated with his Bachelor of Science degree one year prior and was considering graduate school. They had moved to a nice apartment in lower Manhattan after they were married and lived the life of a young married couple, working, going to school, and traveling when they could get away. Life was good.

As she stared at the smiling doctor providing what she imagined was pertinent information about the care of her body while this life was forming inside her, she could barely make out the words. She was sitting outside of herself, watching what was going on in the room but not really a part of it.

Kyrie was 27 years old.

CHAPTER 23

The Power of Him

"Open My Heart" - Yolanda Adams

Silent and pensive defined her disposition for some time during the pregnancy. Kyrie immersed herself in her day-to-day routine, but she functioned outside of herself, her body performing the motions, her spirit disengaged. The concept of motherhood overwhelmed every measure of her thoughts, although she could not make sense of it at all. Her single thought was, I am not ready for this. She was deathly afraid of this life forming inside of her, and she didn't know who would understand that. Kyrie didn't even feel like she could say the words in a way that anyone around her could comprehend.

Shane certainly did not understand her anxiety. For him, having a baby was a normal and expected next step in their life journey.

"Babe, we're married, and we are starting a family. Why are you stressing about this?" Shane asked her a couple of weeks after the appointment.

"I just don't know if I am equipped for motherhood, Shane."

"Equipped? You're not going into a combat zone! What does that even mean? It's not something that people go to school for. My understanding is that it's basically on-the-job training. You learn as you go, Kyrie." Shane crouched down to bring himself to eye level with Kyrie, who was sitting on the couch staring into space. She was looking at nothing and everything as she watched herself in the future make mistakes in a life that hadn't happened yet. "You will be fine, Kyrie. Couples do this all the time and succeed. Single mothers even do it and manage to produce contributing members to society. We have eachother. We will be fine."

She refocused her gaze to settle on him and replied sharply. "Right, but everyone doesn't have my childhood to extract from. I mean, I know my mother loved me and taught me everything she could. I really respect her for giving me all she did given what she was starting with, but there were a lot of omissions in the parenting tool chest. And Man? Sure, he was physically present, which might earn him a gold star in our community given his life choices, but his idea of parenting was knocking the shit out of me with the back of his hand and denigrating me with words as his loving communication method. You do know that I can repeat my history without even trying, right? It's in my DNA! What is going to prevent that?"

Kyrie stopped, her hand flying up and covering her mouth in disbelief. She had said it. She had voiced the fears that had been simmering within her since her urine on the pregnancy test stick had revealed her new reality.

Shane stared at her, his expression sad. "All you have to do is be the kind of parent that you want to be. You are not Pam. And you are definitely not Man. You are going to be fine." She shook her head in disbelief and said nothing. He didn't understand.

Kyrie spent the next several months in the same state of utter confusion, not sharing her news with anyone outside of her immediate family and close friends for fear of not being able to hide her strong feelings of uncertainly and sometimes displeasure, depending on the day. She did not wish to talk about it. In her mind, she wasn't certain that she could go through with it because she didn't have a plan for what it was going to require.

She couldn't end the pregnancy because Shane was so invested and because she didn't have the guts to go through with such a definitive act triggered only by her fear of failing as a parent. She also prayed about it. Although she felt like she was supposed to have the baby, she didn't talk about it because the feelings of doubt evoked a pang of immense guilt within in her that she was unwilling to give voice to. So she spent the next several months processing, trying to evolve to a place of acceptance.

Kyrie didn't share her doubt with anyone other than Shane. She didn't know who would understand her words if she spoke them out loud, and she couldn't deal with judgment, so she pushed the words and the fear that laced them deep down inside of her and moved forward. She took her prenatal vitamins, drank a lot of water, and did everything she was supposed to do, except be happy.

Right before she left work to begin her maternity leave, Bryan called her into his office and delivered yet another blow.

"Sorry I couldn't make it to the baby shower the office threw for you last week, Kyrie. I got pulled into a meeting out of town. I trust it went well, and everyone showed up in grand style to wish you well?"

"Thanks, Bryan! Yes! It was really wonderful! I was so shocked at all the people and all the gifts! Thanks so much for your generous gift. The silk blanket is gorgeous! That was so nice and thoughtful of you and Eileen." Kyrie smiled warmly.

Bryan had treated her so well over the last nine years, grooming and developing her as if he had some kind of personal wager on her success. At 28, she was the youngest manager of color in the entire company and the only black female manager who had not come through the Management Training Program designated for college graduates. Her annual salary had more than tripled in the time that she had spent with the company. She had managed three different operational functions in six years. All of this resulted from Bryan being her mentor, sponsor, boss, and biggest fan. He was in the room where decisions about progression and compensation were made, and she believed that he always advocated for her.

She had not been able to qualify for the company's Management Training Program because the prerequisite was a bachelor's degree, and hers had been "in progress" during the entire extent of her tenure. However, Bryan had ensured that she was equal in compensation, title, and breadth of experiences as any of her peers in the program. He told her repeatedly that she was worth it. She couldn't figure out why this white man did all of that for her, but she was grateful. If she had a relationship with Man, she would tell him that Bryan was the proof that "the white man" wasn't all bad. But there was no relationship. So she didn't.

"I'm happy to hear that it was a fitting celebration, although I'm not at all surprised, Kyrie. Your reputation and the respect your colleagues have for you is unwavering and widespread. Listen, in addition to wishing you the best of luck, Kyrie, I want to encourage you to give some thought to what your next steps might be. Things are changing here, and I will not be around forever." His expression was grave.

"What does that mean? Is there something that I should know?"

"I can't say with absolute certainty, but there is good reason for me to believe that the company is embarking on a significant amount of change, possibly even going public. That might mean a shift for many departments and people, including me. I'm actually ready for it. I'm nearing retirement age, and I have other things I'd like to do. With all that said, I'd like you to be prepared for the reality of me making a decision to move on from here.

"Frankly, you are destined for more than what you are doing right now. I just want you to spend some time while you are home with your blessing, thinking about what you really want to accomplish in your life and how you plan to get there. I'm not saying there won't continue to be opportunities for you here, whether I remain with the company or not, but I want you to be prepared and have options."

They chatted for a few additional minutes, and then Kyrie thanked him and left his office. *My plan.* It was sheer irony that Bryan had confronted her with that insightful challenge because it had already been a source of her pensive demeanor for much of her pregnancy. Despite her success as a young strategic manager overseeing two operations currently, she had become increasingly bored with her role.

Kyrie knew that she didn't want to spend another ten years climbing the ladder of corporate management. She wanted something different and something more. Kyrie wanted to make a difference in other people's lives, and she had been thinking about how she could arm herself with the toolbox to ultimately do whatever she wanted to in life. By the end of her pregnancy, she decided that she needed to reinvent herself. About one week before her due date, Kyrie and Shane were having breakfast in a café not far from their apartment. In a very random moment, Kyrie blurted out the idea that had begun forming in her head.

"I'm thinking about applying to law school."

"Ok," Shane replied as he speared a forkful of blueberry pancakes into his mouth. "When are you thinking about doing that, before or after you pop into the hospital to give birth?" He grinned at her, pleased at his quick wit. Kyrie feigned amusement.

"Ha, ha, ha. Hysterical," Kyrie retorted light-heartedly. "I'm serious."

Shane leaned back in his chair and put his fork down, staring at her intently, a soft smile splayed across his face. She loved his smile. Whenever it appeared, it instantly impacted every inch of his face, making his eyes immediately glisten. His smile both comforted her and excited her at the same time.

"I don't doubt your sincerity," he said. "I trust that anything that comes from your mouth you intend and will do. I'm just trying to understand when you plan on doing this, considering you are about to give birth to an actual human, our actual human, any day now."

She laughed. "Well, first, I'd have to prepare for and take the law school admission exam. The next one given is in three months, so I'd prepare for the exam and complete the application process while I'm on maternity leave. I'll apply to all of the New York schools, and I should have some decisions before it's time for me to return to work." She took a deep breath and added, "I really don't want to go back to work, Shane. If I get in, I want to be a full-time student."

"Sounds like you've given this some real thought. So you would go to law school full-time and not go back to work?" Shane asked, his tone thoughtful.

"I think so. If I get in, that is. I've heard and read that getting in is the first hurdle. I am not sure how I will manage to take care of the baby and study for the LSAT, but I will have to figure it out." She felt the doubt creeping into her heart before it was evident in her tone. Kyrie breathed in deeply. She needed to remain positive.

"You mean WHEN you get in. You know you will do it because you want it. This is exciting, baby. I know you've mentioned the possibility of pursuing becoming a lawyer, but this is a real plan. We will make it work."

Kyrie jumped up and collapsed onto his lap, flinging her arms around his neck and kissing him on the lips, long and passionately. When she came up for air, she was breathless. "Thank you. I love you so much. I just need to invest in myself so that I will have the ability to do anything I want. And more than anything, I want to be able to effectuate change, make a difference in people's lives. I think having JD behind my name will enable me to do that." She leaned into him and felt the baby kick hard.

"The baby approves," Shane murmured softly, grinning and nuzzling her neck. There was that smile again, the smile that made her feel like everything and anything was possible.

"Arrrgg!" She shifted to reposition herself. "Arrrgg!" It was no use. She opened her eyes. Comfort was an unattainable goal these last few months, particularly at night when both a relaxing position and sleep were elusive. Her belly was huge, and lately, she had to remind herself of the vital reason for her extreme discomfort since the baby had ceased its incessant movement. These days, she felt a kick or jab only sporadically, which the doctor said was normal given the baby currently had little to no room to move around in her womb. Any movement was reassuring. She was almost two weeks beyond her scheduled due date, which was disconcerting to her. What if the baby was suffocating in there? Would she even know?

For Kyrie, evidence of the baby's well-being helped minimize her ever-present angst that she was already doing something wrong, even before the child arrived. She changed positions once again and then felt the pressure that her bladder was about to burst and groaned again. This would be her third trip to the bathroom, and it was only 2 am. With a long sigh, she gingerly lifted herself into an upright position. She heard Shane stir beside her.

"You ok, baby?" he murmured groggily, his eyes never opening.

"Yes, just gotta pee, again. Go back to sleep."

She struggled awkwardly to a standing position and walked barefoot into the bathroom. He was so kind, always looking to make her comfortable. In addition to massaging her feet and back on an ongoing basis, he became an enabler in her pregnancy weight gain. Shane gratuitously plied her with Baskin-Robbins' milkshakes at any hour of the night, whenever she even hinted at craving something cold and sweet. She smiled as she lowered herself onto the toilet seat, pulling down her panties without initially flicking on the light switch, eagerly seeking the immense relief that would come with the release of her bladder. It was only after doing so that she reached up to switch on the light and, upon doing so, gasped.

"Shane! Shane! Get up! We need to get a taxi. Either something is wrong, or it's time!" There was a pinkish substance in her panties that did not look like blood.

227

Kyrie's water broke as Shane helped her out of the taxi. That began approximately eleven hours of intense contractions before she agreed to allow an epidural to be administered. The reluctance to accept the epidural was directly attributed to listening to her mother for her entire pregnancy condemn the use of heavy pain medication in the body and its potential side effects. Also, she was more fearful of the needle entering her spine than she was of the pain of the contractions. So while she dug in her stubborn heels to withstand the pain as soon as the contractions began, she also began to experience helplessness that was unprecedented, and she could think of nothing but her mother's arms for solace.

A desire for her mother's presence during her labor was unanticipated and had not been discussed prior with either Shane or her mother. When she mentioned it to Shane, he encouraged her to just call her. Shane had called Pam from the hospital when her water had broken to report that Kyrie was in labor. Pam had asked Shane to keep her posted. He now dialed the number again two and a half hours later. It was about 5 am, and the contractions had kicked into high gear. When Pam picked up, Shane said, "Hold on, Pam," and handed Kyrie the phone.

"Hey honey, how are you holding up?" Pam said when she heard Kyrie's voice on the phone.

"It really hurts, Mommy. I don't know how you did this with no pain medication."

"You just have to visualize the baby being born. Close your eyes and meditate. Focus on the absence of pain. Your mind is powerful, honey."

"Mommy, I'm in pain. How can I focus on the absence of pain? Can you just come here?" Kyrie grimaced and squeezed her eyes tight, bearing down as a contraction ripped through her.

"Come? Come where sweetie?"

"To the hospital. Please, Mommy. I just need you to come here."

"Hold on, your father is talking to me." Pam put the phone down, and Kyrie heard her and Man have an exchange that she couldn't make out. Pam must have covered the phone's mouthpiece. The muffled voices lasted for several minutes before Pam returned to the line.

"Kyrie, it's 5 am. There is really nothing I can do there. Plus, your father is not feeling well. Tell Shane to call me back in a little while to let me know how you are doing. And Kyrie baby, listen to me: God is in you, and He doesn't give you anything more than you can bear. You can do this. Just believe it and say it because your words are powerful. I'll come in a few hours."

The next thing Kyrie heard was the dial tone. She closed her eyes. *God?* She could count on one hand how many times her mother had mentioned God to her. Her grandparents had raised Pam, her Uncle Will, and Aunt Michelle as Christians. In fact, her grandparents were very religious and active in their church. However, Pam had not raised her children in the church or practiced any organized religion. In fact, while Kyrie wasn't really clear on Man's position on God, he expressed open disdain about anything that had to do with the church or Christianity, which he referred to as the "black man's oppressor." Now Pam was telling her to call on God to help her push this baby out? Kyrie handed the phone receiver back to Shane and then awkwardly navigated herself to an upright position.

"What did she say?" Shane looked at her expectantly, his eyes filled with worry.

"She's not coming, at least not right now. It's fine. Help me up so I can walk around the room." As she swung her legs around the side of the hospital bed to stand, another contraction wracked her body. She cried out and bit back the tears. "I'll get through this."

After several more hours of hard labor, the doctor came in to talk to Shane and Kyrie.

"Kyrie, please listen to me. You are doing an amazing job. Your strength and resilience through this birthing process is admirable. I respect your reasons for refusing the epidural and would never attempt to convince a birthing mother to compromise her commitment to natural childbirth unless the unborn baby is at risk. We are approaching that potential reality now."

"Is the baby hurt?" Kyrie asked urgently.

"No, the baby is fine right now, but I have reason to believe that your baby could be subjected to some stress if this goes on much longer. The monitor is showing me that your contractions are significant in strength, but you are not dilating. One reason might be that your body is subconsciously tensing up to defend against the pain and preventing the dilation from occurring. I don't want to be forced to perform an emergency cesarean section without you giving your body a real chance to do this. Plus, you could be enjoying what is left of this labor experience. Please, consider the epidural." The doctor looked at Shane, and he nodded his head. He turned to Kyrie.

"I'll be right here with you, baby, when the anesthesiologist comes in. It will be ok. You can do this."

Kyrie squeezed her eyes shut as another contraction tore through her, this one more painful than the prior ones. She began to talk to God. She wasn't quite sure what to say, so she just began to plea.

"Lord, I am grateful for the strength that you have given me up until this point. I don't know if I can take any more, so please help me, Lord. Walk with me, oh Lord. Give me the strength and the wisdom to make the right decision about this. I'm asking you for your guidance. I know that women have been doing this for a long time, but it feels so foreign to me. I don't know how to do this, God, and I just want to do it right." She opened her eyes, the tears flowing. And then, instantly felt a calm settle over her body. She could do this.

She grabbed Shane's hand and squeezed it tight. "I'll take the epidural. Please don't leave me." And he didn't. Then she continued to pray.

As soon as the epidural was administered, Kyrie lapsed into the best sleep she had had in weeks. When she awoke two hours later, she was fully dilated and able to start pushing. A short while later, their daughter was born. They named her Rhythm. Kyrie thought she was the most beautiful being she had ever seen.

Her mother arrived at the hospital several hours after Rhythm was born. As Pam walked into her hospital room, gregarious and happy, Kyrie looked down at the tiny bundle swaddled on her chest and swallowed her frustrations about her mother deep into the bowels of her gut with the rest of the built-up resentment contrived from the past and smoldering doubt brewing for the future. At that moment, she decided to accept her mother with all her love combined with her failures, and she promised to teach this baby to find her strength within. She also promised to never mistreat her and to give her a life different from what hers had been, a life dysfunction-free.

"I escaped my personal hell and survived to live, and lived to reflect," Kyrie whispered to Baby Rhythm. "I can do anything through God." She looked up and caught Shane staring at her. She thought she saw something different in his eyes.

"What are you thinking about?" she asked him while immediately turning her attention to the baby stirring in her arms.

He smiled. "How awesome God is, and how amazing you are."

"Wow, I was actually thinking the same thing," she replied, smiling softly.

It is going to be all right. It is going to be all right.

CHAPTER 24

The Road Not Traveled

"My Life" - Mary J. Blige

"I've derived strength in the reality of my story while all along rejecting that narrative; wishing that it wasn't mine." - Kyrie

The office was chic and pretentious. It was located in an upscale Manhattan community on the upper west side, tucked away within a residential apartment building that screamed opulence and white privilege with its numerous doormen and wealthy residents. The lobby was elegantly decorated with leather and elegant fabric upholstery. Oversized centerpieces of elaborate floral bouquets overflowing from decorative vases graced ornate tables throughout the lobby; they were swapped out weekly and always seasonally appropriate.

As it was a residential building, its inhabitants sauntered through the building's lobby casually, relaxed gaits exemplified by their status, which often afforded them non-hurried living. In Kyrie's mind, the possession and control of time was their most invaluable asset. Their incomes were not predicated on a standard eight-hour employment obligation requiring their physical attendance. Kyrie imagined what their lives might be like.

People had always intrigued her. She had been coming to the building weekly for close to five years now and had not observed a black, brown, or person of color cross her path once. Nevertheless, she had learned that at least one African American celebrity owned an apartment in the building, so she held tight to her belief that access for those that looked like her, to whatever experiences lay behind these walls, was attainable. Still, consideration of the accumulated wealth within the building's structure both baffled and awed her at the same time.

She strode into the inner office, walking briskly. As usual, she was running about five minutes behind for her fifty-minute appointment. She sighed. She looked forward to her weekly visit most of the time, but she questioned whether she should have canceled today. She would return to her waiting driver to go back to work in just about forty-five minutes. She needed to be prepared to focus on the balance of the day after this session.

After law school, she started her legal career as a prosecutor with the Manhattan District Attorney's office. She enjoyed being an Assistant District Attorney. She had started in the Trial Division, where she spent the first two years prosecuting misdemeanor crimes and, after doing well, major felonies. Having developed a stellar reputation in a short period of time, she moved to the Violent Criminal Enterprises Unit, where she spent the next five years investigating and prosecuting interstate gun traffickers, armed street gangs, and narcotics dealers.

Although she enjoyed the work, the long hours and unsavory characters had been challenging, so she quickly accepted when she was asked to move into the office's Conviction Integrity Program. In that role, she managed the investigations of post-conviction claims of innocence and prevented wrongful convictions from standing. Kyrie relished the decision-making that went into determining what cases deserved a second review. She committed herself to getting to know the people behind the case file number and rap sheet.

There were also the cases where the evidence was circumstantial, or the charges were against a youth offender, and she knew that her lens, that of a black female who had grown up as she had, was valuable.

She recognized that mass incarceration was an issue that impacted men of color disproportionately, and she vowed to always be a part of the solution, not the problem.

After 10 years as a prosecutor, where she had built a strong reputation of being tough as nails but fair, she was encouraged and highly favored to run for election for a seat on the New York State Appellate Division judicial bench. She had won that election in a landslide victory several months before, and given her freshman status on the judicial bench, she now had to be prepared for unknowing cell phone cameras snapping pictures of her when she least expected it. This meant she could do without getting emotional during her afternoon therapy appointment.

Dr. Clayton Grifford put down the notebook he had been writing in when his assistant ushered her into the cozy room and closed the door behind her. He had suggested that she address him as "Clay" early on in their relationship, but she had called him "Dr. Clay" once, and it stuck.

Dr. Clay sat back in his leather chair and pushed his glasses closer to his eyes while he waited patiently for her to remove her coat, turn off her multiple devices, and get settled. His mahogany pipe was gleaming, protruding from the corner of his mouth where it always was, every week, unlit. It was a constant, a part of his uniformed look. It went well with his salt and pepper close cut, sweater vest, and plaid polo. Kyrie wondered if he actually smoked a pipe or if he just included it to complete the look and effect. He reminded her of Cliff Huxtable, that is before Bill Cosby's sexual abuse scandal tarnished an unaware Dr. Huxtable forever.

She liked talking to Dr. Clay, whom she had started seeing first as a marriage counselor, as she and Shane realized that it was helpful as they morphed from teenagers cohabiting to adults in a marriage to have an objective third party to hash things out with. While that had been valuable, Kyrie had quickly determined that she needed her own outlet and that she had her own inner strife to work through. She started coming alone and had continued doing so for long after the marriage counseling paused. She wondered after she had been seeing him for several years if her comfort level with talking to him was at all related to the reality that he reminded her of someone's father, with his mellow tones and kind and patient demeanor. Just not her father.

"Hello, Kyrie. How are you doing today?"

Kyrie leaned back into the plush leather sofa. "I don't know."

"What's going on?" The doctor's voice was gentle and encouraging.

"I'm feeling unsettled, unsure. I have this event in the next couple of weeks sponsored by the New York State Bar Association. They want me to talk about how my experiences growing up in an inner-city in a less than affluent household impact my worldview and cases that come before me. The closer it gets, the more anxious I feel. Today, I was thinking about what I would talk about, and I started hyperventilating."

"I believe you mentioned it to me. My sense is that you generally feel at ease speaking before large audiences. Why is this particular event having such an effect on you?"

"I really don't know, Dr. Clay. I've been trying to figure that out."

"What thoughts have you had about it?"

"Well, for one thing, I'm not quite sure why I was asked to participate. I mean, I am proud of my accomplishments. I really am. It is certainly an honor being recognized as one of the preeminent legal minds in the country – those are their words, not mine. But I don't know that my accomplishments give me standing to talk to a room full of equally successful and prominent people. I just don't know that I...that I…" She stopped, attempting to gather her thoughts, and then lapsed into several moments of silence. She really wasn't sure what she was feeling.

"Why was it important for you to point out that 'preeminent legal mind in the country' was someone else's words and not yours? Would you not use that phrase as a way to characterize yourself?" Dr. Clay asked her.

"I just didn't say it, that's all. And honestly, it does sound a bit presumptuous. We make haste to praise and label people as iconic in this country and likewise annihilate feeble idols with little regard and at the same speed of motion."

Dr. Clay raised his eyebrows. "Are you now referring to yourself as a feeble idol?"

"No, I'm not. I'm merely suggesting that if this society was not so needy for instant gratification, we would give people time to build a substantive track record of accomplishments demonstrated by more than a professional title, some significant level of wealth amassed, or what is usually the case in our current social media and reality TV show age; an inordinate number of followers and eyeballs trained on a person's every move and tweeting about it. We would allow for folks to actually get to some legacy building before we hoist them up on the world pedestal and decree them "most popular.""

"How does having been chosen for this honor make you feel, Kyrie?"

"I just don't feel good about it. I feel like a fraud, an imposter - for so many reasons. I want to be worthy of the praise, as judged by myself and God. For me, it's not valuable to boast about how I dragged myself up by my bootstraps, how I've prevailed because of what I've been able to do for myself. I'm looking to attain something more. I like to think of it as the 'depth of doing.' The level of action that I'm talking about requires time, patience, and effectuating real positive change that is quantifiable, tangibly measurable by more than likes, follows, or notoriety. It should be measured by impact."

"Hmm." Dr. Clay leaned back, quiet for a moment. "Your words are powerful, Kyrie, but fairly generalized. I am asking you to tell me how you feel about yourself. Are you worthy of the praise and accolades of your peers, Kyrie?"

"You are right. I did start by making a generalization about how society validates accomplishments. While I don't put myself on the same pedestal as a celebrity or social media personality garnering attention because of the shoes and sunglasses I wore out at dinner last night, I also don't necessarily believe that I have earned the right to stand before hundreds of lawyers and pontificate about how valued I am because of my underserved beginnings. I haven't struggled that much. Some people have had to endure much worse than me."

"That's certainly one perspective, but go on. Why do you think you were even chosen?" Dr. Clay asked.

"You know, all of the standard accomplishments. Sure, I finished college and attended law school full time with a young baby – so what? I also had a great husband at home supporting me and taking care of our child and our family. Sure, despite the odds and my beginnings, I worked hard. I was appointed as one of the very first African-American female judges on a federal court in my circuit. Still, most don't even know or care why that's important.

"By no means am I saying that any of this is inconsequential, but what has my impact truly been at this early stage? What have I done to change the lives of others? Am I feeding the poor? Are my actions halting or even spotlighting racists sitting in control seats where they are killing our black men's spirit with their constructed barriers to access the American standards of success? What about those who are hunting black folks like prey and slaying us in the streets of this land of the free, some carrying out executions in the name of law and order? What am I doing about that? Am I saving thousands of little black and brown kids that are intellectually perishing in the inner cities because they are being raised by young parents focused on fashion and pop culture and not social and political inequality or education? Am I taking proactive steps to counter gang violence and black-on-brown-and-black crime? What have I really done to warrant praise and honor besides recognizing that I have so much more to do?" She stopped to take a breath. She was so frustrated, and she couldn't even identify why this was upsetting her so much.

"Kyrie, there is a lot there, but I want to go back to something you said a few moments ago. You said, 'I haven't struggled that much. Some people have had to endure much worse than me.' I'm wondering if you are acknowledging your struggles at all. Can you expand more?"

"I meant that a black woman succeeds, and she is praised because she succeeded as a black woman, but usually, both her supporters and detractors are unaware of what that actually looks like, what it means. I accept that narrative of myself articulated by others all the time, and they don't even know my story. I can't even count how many times someone has said to me or about me, 'You have two strikes against you; one is that you are black, and the other is that you are a woman – and you've accomplished so much.' Comments like that take for granted that black women who succeed do so despite the very physical characteristics that make her a black woman and her individual experiences. That represents a tough road not traveled by our non-black counterparts.

"And let me tell you something else. The disrespected "angry black woman's" reality is generally taken for granted, both the one from the impoverished government-assisted household as well as the one from the middle class two parented college-educated household. That's because often, these very distinct narratives are viewed as a unilateral experience without real understanding. Every black woman's reality is not homogeneous. To be honest, I don't generally feel comfortable spotlighting any dramatic dysfunctional reality as my own because I just don't think it's worth focusing on when there are much worse experiences out there."

"Hmm." Dr. Clay murmured thoughtfully. "It sounds like your anger right now may be driven more by your reluctance to claim and respect the impact of your own narrative, not so much from your annoyance about society imposing only a single narrative on all black women." Dr. Clay waited for his words to register. When Kyrie said nothing, he continued.

"Kyrie, do you recognize that you have been subjected to an inordinate amount of trauma in your life, and you are certainly impacted by that history every day, including today? That is a fact whether you claim the experiences as yours or choose to ignore them. However, the road to growth and increased emotional stability depends on your ability to own your experiences and acknowledge how they have shaped you and continue to impact you daily. Only then can you begin to understand yourself. What do you think about that?"

Kyrie opened her mouth to disagree. She stopped abruptly, remaining silent. She closed her mouth and then reopened it again to speak, but no words came out. She decided to remain quiet and wait for Dr. Clay to continue, although he had asked her a question. When he said nothing, she offered only, "I don't know."

"Kyrie, I'd like you to give some thought to how little you talk about your childhood experiences with your father and how they have shaped you as well as your relationship with your mother and the resentment that you have acknowledged in just a few of our sessions although you have harbored it for most of your life. Your feelings triggered by your mother's apparent apathy about your father's interactions with her, with you, and with others, they are real. Those feelings matter. Further, her failure to own the role that her silence and inaction played while you endured treatment that was verbally abusive, emotionally abusive and at times, physically abusive; those feelings also matter."

Kyrie winced each time he said the word "abusive" and cradled her face within her hands, covering her eyes as if shielding them would block out his words as well as hide her shame. She said nothing. Dr. Clay paused for a few moments and then continued.

"It took us more than three years of engaging in this therapeutic process, for you to begin to touch on the details of your life before you left your childhood household and the effect the experiences and the continued family dynamic has played in your life, and moreover, how it continues to have an impact on your life today. I've observed how difficult it has been for you to acknowledge this story as your own. I can certainly see where the experiences are painful to recount but can you talk to me a bit about why you seem to be interested in downplaying the existence of them?"

Kyrie hadn't even realized it, but she had begun softly sobbing into her hands. She grabbed some tissues from the conveniently placed box on the side table next to the sofa and blew her nose while she attempted to quell her tears. She wanted to answer. She was searching for the words. She looked up to the ceiling above Dr. Clay's head and was momentarily 17 years old again, staring at the roach crawling aimlessly back and forth in the corner of the room behind Man's head. Dr. Clay's characterization of her experiences had conjured up the old but familiar feelings of helplessness, powerlessness, loss, and derision for what she had seen as a weakness within her for so long. And then, almost in the same moment, she felt the surge of adrenalin that had forced her out of her bedroom window and down the fire escape that night. It was only then that the words came.

"He's never acknowledged it. Any of it. He's never said anything to me to own where we are and express an interest in moving forward in a new relationship. He's never said, 'I did the best I could with what I had. I wasn't ready to be a dad. I was dealing with a lot. I was making the wrong decisions and got tied up with drugs and crime because I was disappointed in my inability to provide for my family. I'm sorry I wasn't able to do better. I didn't treat you right. I treated your mom badly and did it in your presence. I'm sorry that I hurt you. I'm sorry I didn't show you unconditional love. I'm sorry I didn't respond to your needs by talking to you. I'm sorry I didn't listen to you. I'm sorry I didn't hear you. I didn't focus on you. I hurt you until you ran away, and I am sorry I didn't try at all to get you back.' He's never said ANYTHING!" Kyrie was sobbing uncontrollably by this point, but she continued.

"And then there's my mother. I've tried to talk to my mother a few times over the years about what I went through. She refuses to hear me. She shuts me down and denies that either of them did anything less than love me. So yes, I've learned not to talk about it, which I felt was the best approach for me. I've been ashamed of the experiences and so very disappointed about the absence of meaningful relationships with my mom and dad for both myself and my children. The truth is, the longer I hid my story, the easier it was for me to pretend it didn't exist. At the same time, I've subconsciously found strength in the reality of my story while all along rejecting that narrative. I have never wanted these experiences to define me, but I do know that they have made me the survivor that I am."

Dr. Clay was quiet for a few moments. "These are all very honest observations, Kyrie. I believe that through your silence, you've allowed your mother, your father, and your siblings to create their narrative for you. However, there is power and healing in acceptance of your story. There is growth in the cognizance that these experiences, as painful as they are, created the strength and power of the woman, the wife, the professional, and the mother that you are. You have carried a tremendous amount of weight on your shoulders your entire life. You still carry it. You have survived a great deal of trauma. Own that. It is irrelevant that others have experienced worse. You might find that you will experience an intense catharsis from examining these experiences as well as your feelings about them, talking through them, and claiming them as yours. I would encourage you to push the envelope and start grappling with those stories. How does that sound to you?"

Kyrie nodded her head in agreement. She didn't trust her voice at that moment.

"Good. We can use your time here for that or not. These sessions are yours. How you spend them continues to be up to you. Another option is writing. You've mentioned you used to write letters to your best friend in high school about what you were going through at the time and how you were feeling. You've also shared that you have sometimes used letter writing with friends and loved ones when you need to express your feelings in an uninterrupted space. With that in mind, another suggestion for you to think about is starting to write your stories and your feelings down. You can approach it in whatever way that speaks to you most effectively. Whatever method that will foster honest acknowledgment and reflection of your story, the negative as well as the positive, is the one that I encourage."

Kyrie remained silent but again nodded her head up and down slowly in assent. She choked back another sob, grabbed a few more tissues, and took a couple of deep breathes in an attempt to calm herself. Her commitment to remain emotionless during this appointment had clearly been a colossal failure. She pulled a makeup wipe out of her bag to blot away the tear streaks on her face. She would have to reapply her makeup in the car on the way back to the courthouse. She opened her mouth to ask Dr. Clay how she should start this process and noticed that he was looking down at his watch.

"Well, all right then. This is certainly a good start to a new stage of reflection and self-awareness. You are on a road you have not traveled, but I believe it's the right path and the right time ." He smiled patiently at her, but with clear dismissal, in his tone, he continued, "You take care of yourself, and I'll see you next week."

She stood and quickly exited the office and then building, ducking into her waiting car. She was no longer glancing around her to speculate about and create any stranger's stories. It was time to start looking at and accepting her own life's story. Starting right now.

Kyrie was 37 years old.

EPILOGUE

"Brand New Me" - Alicia Keys

"Freedom" - Beyoncé & Kendrick Lamar

The ride to the gala had been like surfing on an emotional wave. As she now sat at her table, finalizing her remarks in her head, she recalled the tension leaving her body as she had imagined Lauryn Hill was her BFF girlfriend sitting next to her, their voices singing in harmony. She smiled. That song calmed her. This ability to transport herself to an emotionally grounded space during periods of frustration or angst had not always been a reality for her. It was the result of a lot of growth, self-reflection, and acceptance. The music's power in her spirit always helped. She would've never imagined that heavy traffic could be a gift, but sometimes, she just needed a little extra time.

"Everything is as it should be," she whispered in her mind as she sat, taking in the guests in the venue around her.

The ballroom was massive and packed, a sea of multiple hues of black, brown, and sprinkles of other races and ethnicities all around her. Amidst the crowd sat the Black elite; physicians, lawyers, judges, top educators, politicians, corporate business leaders, and entrepreneurial success stories. These folks were frequently featured in glossy magazines found in airport terminals, the reading material for weary travelers. Entrée into this social group symbolized a certain standard of achievement attained, excellence recognized by this black elite community and, to a certain extent, America beyond.

While she knew and genuinely liked many of the folks in the room, there was an air of pretension that she despised which fit many of the inhabitants like a caterpillar's silk cocoon. She pondered whether some of them merely ignored the poverty along their driving routes. *That shouldn't matter…they know it's there even if they don't allow themselves to ingest the brutal realities of it.* But then, who was she to judge? *"Am I really doing enough to make a difference?"* She sighed. She never felt that she was doing enough. She suspected that proceeds from events such as these failed to reach communities like the one she had stopped in a few miles away and the one she came from. There were millions of kids in communities all over the country that would likely never be in a position to vie for a college scholarship because they could barely read and didn't know to care.

Shane's voice coaxed her out of the contemplative fog she had been in from the moment she sat down next to him in the banquet hall. "Babe, where are you because you are damn sure not here," he whispered, his tone light.

She smiled warmly and squeezed his knee underneath the table, signaling that she was good. To the unsuspecting observer, she had been engrossed in the evening's program with rapt attention. However, she was really not present at that moment at all, and Shane could not be fooled. Whenever she was in a room full of people, she was always very interested in the potential of the narratives around her, mostly being stories that she would likely never know but were valuable, nonetheless. In this moment, she was focusing on herself.

She and Shane had brought four children into the world before she turned 35 years old. Rhythm was the eldest, age 20 and in her Sophomore year at Williams College in Massachusetts. A set of identical twin girls, Lyric and Harmony, were born five years after Rhythm blessed them with her presence and were now 15 years old. Then, the prodigal son, arriving two years after the twins and currently 13 years old. They had named him Chord and decreed him to be their last child. Kyrie knew the names they had chosen were a bit cliché, but she didn't care. For those who inquired, she shared that her decision to pursue a legal career instead of her lifelong dream of a music career was solidified by her commitment to motherhood and financial stability. They had named their children to honor her adoration of harmonious melodies, meaningful lyrics and soulful rhythms underpinned by beautifully executed chords, which also saluted Shane's equal love of music. While she was proud to say that her children did not entirely define her, motherhood was one aspect of who she was, and her children certainly were apart of the soundtrack of her life. She loved them with every ounce of her being.

Five years had passed since the day she walked into Dr. Clay's office, still asleep. She had departed roused, awakened by the power of the importance of giving voice and credence to her truth. Therapy fostered self-reflection had helped her slowly come to terms with that truth, and she would be forever grateful. On the heels of that emotional session, she had embarked upon a journey led by Dr. Clay's gentle prodding. She had commenced writing a journal of sorts, peeling her soul bare in the sanctity of the private lines and the parchment the words relied on.

Little by little, her vulnerabilities were revealed unabashedly, the stories and experiences of the previous four and a half decades filling the pages to the extent that she could recall them. And when her memory provided only bits and pieces of events that she was certain actually occurred, she swapped out the missing peripheral details for the resulting feelings that had remained with her, despite the absence of a full picture. The process proved to be life-altering for Kyrie. It gave her perspective of a life that she had stored in a box, only opening it up a crack at a time and primarily hiding it from outsiders until the writing process started. That journey fostered acceptance of the things that she couldn't change and the people that would always be there, some unchanged. Through therapy and that writing process, her awareness was heightened with respect to how she reacted to the things that she had no control over. Refining those reactions and learning from them remained an area of growth for her, but she acknowledged that she was getting there. She accepted that she was a work in progress.

The day that she swept into the ballroom of the Four Seasons, she had been reflecting on all of that. In the background of that reflection was also the ongoing self-mediated debate about her place in the world and how she contributed to it. For the second time in the last five years, she had been asked to put herself and her life experiences on display as an inspiring example of success. This time, she was the Diamond Honoree and recipient of the "2021 Woman of Distinction" for an inaugural fundraising event hosted by the very first ever combined organizational committee consisting of two prominent Greek sororities, the Eastern Region of Jack & Jill of America, and The Links, Inc.

She had left Shane still slumbering earlier that morning to grab some long-overdue catch-up time with Malyka. They had spent the day together with all of their kids, respectively, and then all dressed for the evening event at Malyka's house. Rhythm had driven down from school and arrived at Malyka's house to help her younger sisters don their cocktail dresses and Chord's tuxedo and then had driven them to the event. Malyka and her husband were also in the ballroom as Kyrie's invited guests to the evening's festivities along with her mom, Pam, and several sister-friends that were fixtures in Kyrie's life. Man had passed away a few years prior.

Since Kyrie's return drive to the hotel was solo and devoid of friendly banter or her children to distract her, reality had threatened to overwhelm her senses with its stark reminders of much of what was wrong about the socio-economic divides within American society. To some extent, even events like this one illuminated a spotlight on inequities existing within the racially homogenous communities of color. Inequities pained her intensely, but she would not let her observations distract her from her task this evening. Kyrie was fine-tuning her remarks in her mind as she sat in the ballroom reflecting upon her life, as she often did of late because it was incumbent upon her to pull from it.

Now, her close friend and long-time mentor, Cherie Marie Freeman, was at the podium addressing the room with her wit and candor. Cherie was well known in this space, President of her sorority's regional organization, Associate mother of New York City's

Metropolitan Jack & Jill chapter where she had strongly advocated for and ultimately sponsored Kyrie's membership into some years prior, and recently appointed as General Counsel of the Federal Trade Commission. Cherie was at the podium offering funny anecdotes about their relationship as she weaved her way through a thoughtful but lengthy bio and introduction. Kyrie smiled and readied herself to stand. It was time.

"...so ladies and gentleman, as you may be able to tell, I truly love this woman. I've had the unique pleasure of having enjoyed an over twenty year relationship with Kyrie and can say unequivocally, she is nothing short of a class act. I could remain here for another twenty minutes parading her numerous professional accomplishments for you, as I've only mentioned a few. I won't do that because she would kill me, but what I will say to you is this; more important than all of her professional achievements, Kyrie is a devoted wife, super mom to four gorgeous and wonderful children sitting right here in this room, superior legal mind, community service leader and budding philanthropist. Above all, and this last adjective I'm adding without her prior approval, Kyrie is a survivor, which makes what she is and has accomplished that much more impressive. Ladies and gentlemen, please help me welcome to the stage our 2021 Diamond Woman of Distinction Honoree, my dear friend, my sister, the Honorable Kyrie Graves-Meadows."

The applause was overwhelming, but as Kyrie made her way to the stage, all she heard was the word survivor reverberating in her heart and mind, as if it was echoing through the public address system. Cherie hadn't prepared her for that, although she wasn't surprised, given the insight Cherie had into her life. In addition to being her first mentor in the legal profession, Cherie was a close friend who knew more than most about Kyrie and often referred to Kyrie in their private conversations as a survivor.

Kyrie pondered that word as she walked to the stage, her breathing calming and the beating of her heart slowing to a melodic pace. Unlike any other time in her life, and quite antithetical to the first time she was ever asked to address a crowd of her peers, she felt at ease with herself. She felt comfortable. Kyrie accepting Kyrie, she thought.

"Thank you, friends, honored and distinguished guests. Thank you so much, Cherie, for that glowing but lengthy introduction [Laughter from the crowd]. *Cherie has been a big sister to me for over two decades, and those of you who know Cherie well also know that she loves to talk and does exactly what she wants to do, so going on ad nauseam was more about her having unfettered access to a microphone than it was about sharing my accolades – but I won't digress.*

The crowd laughed, and heads were nodding in agreement all over the room. Cherie was respected and adored by many in this circle. Kyrie turned to where Cherie was sitting and brought her hands to her mouth to blow Cherie a kiss, holding her gaze for a few moments and smiling warmly. Turning back to the crowd, she continued.

"In all seriousness, I am humbled by Cherie's words as I have overwhelming gratitude to be standing before you today, recipient of your 2021 Diamond Woman of Distinction Award.

"When I was asked a couple of months ago if I would accept this honor, I was struck with the query of what it meant to be called a 'woman of distinction.' Doubt besieged me. So I went to my standard 'go-to' when I need clarity; I turned to the dictionary. You laugh – but yes, I have loved and had a deep respect for the dictionary since I was a child. You will often find me looking to define the most simplistic of words as a step one in my processing. So, 'distinction.' The definitions consistent with this context were: excellence that sets someone or something apart from others; a decoration or honor awarded to someone in recognition of outstanding achievement. Well, I had to sit with that for a bit because until quite recently, I struggled with the concept of "distinction" as it applied to me. While I am proud of my accomplishments, I am always struck by the reality that I have not done enough, so how can I claim 'outstanding.'

"My standard is fairly high because my lens focuses on and assesses how much more I have to do. I believe that when we leave this earth, our worth will be assessed not by the money in the bank, not by how classy our closets are, not by how expensive our houses, cars nor how red the bottoms of our shoes are. Instead, it will be measured in impact. How did I effectuate positive change? In what way did I move the needle to better my family, my county, my city, my state, my country, my world? So when I think about my impact thus far in that context, I come out at the same place every time. Sure, I'm doing all right for myself, but I can do so much more for others. I can move the impact needle, and I will do so much more.

"At the same time, as I deepen my bench with respect to the extraordinary people, primarily women, in my life feeding my spirit, challenging me, growing me, and sometimes checking me, I am constantly widening the lens through which I view myself and the world. I will tell you, introspection is a difficult but also invigorating process. The difficult part is that it requires a level of honesty and acceptance of truth, including the segments of our being and our narratives that we are not happy about, the parts that we most want to omit or forget. The invigorating part is that once you work through acknowledgment and ultimately accept all of the components that comprise you, self-awareness fuels growth, and that growth is electrifying!

"My life has been riddled with many such segments that have been undesirable, untenable, and just plain difficult. As recently as five years ago, I wanted no parts of the distasteful aspects. I refused to claim the ugly chapters of my narrative; I didn't want to discuss them and ultimately realized that my denial was fueled by the reality that I didn't want the bad elements to define me. Thinking about them hurt. Talking about them made me feel weak. However, recently I've come to realize something that may seem like a given. Someone from that bench I mentioned, a sister that is very dear, said the following: "Kyrie, sometimes gifts come in beautifully adorned boxes wrapped in elaborate silk bows, but sometimes they come in brown paper packages tied up with string. But, a gift is a gift, regardless of how it is wrapped." The inherent conflict here is that we tend to evaluate a gift's very status by its presentation, making it really difficult to actually see its value, particularly when its presentation is unsightly. My strength and willpower have been sown and nurtured by so many toxic elements. Nevertheless, I stand here before you today able to say, I own it and am better for it, and seek to help others through it.

"Leaving my home at 17 to start my life as an adult while still a child was scary. It made me extremely uncomfortable and intensified my already weakened emotional stability at the time. The catalyst that prompted my unexpected journey was a childhood and adolescence where drug use, domestic violence, and dysfunction were commonplace. Even shedding the guilt and shame of owning that reality has been a journey for me. I should mention here, my experience is not a unique one. Globally, 275 million children witness firsthand violence at home.

Further, 1 in 3 women and 1 in 7 men will experience domestic abuse in their lives. There are many more alarming statistics, and I would never label any kind of abuse as positive. It's a heart-wrenching reality, and even as I stand before you today, it is difficult for me to acknowledge that the verbal and physical abuse that traumatized me through much of my childhood could have resulted in anything

251

beneficial. However, I know now that those experiences left behind seeds that cultivated flowers of strength, resilience, power, independence, and ultimately emotional maturity that has been extremely valuable. Those seeds certainly didn't fully reveal themselves for a long time, and they weren't wrapped in a bow. However, I now see them as a part of a full bouquet of gifts that I cherish today.

"The young men and young women that I interacted with growing up were also gifts, both the ones that nurtured me, the ones that took advantage of me – and even the ones that didn't treat me with the most kindness and respect. They all taught me real-life lessons about courage and trust. One poignant lesson was that trust not earned is not dependable. Those gifts taught me to bar unfiltered access to my heart and physical proximity without time earned trust and regard.

"The circumstances during which I entered law school were yet another gift. I entered law school several years older than the average full-time day program law student, with a young child and supportive husband at home. The gift of that reality spurned an immeasurable work ethic and degree of patience that I would've never realized but not for the heartache that was gifted to me over the three years that I spent twelve to fourteen hours a day away from my young child, a baby turned toddler, missing her so much it felt like my insides were melting. Likewise, it was a gift for me to be summoned to the Admissions Dean's office during my first week of law school and told by a female administrator of color that because I had earned a C in an accelerated pre-entry summer law school class and she was aware that I had a small child and was a single parent that I should delay my entry to law school or transfer to the evening program. The single-parent narrative was her erroneous, biased assumption.

"That Dean of Admissions sought to further validate her point of view by spewing statistics that supposedly validated that people 'like me' were not likely to succeed in law school competing with the average law student that didn't have my obstacles. She further asserted that it was likely that I would not pass the bar exam in 3 years. That Dean's view of me was supported by ignorant stereotypes and unconscious biases, and she failed to take the time to talk to me first or even read my admissions file. Her ignorance was a gift, as was the maturity and self-control that I had garnered from the adolescent experiences that gave me the wherewithal not to disrespect her at that moment while I told her what I thought of her assumptions. The ultimate gift there was the vigor I realized existed within me after her affront and my determination to succeed, notwithstanding her uninformed judgment of me.

"Finally, my parents were mere teenagers themselves when they began their parenting journey, encumbered by difficult life conditions and sometimes poor choices. I now recognize that they were parenting in the only way they knew how which meant they passed on their personal strengths that they relied on the most. My father introduced me to the world of books, albeit forcibly, unlocking unlimited words and pages for me to lose myself in. And in all honesty, I learned from him the power of standing up for myself in the face of seemingly insurmountable challenges; this has been an invaluable attribute. Through her unwavering motivation and positivity, my mother instilled in me the commitment to seeing the light at the end of the tunnel, even when there is a mountain of debris in the way. She epitomizes the very beacon of hope to this day.

"During the course of my life, unwrapping these brown paper packages often felt untenable. Still, the experiences within fostered profound strength and unequivocal commitment in me to parent my four children with intense and overt expressions of love, incessant positive dialogue, unwavering acceptance, and a refusal to allow any breach of toxicity into our family dynamic. I tell you, I thank God for that gift today.

"As women and, more broadly, as human beings on this great earth, we all are given varied sets of circumstances, all different from each other. One shared commonality is that our struggles, however varied, can feel insurmountable and beyond our control in the moment. As I accept this honor today and acknowledge that I, the Honorable Kyrie Graves-Meadows, am certainly a woman of distinction, my message to you is - a gift is a gift – whether it is one that you or I asked for or one that was gratuitous; whether it is one that we are immediately grateful for or one that we begrudgingly or unwittingly accept. It is a gift regardless of if it comes in the form of a really annoying boss or a relationship with a partner that's not the best fit for you. In the latter case, hopefully, you recognize the bad fit and get out quick – keeping only the gift of the lesson, so you don't repeat it with the next relationship. We learn and grow from all the gifts, notwithstanding the pain, happiness, and even trauma associated with its very fabric. Every experience, obstacle, and decision – good or bad- is a gift that manifests itself in the whole that makes me distinct, and you as well. All of the experiences that life has gifted me have been part and parcel, an integral component of what has made Kyrie, Kyrie."

"So, today, I claim them. I own them. I thank God for them. Sure, it's a rose-colored glass half full view. It's a manifesting positive attitude view, but what's wrong with that? I challenge you all to endeavor to appreciate every morsel of your truth that makes you distinct. Also, own the positive impact that even our very survival and growth might have on those that we allow in. That positive impact is possible not despite the gifts, but because of the gifts. Cherish not only the gifts adorned with silk ribbon but also those gifts in brown paper packages. Thank you."

THE END

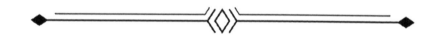

Made in the USA
Middletown, DE
18 May 2022

65900139R00146